# Forbidden Desire

11/08

"I can feel the blood racing through your veins," Ian whispered as he brushed aside her long, thick hair and gently kissed the pulse of her neck.

"It's the ultimate aphrodisiac for you, isn't it?" Catherine murmured as she wrapped her arms around him, signaling her acceptance.

"You know my weakness," he whispered as he lowered his mouth to her neck once more. "Give me what I want. Let me leave my sanity and indulge my senses once more. You were made for this, you know. . . ."

"Ah, darling, if I really believed that, I'd be terrified," she breathed in his ear, giving him a soft kiss. "But tonight I'm yours. Let's make each other very happy while we can."

Catherine really didn't remember how she and Ian arrived at his bedroom door, but she did remember being carried across the threshold and entering a world of pleasure where sensual passion ruled and nothing prevented her from indulging her most forbidden fantasies. . . .

# DEVOUR

## Melina Morel

A SIGNET ECLIPSE BOOK

SIGNET ECLIPSE
Published by New American Library, a division of
Penguin Group (USA) Inc., 375 Hudson Street,
New York, New York 10014, USA
Penguin Group (Canada), 90 Eglinton Avenue East, Suite 700, Toronto,
Ontario M4P 2Y3, Canada (a division of Pearson Penguin Canada Inc.)
Penguin Books Ltd., 80 Strand, London WC2R 0RL, England
Penguin Ireland, 25 St. Stephen's Green, Dublin 2,
Ireland (a division of Penguin Books Ltd.)
Penguin Group (Australia), 250 Camberwell Road, Camberwell, Victoria 3124,
Australia (a division of Pearson Australia Group Pty. Ltd.)
Penguin Books India Pvt. Ltd., 11 Community Centre, Panchsheel Park,
New Delhi - 110 017, India
Penguin Group (NZ), 67 Apollo Drive, Rosedale, North Shore 0632,
New Zealand (a division of Pearson New Zealand Ltd.)
Penguin Books (South Africa) (Pty.) Ltd., 24 Sturdee Avenue,
Rosebank, Johannesburg 2196, South Africa

Penguin Books Ltd., Registered Offices:
80 Strand, London WC2R 0RL, England

First published by Signet Eclipse, an imprint of New American Library,
a division of Penguin Group (USA) Inc.

First Printing, October 2007
10  9  8  7  6  5  4  3  2  1

Copyright © Carol Kane, 2007
All rights reserved

SIGNET ECLIPSE and logo are trademarks of Penguin Group (USA) Inc.

Printed in the United States of America

*To Sophie Brunson, for never doubting*
*I could write a paranormal, and for being*
*kind enough to read all those pages!*
*Thank you for your belief in me.*

# Chapter One

*Touraine, France, Summer 2005*

Paul DuJardin always found something new to admire about the Château Montfort. Even though modern owners had transformed it into a chic and expensive château-hotel, it retained enough of its eighteenth-century charm to weave its spell.

Paul had a particular reason to be fond of the place: It had provided him with the subject matter for a very successful book in his native France, with foreign sales in his future. For all its elegance and fine architecture, the Montforts' ancestral home had been the scene of terrible tragedy at the time of the French Revolution and the source of endless speculation ever since. In 1789, people claimed one of the Montfort counts had turned werewolf and killed the beautiful young countess, Marie-Jeanne. The legend was born.

"Paul, what about a nice shot of you in the back garden, near the scene of the crime?"

"Fine." The Frenchman nodded his assent and followed

the photographer, who had been sent by his publisher to get a jacket photo for the German edition of the book.

Paul had very little vanity, so he hadn't done more than get a haircut and put on a new shirt with a pair of comfortable jeans and loafers. He blended in with the tourists who sauntered all over the grounds, going to or from the golf course, the pool, or the tennis courts.

When he and the photographer arrived at the spot where the young countess had met her death over two hundred years earlier, he found a pretty blonde standing very still, looking down at the discreet marker, probably trying to decipher the French dedication. She glanced up at the arrival of the two strangers.

"Hello," she said. "This isn't a restricted area, is it?"

"Not at all, mademoiselle. Were you trying to read the inscription?"

She smiled at that. "Actually, I read it. It says that Marie-Jeanne, the Countess de Montfort, was slain here by the Montfort werewolf. That's why I came here—to visit the Château Montfort and learn more about the story."

The photographer, a tall man with a sun-lined face, gave Paul a grin as he took out his camera and motioned to him to stand near the sundial to the left of the marker. "Another customer," he joked.

The young woman glanced at the two men, probably wondering why they had come here for a photo. Paul could almost hear her speculating about his identity. An actor? No, too ordinary. A model? Hah! Even less likely. Still, the young woman remained, watching their activity as if she found it entertaining.

When the photographer had gotten his picture, shown

the results to Paul through the viewfinder, and received his approval, she smiled and asked if one of them would take *her* picture at the same spot. The professional, whose fee normally ran to several hundred euros, grinned and reached for the camera she offered. Paul intercepted it and said politely, "I'll do it, mademoiselle. How would you like to pose?"

Three hours later, the photographer had long since disappeared, but Paul DuJardin and Julie Buchanan still lingered in the gardens, talking about her link to the Montfort history and the old days of prerevolutionary France when the Montfort counts ruled their lands and the beautiful and doomed Marie-Jeanne ruled the heart of her husband.

"Well, monsieur, as I said earlier, I'm a direct descendant of Marie-Jeanne's younger sister, Manon, and in the family we've always considered Count Jean the murderer. Although some doubters have always suspected his cousin," she added.

"Call me Paul," he said with a smile. "Americans always use first names, yes?"

"Yes. Americans are very casual about that. How do you know?"

"I spent time in New York as a university student. I love the United States," he said.

"Ah, that's why your English sounds so American."

"Sure. I was all over the place. And I watch American movies in English."

Julie smiled at her companion and thought he was the most attractive man she'd met in months. Paul DuJardin had a look that was a cross between a young Louis

Jourdan and a really fit runner. This man was a serious athlete, Julie figured. He probably played a mean game of soccer with his buddies on weekends.

"How did you come to pick the Montfort werewolf as the subject for your book?" she asked. "Have you always been interested in things like that?"

"Like what?"

"Like, uh, werewolves."

Paul nodded. "European folklore is filled with strange creatures. And in France, especially in this region, we have our werewolves. The Montfort was always the most interesting for me," he explained, "because of the love story of Count Jean and his countess. That was so rare in an arranged aristocratic marriage of the time. Here was a young girl of the *haute bourgeoisie*, married to a noble-man in order to increase her family's social standing, and to everyone's surprise, he falls in love with her. It caused a shock among the upper crust."

"Yes," Julie said with a nod. "That's why some of my family had doubts. But he was accused of the crime, and of course, there were the peasant girls who said he rav-ished them and roamed the woods in the form of a large gray wolf. Lots of peasant girls," she added.

"Ah," said Paul with a grin. "The old accusations, bought and paid for by the guilty young cousin, Raoul."

Julie laughed. "You're very partisan."

"I spent a long time researching the historical records. I put my money on Raoul."

"All right," Julie told him. "Why did Count Jean dis-appear shortly after he was arrested for Marie-Jeanne's murder, right after Raoul was found hanged by the side of the road?"

Paul looked deeply into her beautiful blue eyes and said playfully, "You'll just have to read the book. And since it's getting late and I've kept you from whatever you intended to do today, I'd like to take you to dinner to make up for it."

Julie had been hoping he'd say something like that. Then she remembered she was talking with a man—a very attractive man she had just met—who wrote books about werewolves, and she was alone in a foreign country and didn't know the area well. Would it be a good idea to get into a car with him and end up God knows where?

Sensing hesitation on her part, Paul said helpfully, "Are you staying at the château? The restaurant that overlooks the garden is one of the best in Touraine. You choose the time and I'll meet you there."

That worked. "I'd love to have dinner with you," Julie replied. "How about seven o'clock?"

"Great. I'll meet you in the lobby."

"Oh, they have a dress code," she remembered, with a glance at his jeans.

"I'll be presentable," he promised. "I'm staying with a friend who lives nearby. See you later."

When Julie arrived for dinner, she found her new friend waiting in the foyer, deep in conversation with the hotel's director. They appeared to know each other, and Julie caught snatches of conversation about fishing. So this Paul DuJardin was an outdoorsman, too, in addition to being a writer. A man of many talents.

"Julie, I don't know if you've met Georges. He's the man responsible for keeping the château worthy of its five stars. Georges, Julie Buchanan, a descendant of Manon de LaVillette, Marie-Jeanne's sister."

This struck Julie as faintly ironic, since Manon had been dead for over one hundred and fifty years, but apparently Marie-Jeanne was such a presence at the château that any connection to her was significant. It rated a respectful look from Georges.

"Delighted to meet you, mademoiselle. I hope your visit has been pleasant."

"Oh, yes. It's even better than I expected. I can't wait to tell the family."

"Then I'm very pleased. If I can do anything to help with information, let me know. Although," he said with a warm smile, "you're in good hands with Paul. He's an expert on the Montforts."

"Thank you."

Julie didn't know if it was the new dress she was wearing or the good-looking man at her side, but she noticed a subtle increase in attention by the staff as she and Paul were escorted to their table near a large window overlooking the gardens.

"It seems as though everybody knows you here," she said after ordering. "Am I the only person who doesn't realize who you are?"

"I'm just who I said I was. A writer."

"Then you must be a very successful one."

"I've had a few books that racked up good sales."

"Don't tell me you're a regular on the French bestseller list."

"The last two did quite well," he said with a smile. "The one I wrote before the Montfort book is about to be turned into a film."

"Congratulations."

"Thank you. Do *you* write?"

"No," Julie said. "But I've worked as a translator. French to English. I'm actually a history professor at a small college in New York."

"A translator," he said. "What have you worked on?"

Julie named four books. Paul knew three of them.

"I'll give you a copy of *L'Affaire Montfort*."

"To translate?" she asked playfully.

"To enjoy," he replied. "With your family connection, you ought to find it interesting."

"Let's see if you can convince me Count Jean was innocent," she said. "I'd like to believe it."

Paul smiled. "After you finish *L'Affaire Montfort*, I might even convince you to believe in werewolves."

Well, thought Julie, that was a stretch. But she certainly enjoyed his company and liked his rugged good looks. She hoped against all odds that this wouldn't be the last time they met.

# Chapter Two

After Julie returned to the United States, showed her family the photographs of the Château Montfort, and told them about her chance meeting with the good-looking French author and his information about the Montfort legend, she settled into her regular late-summer routine and prepared to spend time with some cousins before the return to work in September.

Paul lived three thousand miles away. There was no reason for her to hope to see him again. She had spent two days with Paul in the beautiful countryside of Touraine, enjoyed every minute of it, and even gained some insights into her family's history, but that was a delightful gift of fate. Men who lived half a world away didn't keep in touch. Men who looked like Paul usually had girlfriends who resembled French movie stars. Either way, she put no faith in his promise to call her.

Well, Julie thought, at least if she ever saw him again, there was no need to feel embarrassed. They had truly enjoyed each other's company, discovered things in common, and done nothing immoral, irrational, or illegal. That was good. Sure.

Paul had such a wonderful smile, she recalled. He probably melted hearts all across the country with it. And he looked great in jeans. He was born to wear jeans. Wranglers, French jeans, or even trendy Italian jeans.

Shit, she would never hear from him, she thought morosely. He probably used his cell phone to have long, exciting conversations with girls named Giselle, Delphine, or Marie-Chantal. Or even Clarisse, Mette, and Graziella. Not with history professors named Julie.

It came as a heart-stopping surprise one morning four weeks after their meeting when Julie answered her phone and heard Paul's voice.

"Julie, do we have a bad connection?" he asked. "You sound muffled."

She recovered and said, "Oh, no. It's the way I was holding the phone. How are you?"

"Great. I'm coming to New York next week and I'd like to see you, if that's possible. It's a business trip. I won't be there very long, but if you're free on the day I am, we could have lunch. There's something I'd like to discuss."

"Well, that's terrific. Which day do you have in mind?"

"Wednesday," he replied.

Julie didn't care what day he said; she'd make time.

"I think I could arrange that. Where would you like to meet?"

Paul mentioned an Italian restaurant in Little Italy, an old favorite. Julie knew it.

"All right," she said. "When?"

"One o'clock."

"I could do that," she said.

That night, Julie's dreams spun into swirls of fantasy, taking her back to the gardens of the Château Montfort. She walked there with Paul, arm in arm, but in her mind she heard a strange voice, a male French voice telling her he was glad she had come to discover her heritage. It pleased him, he said, more than she could know.

"It is beautiful," she admitted. "It must have been paradise when Marie-Jeanne and Count Jean lived here."

"You have no idea. Sleep well, *ma chère*. We will speak again," he murmured. And then he was gone.

On Wednesday, Julie arrived at the restaurant in her favorite summer linen suit, greeted Paul warmly, and went in to lunch. He looked just as good in New York as he had in Touraine—not one of those guys who seem out of their element in a foreign country. His tan skin brought out the amber glints in his dark eyes. He was an outdoors kind of guy, the type of man she found appealing.

After a simple lunch and wine, Paul sat back and gave Julie a look that signaled personal interest and something she couldn't quite understand. When he spoke, she realized what he had in mind.

"After you told me you worked as a translator, I was curious enough to buy those books in English. You did a superb job."

"Thank you." Somehow that was *not* what she had thought he might say. Nice that he admired her talents, but Julie hoped for something along the lines of "You look gorgeous in sage green. The color was made for you."

"It's true," he said, leaning toward her. "I read them all in the original, and you managed to convey the author's style. That's very hard to do."

"I studied in France and became fluent. It led to several jobs in the field."

"Are you working on anything now?"

"No. I wanted the summer off."

He looked straight at her and she felt a sizzle of excitement at the expression in his beautiful dark eyes. It went straight through her.

"Could I convince you to take on a new assignment?"

"Not *L'Affaire Montfort*," she exclaimed.

"Yes. We sold it to an American publisher. Now we need an English version. I specified approval of the translator," he said with a smile.

"Well, it's very flattering that you would entrust me with something so important. . . ."

"And I hope you'll say yes."

"I read it," Julie told him. "It was awesome. But are there really werewolves alive today?"

"Yes," he replied. "And even living in New York."

"Do you think this Montfort guy will sue?" she asked nervously. "You practically called him a werewolf."

"I said he was the descendant of the notorious Montfort family, who produced several werewolves. So far we have no proof he's taken that route."

"Do you think he might?" she asked.

"There are many things that might happen to all of us," Paul replied suavely. "Let's say we are very interested in the outcome."

Julie glanced at him with a mixture of diffidence and curiosity. "You keep track of them?"

Paul leaned across the table and reached for her hand. "Yes," he said softly. "And sometimes we hunt them. I work with a partner," he added casually.

Julie didn't know if it was the wine, those gorgeous dark eyes with a hint of playfulness, or her raging desire to spend more time with this really attractive man, but she told him she'd do the translation—just as long as he realized she had a full-time job, too. She held her breath at the possibility that this was the kiss of death.

"Could you get it done within the year? They're thinking of a 2007 pub date," he replied.

She nodded. "You've got yourself a deal," she said.

# Chapter Three

*Alsace, France, Winter 2006*

"Are you certain we'll find him here?" Paul asked softly as he and his companion made their way stealthily into the woods. He knew their source was adamant about it, but so far they had been walking for half an hour without sighting so much as a rabbit. On this cloudy night in Alsace, only an owl had broken the silence with its shriek, an ominous backdrop to their expedition.

Catherine Marais suddenly paused and put her hand on his arm. Paul stopped, turned, and looked expectantly in her direction. To his surprise, she was studying the sole of her boot and scraping it against some grass. She then moved back to get a better look at what she had stepped in. Animal droppings. The kind a large animal might leave. The kind a large wolf might leave.

Paul squatted down beside her and looked carefully at the scat. It was lupine. Catherine held her Beretta at the ready, prepared to engage the enemy. He stood up and reached for his own weapon. Both hunters felt an adrenaline rush: He was here; so were they. They were ready to rock and roll.

Now Catherine's senses quivered; her eyesight focused on the direction of the soft sounds in the distance, the hint of a creature making his way through the woods, slowly, steadily heading toward his trackers. She could almost swear she smelled him now. This close, he could certainly smell them.

Paul quietly moved away from his partner, both of them getting ready to shoot at the first sign of attack, both trying to give the other a better field of fire.

Now the sounds came closer; Catherine glanced at Paul and nodded. *Get ready,* she seemed to say. *Hit him fast.*

Before Paul could even respond with a tilt of his head, the largest wolf he had ever seen leaped out from behind a stand of fir trees and knocked him to the ground, snarling, growling, tearing at Paul's heavy padded jacket.

Desperate to protect his neck, Paul punched and kicked his attacker as he fired wildly, hoping at least to startle the wolf into suspending the attack, however briefly, till he could get to his feet and fire again. Undaunted, the great gray wolf hung on, intent on tearing flesh from bone.

With exquisite deliberation, Catherine blocked out the shouts of her friend, the pounding of her own heart, and took aim. With the thrashing of both man and beast, she had to be accurate. Aim wrong and Paul was dead by her own hand, with the werewolf still alive and lusting for *her* blood. She couldn't allow that to happen. If it did, she wouldn't live long enough to regret it.

"Aaaagh!"

The scream came from Paul as the bullet tore into the wolf, sending it momentarily into the air before it landed with a dull thud inches from its intended victim.

"I got it!"

"Shoot it again. Make sure," Paul said unsteadily as he tried to rise to his feet, still shaking. The bastard had torn his jacket but hadn't penetrated his Kevlar vest. Bruises were already forming. His breath exploded in gasps as Catherine helped him to his feet, still not taking her eyes off the dead or dying wolf.

She prodded the animal with her foot and received no response, but she was too experienced to be satisfied with that. It could be trying to lull them into complacency by playing possum. That little stratagem had nearly ended her career on her first time out. Damned German werewolf made her think she had killed it, and a second after she put down her weapon, it rose and lunged at her throat. Fortunately for her, she had an intelligent partner who knew all the tricks. He shot the wolf as it rose, the wolf's final action.

With that in mind, Catherine aimed her Beretta and shot her prey three times, once in the head, once in the chest, and again in the head. *Ah,* she thought, as she saw the beast open and close its eyes just before the bullets tore into it, *nice try. Too bad you were too slow.*

"You loaded the silver bullets?" Paul asked with a smile as they stood over the werewolf.

"New ones from the Institut Scientifique," she replied. "Guaranteed to do maximum damage."

"Ah, good. Those boys are always improving the equipment."

Catherine smiled. She considered them so single-minded. They thought only about the werewolf—how to hunt it, how to find it, how to kill it. A dedicated associate herself, Catherine had a life beyond that. In the family château, for example, in the great cities of Europe, in every high-end shop on several continents.

Born into a noted family of werewolf hunters, Catherine had entered the services of the Institut as a protégée of the director after she and her friend Paul DuJardin tracked a vicious French werewolf and provided the information that led to its liquidation, and this on summer vacation from the university. After that episode, Catherine and Paul received invitations to join the "company."

"It hasn't begun to revert back to human form," she remarked. "I wonder how long it will take."

As Catherine said the words, Paul swore he saw the fur on a paw start to recede.

"It's beginning," he said as he rubbed his sore shoulder. "Let's go. We can't be here when they find him."

"Can you walk to the car?"

"Yes. I'm not badly hurt. It just knocked the wind out of me."

"You ought to get to one of our doctors just to be sure," Catherine said as she put her arm around him to steady him. "They carry all kinds of bacteria in their saliva."

"I'll be fine," he said as they headed back out of the woods, to the waiting car. "You worry too much."

By the time they returned the vehicle to the associate who had rented it, took the train from Strasbourg to Geneva, and reported back to the Institut, Paul was running a fever that took nearly a week to abate.

When he finally recovered, he found Catherine seated

by his bed in the Institut's private clinic, reading a Strasbourg newspaper. The place looked sterile and impersonal, very efficient and quite well organized, a kind of tribute to its Teutonic roots.

"One of the town's leading citizens was discovered dead in the woods," she said with a glimmer in her eye. "Stark naked and shot full of holes with silver bullets. Guess what they suspect?"

Paul managed a weak shrug.

"Kinky suicide sex pact with some unknown lover. Apparently this one had a reputation for the wild life."

"Very convenient," he murmured. "But there was only one body. How do they explain that?"

"Kinky but stupid," she replied. "The police claim to be looking for the shooter. They're questioning his wide circle of friends. To be continued."

"One of our friends is in charge of the investigation?"

"Absolutely," she said with a smile. "Oh, and by the way, the doctors said you're lucky to be alive. This boy had a vicious genetic makeup. Its saliva was loaded with unusually dangerous antibodies."

Paul almost expected to hear "I told you so."

# Chapter Four

*New York, Autumn 2007* ——

In her office in the history department of James Miller College, Professor Julie Buchanan sat with a heap of undergraduate papers and a hot cup of coffee. She needed caffeine for this; it was almost a requirement if she hoped to get through the pile this evening. They were beyond dull. They were hopeless. They combined an almost total lack of cohesion with a shocking unconcern for grammar, not a winning duo in anybody's book. And she had to correct them and grade them. Ugh.

Julie worked at the papers with stoic determination, wondering if any of her students had ever researched anything in a library—a real library and not some virtual place. She didn't think so.

At around six thirty she gave a little start when her cell phone rang, and she quickly picked up, grateful for the distraction.

"Hello, Julie, it's Paul," said her caller with that sexy, husky voice she found so French. "I'm sitting here at the café with an after-dinner drink and looking out onto Lac Léman. It's wonderful. I'm sorry you're not here to share it."

"I'm sitting here in my office, staring at a bunch of papers written by morons. It's horrible," she cheerfully replied. "How nice of you to call me and gloat."

She heard him laugh. Then he said more seriously, "*L'Affaire Montfort* is coming out next week. I wanted to let you know. I also want you to come to my first signing."

"Great. Where's it going to be?"

"Manhattan," he replied. "Fifth Avenue. Friday."

"What time?"

"Six thirty. Can you come?"

"Sure. My classes end at twelve thirty. Send me all the details in an e-mail, and I'll be there. Will you be in New York long?"

"Perhaps a week. I'll be doing signings in Philadelphia, Chicago, and San Francisco, too." Paul hesitated. "You know," he said, "I think I ended the book too soon."

"What makes you say that?"

"Because our people have picked up a trace of a mature Montfort in Manhattan." He let that sink in. "They go through a growth period before they become capable of controlling their ability to change. He's nearly ready."

"You're kidding. Are they sure? I mean, there have to be people called Montfort all over the place without being one of *the* Montforts." She paused. "They really believe it?"

"They feel he's one of them," Paul replied. "I can't go into details, but I'm telling you this because of your link to the book and to the history of the family. We don't like to leave anything to chance. The really dangerous thing about the werewolf is the instability. If he can't successfully control his inner wolf, the lupine side takes over and starts to control the man. You can guess the results."

Julie shuddered. "And then he goes on a killing spree, right?"

She shook her head as if trying to ward off a sense of disquiet. "Just because the eighteenth-century Montfort werewolf killed my many-times-great-aunt doesn't mean this modern Montfort poses a threat to me. He's probably just some guy who works on Wall Street or for the city. And how many of them have there been since the famous one who killed Marie-Jeanne? None, right?"

"None that I've found. That doesn't mean they don't exist."

"Well, if some furry guy pops up and threatens me because I translated your book, I'll call the cops."

"If some werewolf threatens you, call me or Catherine," he said. "We're both better equipped to handle this. The police will only file some paperwork and promise to look into it—then get called away and forget all about you. Manhattan is huge; the cops are busy. They don't believe in werewolves. We, on the other hand . . ."

"Ah, well, I get your point," Julie said with a smile. "Okay. So if something furry comes calling, I'll send you an SOS."

"Catherine is looking forward to seeing you, too," he added.

"And I'd love to see her again. We can go shopping. She has every store in the known world on her BlackBerry."

He chuckled at that. "She is certainly a shopper. Hermès sends her birthday cards."

"See what I mean? She's amazing."

On his side of the Atlantic, Paul looked out on to the dark surface of Lac Léman, twinkling with the reflection of hundreds of lights, and he sighed. "You understand what I'm doing, don't you? This book is provocation. No Montfort with any sense of pride will let this attack pass unchallenged. They're a touchy race—always have been. Our werewolf is going to manifest itself, perhaps even earlier than we predict," he reflected. "It's coming of age and it has to be struggling with its sense of control. They all do."

"Well then, we'll be ready," Julie said. "Call me as soon as you arrive. I can't wait to see you again—and bring out the book."

"I'll e-mail you with all the details," Paul promised. "See you next week. Ciao."

"Ciao."

When Julie pressed the button to end the call, she put the phone back in her bag and took a long sip of coffee. She had spent all last year working on the translation, which contained the account of the notorious attack on her ancestor, the beautiful, the tragic, the adored Marie-Jeanne de Montfort. It taught her more about her history than all the family stories combined.

Marie-Jeanne de LaVillette was a charming girl whose social climbing parents owned vast vineyards in Touraine, and her union with Count Jean would have been absolutely splendid if two things hadn't happened, namely the French Revolution and Marie-Jeanne's murder.

Local gossip attributed it to the werewolf, and the

story took root. In any case, a lovely young wife and mother met a horrific death in her own garden, the husband was accused, and her sister, Manon, and her grieving parents escaped the Revolution by fleeing to England. That was where Manon married Mr. Angus Buchanan and started a family. Julie was their descendant.

Julie found it more and more difficult to believe Count Jean ever murdered his wife, but the LaVillettes, Marie-Jeanne's parents, thought he had, and they hated him for it. Their hatred was so implacable it still caused lively discussions whenever the present-day Buchanans brought up the old family history. Only the dead really knew, and they were long past revealing it.

When she had first met Paul and had agreed to work with him, she felt an attraction for him that drew her into the outer reaches of his world. Julie still didn't know all he did, and some part of her didn't want to. His partner, a striking Frenchwoman from an aristocratic family, would have caused heart-stabbing jealousy in Julie if the woman hadn't sat her down at a chic restaurant early on and explained that she was delighted to meet her and happy for Paul. What they had between them was business and a long-standing friendship. Their romances were with others.

Julie found she liked Catherine Marais much more than she had expected to when she realized Catherine told the truth. That settled, they became friends, even though it still amazed Julie that she now had a friend with a listing in the *Bottin Mondain* and the *Almanach de Gotha*. Go figure.

The evening she spoke with Paul, Julie found herself thinking nostalgically of her trip to the Château Montfort in beautiful Touraine, the Garden of France. It had all

seemed bathed in sunlight, their meeting, the charming
landscape, their attraction . . .

Paging through the book she had spent so much time
translating, she recalled the dozens of yellowed docu-
ments Paul showed her back at the château's archives,
the odd, dusty scent of the room, even the feeling of awe
as she first touched the parchment. Somehow it all made
her feel closer to Marie-Jeanne, even though she knew
her only from family lore, from the pages of testimony
to her brief life and her dreadful death. There was no re-
maining portrait of either Marie-Jeanne or her husband.
All had been destroyed during the turbulence of the
Revolution.

*What were you really like?* Julie wondered as she lay
in bed, thinking of Count Jean de Montfort. *If you loved
that woman, how could you kill her? And if you didn't kill
her, what actually happened that night so long ago?*

Paul had made a good case in his book that Count Jean
wasn't the killer, but who could know the truth of it after
two centuries? So much was speculation, and all the prin-
cipals were long gone.

Later, in her dreams, Julie returned to the beautiful
gardens of the Château Montfort, alone, dressed in a
white muslin dress of eighteenth-century style, her long
curly blond hair pulled back by a blue silk ribbon. She
wandered through the familiar spaces, breathing in the
scent of summer flowers, feeling the late-afternoon sun
on her face, searching for her lover.

On the path leading back to the château, she saw
Catherine with a basket, clipping flowers. The young
woman waved a greeting, called to her, inviting her for
tea in the salon.

"I'll be there as soon as I find Jean," she replied. "I know he's near the grotto. I heard his voice before."

"Oh, be careful if you go there," she called back. "The cook warned me . . ."

Julie tried to hear what Catherine said, but it was useless. Overhead, an Air France plane roared its way toward the Atlantic, making too much noise to hear the Frenchwoman. Julie shrugged and went off in the direction of the grotto, leaving her friend waving frantically, trying to warn her away.

Julie loved Jean. Her heart began to beat faster as she walked toward the grotto, expecting to find him there. Suddenly the air changed. No longer did the scent of flowers waft over the garden; an evil smell began to foul the atmosphere. As she took another step, a strange, dark creature leaped out of the bushes, barring her way, its yellow eyes fixing her with their glare of unspeakable malice.

"Jean, help me!"

Instead of Jean de Montfort, a snarling beast stood there growling at her, taunting her, daring her to take another step toward her lover.

Then the animal—a wolf, a huge silver wolf—lunged at her, its fangs flecked with foam, its teeth as big as golf tees.

Trying to escape it, Julie ran, and then fell, helpless beneath its paws, the terrifying sounds of its growls echoing in her ears.

With her heart racing so hard she thought she would die of fright, Julie woke up in her own bed, soaked with sweat and gasping for breath. She sat there for a minute in the dark, struggling to regain her composure, listening to her frantic heartbeat. It was all right. She lived in

America. There were no werewolves stalking her, she told herself desperately. They were all back in France, circling the Château Montfort, and she was safe in her own apartment. It was over.

Lying back down and seeking a cooler spot in her bed, Julie experienced a strange, fateful feeling as she fluffed her pillow and then drifted off to sleep once again. The last thing she remembered in a cascade of fleeting images was the sight of someone dropping thirteen gold coins into her outstretched hands, the *treizaine* of aristocratic France, given to Buchanan brides for over two hundred years.

*Fat chance,* she thought with amusement before succumbing to sleep. *Not this Buchanan.* She didn't even have a steady boyfriend. Still, the image of the golden coins seemed to hold out a kind of comfort to her, as if someone really stood watch over her, a benevolent guardian angel of sorts.

She slept better that night than she had in a long time.

# Chapter Five

Paul harbored mixed emotions about his latest expedition, for he loved to visit New York. He had spent a year there as a student and fondly remembered that time in his life. Now an established writer in his late thirties, he could afford to indulge his passion for things American, like gadgets and Ralph Lauren blazers. And pretty translators.

Home Depot and Madison Avenue ranked as two of his favorite places, with detours to New Jersey malls whenever possible. He loved the energy, the mix of people, and the opportunity to observe uncensored humanity at leisure. He even subscribed to the magazine *Weird New Jersey* and had it airmailed to one of the Institut's drop boxes in Paris.

Catherine found his enthusiasms endearing. Then again, she was as conversant about the Jersey Devil or Transylvanian werewolves as she was about eighteenth-century art or Fabergé eggs, two of which adorned her salon in Paris.

With centuries of werewolf lore in her blood,

Catherine Marais had many interests that set her apart from her peers in Paris and the château country. Some of her hobbies won admiration, like her expert marksmanship, and some remained hidden, like her vast knowledge of werewolf lore ranging from Russia to southern France. People always found Catherine attractive, polished, and oddly exotic, as if she might suddenly confide wonderful stories of strange places in that disarming voice of hers, replete with a lilting irony that charmed her listeners.

Her relatives swore she embodied all the characteristics of her most intrepid ancestors, including a fearlessness bordering on hubris. Her mother expected her to have a short life like her father and wished she had never gotten caught up in the family tradition. How embarrassing, after all, to keep making up lies to explain her daughter's periodic disappearances. Catherine was a freelance writer, always hunting some story in far-off places. With a degree in journalism from Columbia University, this served as a plausible cover; oddly enough, her stories never seemed to appear in any publication her mother's friends read. Of course, *HELLO!*, *Harpers Bazaar,* and *Point de Vue* didn't feature many werewolves.

"We're going to be working with Ian Morgan," Catherine said to Paul as they caught a cab into Manhattan from Kennedy Airport, having survived the rigors of international arrival, passport checks, and new security measures.

Paul merely nodded as he scanned the passing urban landscape from the backseat of a yellow taxi. "Ah, yes. Your favorite partner on the dark side."

Paul knew Ian, liked him, and had even worked with

him on another assignment, but he worried about Catherine's growing passion. Ian had the attraction of the forbidden, and Catherine loved to push the limits.

"Very well preserved," Paul added drily. It was an inside joke.

"You can be so bourgeois," she murmured with the trace of a smile.

"Sorry. I keep forgetting how broad-minded the aristocracy is. I'll try to keep up."

Paul and Catherine exchanged amused glances; this banter surfaced constantly with them, she the aristocratic daughter of the Countess Du Vallon, he the son of an enterprising inventor from Provence. They shared a history going back to their student days, a sense of humor, and a passion for hunting things that were better left unnamed. They worked as a team of seasoned professionals.

"Karl von Hoffman thinks Ian is a good ally," Catherine asserted. "He knows the history, wants to help us, and will let nothing stand in his way to achieve success."

"He certainly has motivation," Paul agreed. "But does he have any new information?"

"According to von Hoffman, the last Montfort is alive in the Big Apple. Ian is convinced he knows who he is. If he's right, we can bring him down, all of us. And remember, he's reaching maturity and can become a time bomb if he fails to control his nature."

"Well, we have to be absolutely certain," Paul demurred. "I mean, we can't just take the word of a—"

Catherine flicked him a glance that silenced him. They were not alone; the driver, who might or might not speak fluent English, appeared to be listening.

"Lady, you like go see tourist places in New York?" he asked with a gold-toothed smile. "I make you and husband a good price. Three hundred dollar for private tour."

"No, thank you," Paul replied. "We've lived here. We know all the spots."

"Okay. But you gonna miss things. I know where get good deals on Louis Vuitton handbags, Tommy Hilfiger T-shirts."

"We'll take our chances," Catherine said. "By the way, how long have you been driving a cab here?"

"Four month," he replied.

"And before that?"

"Worked as engineer in old country."

"Which was . . . ?"

"Russia."

Catherine's dark eyes went to his ears, doing a kind of reflex check. Paul shook his head in amusement. She viewed all Slavs as potential werewolves, and she always claimed the ears were the giveaway.

"Relax," he said. "They're not pointy."

"Lady no want Louis Vuitton copies? Good deal."

"Thanks," she said with a smile. "I've already got the real thing."

"You pay too much," he said, shaking his head in sorrow. "You waste husband's money."

"Sorry," she murmured as she studied the relationship of his ears to his head. This one lacked the famous von Hoffman ratio, improvised and named after her old mentor. Most likely not a werewolf. The proportions were all wrong.

"You never stop, do you?" Paul asked with amusement

as he watched her. He could almost hear the calculations going through her mind.

"Not while I'm still alive," she replied with a smile.

"Julie, it's Catherine Marais. How are you? Paul and I just arrived in New York, and I had to call to say hello."

On her end of the line, Julie smiled as she greeted her friend. "Are you all set for the launch of the book?"

"As ready as I'll ever be. We really have high hopes for this one."

"Yes. I can't wait to see who shows up."

Catherine laughed. "My thoughts exactly. You'll be with us at the bookstore, won't you?"

"Of course. Paul called from Geneva to invite me."

"Good. There's somebody who wants to meet you. I wanted to be sure you'd show up."

"This sounds mysterious. Who is it?"

"It's an old friend who insisted on meeting the translator," Catherine said. "I sent him the final draft and he loved it. He thought you did a superb job."

"Well, thank you. Does he have a manuscript he wants me to work on?"

On her end of the line, Catherine gave a faint smile as she said, "No, he's not a writer. But he has an appreciation of language and nuance, and he liked your turns of phrase."

"Well, he must be a man of discernment and taste," she said playfully.

"Actually, he is."

Julie paused. Catherine was an elegant woman. This was probably someone from her circle.

"Is he a friend of yours from France?"

"No. Ian Morgan's a New Yorker. I've known him for several years. He's quite charming," she added, with a hint of lots of experience with that charm.

"Well, then, I'll try to be on my best behavior," she promised.

"Just be yourself. He'll be delighted to meet you."

"Okay. Well, I'll be looking forward to the book signing," Julie said. "We'll have a lot to talk about."

"Absolutely," Catherine agreed. "*A bientôt.*"

After she hung up the phone, Julie wondered who this Ian Morgan was, besides being a friend of Catherine. He had to be somebody special or Paul wouldn't have sent him a prepublication copy of the book. Perhaps he didn't read French; otherwise he would have had the original. And how did he rate an early copy? Oh, he must be a very *special* friend, she thought with a smile. Like Catherine Marais would ever lack male admirers.

Catherine never needed to drape herself around a man to let the world know he was hers. Men just gravitated to her. It was probably genetic, some aristocratic French talent passed down from generation to generation, like knowing just how to address anyone with a title.

Julie didn't really care who the mystery man was. She'd be polite, but it was Paul who occupied the center of her thoughts, ever since the day she met him at the Château Montfort. He had such a way about him without being either pushy or arrogant. He made a woman know she pleased him, and he was more than willing to please as well.

So far there had been meetings and phone calls focusing on the work she was doing, but never enough time to start a serious relationship. Sometimes Julie wondered if he had a girlfriend in Europe. Or, worse, several. Well, she didn't want to go there. But the last time they were together, they had taken things a step further and spent the night together. Between darkness and dawn, she was the only one who counted.

Oh boy, what a night. Nobody had ever made love to her the way he did. Not that she had a vast list to compare him with, but Julie smiled as she remembered how tender he was—and how thorough. That night was magic, and she felt vulnerable, hoping it wouldn't be the first and last.

On one level Julie couldn't wait to see her friends, especially Paul; on another she couldn't shake the sudden feelings of dread this brought on, as if she and they might provoke the anger of dark forces that lay just beneath the surface of reality, patiently waiting to destroy those whose hubris dared to threaten them. Not a comforting thought. And Paul and Catherine were on the front lines, of course.

But if it brought her closer to Paul, let the dark forces just try.

# Chapter Six

The next day, as Julie finished a class and headed for her small office, she found a surprise waiting for her: a man relaxing in the chair opposite her desk, paging through a history of nineteenth-century New York. When Julie entered, he turned around and gave her a broad smile.

"Paul! What a shock. I didn't expect to see you until the signing. I'm thrilled."

He rose, wrapped her in a warm embrace, and kissed her on both cheeks, in the French style. "I couldn't wait," he said. "And I was curious to see your school."

"Did you have any trouble getting in?"

"No. The security guards asked me what business I had here, then escorted me to the administration building to get a temporary ID after checking my own identification. Finally, someone took me to your office. They were very pleasant," he said with a smile. "But I have to say, things have changed since I was a student. In those days, I don't remember so many security guards. Then again, circumstances have altered, haven't they? One has to be so careful."

"Yes, even in a small place like this. Well," she said with a smile, "would you like to take the grand tour?"

"I think that would be delightful. For starters, is there a place where we could go for coffee?"

"Starbucks," she replied. "You can indulge your passion for cappuccino or latte right on the premises now. They put in an outpost last year. We're very *tendance*," she teased.

"Amazing."

"Ah, yes, James Miller College is small but cutting edge. We also have a lab in the economics department that includes a replica of the big board at the New York stock exchange. One of the few in the whole country."

Paul raised his eyebrows in an expression of admiration. "That's what I've always admired about America. You go for the latest. If it's out there, you want it. I love France, but things move much more slowly over there. The bureaucratic red tape strangles progress."

"And to think a Frenchman is saying these things," she said, laughing.

"You'd be surprised," he replied with a smile.

After stopping at Starbucks, Julie took her visitor on a tour of the neatly designed campus grounds, an oasis of calm in the midst of urban New York.

"You know, Julie," Paul said as they paused to watch a group of freshmen play Ultimate Frisbee, "there is always a risk to the work Catherine and I do. We investigate the bizarre, and sometimes it doesn't go quite the way we imagine."

She turned to look at him, concern in her beautiful blue eyes.

"I'm not trying to be dramatic," he said with a self-deprecating gesture. "I'm just a little anxious about what we might provoke during the book signing. I wanted to be sure you understood the possibilities for unpleasantness."

"Well, thank you. That's very nice of you to be so concerned, but in my family we've had lots of strange things happen to us over the years, so I won't be surprised by anything."

Paul looked at her and smiled. "What kinds of things? Disturbing things?"

Julie shrugged. "Not really disturbing, just odd. In a nice way, I suppose."

"Such as?"

She turned over her hands in a gesture of bewilderment. "A stranger helping my great-aunt when she was alone in the middle of a snowstorm and fell and broke her leg; a stranger coming to help change a tire for my aunt on the Garden State Parkway just after her tire blew out and she was stranded; a stranger pulling into the driveway in time to jack up a car for my aunt, after it had fallen on her husband and pinned him to the garage floor. That kind of thing."

"I'd say the women in your family are exceptionally fortunate. They must have good karma, as the hippies used to say."

"No," said Julie, "it's more than that. When my aunt Marie went into labor with her husband out of town and her mother off in New York for the day, she tried to drive herself to the hospital and had to pull into a parking lot because she couldn't do it. And no sooner does she bring the car to a stop than a young man comes to the window, asks her if she needs help, and calls the police. He goes with her to the hospital, calming her down as the cop bundles her into the patrol car, and accompanies her to the waiting room."

"What a prince."

"Yes. Then, when Marie's husband and mother arrive, just after she gives birth, she asks them how they knew where she was."

"And?"

"A young man called to tell them Marie was in the hospital. The thing is, her rescuer didn't know her, didn't know her phone number, and didn't know her mother's number, which was unlisted. How did he do it?"

Paul shrugged. "Maybe the hospital called."

"No. Aunt Marie inquired about that. They didn't even have a male nurse on duty in that wing that night, and nobody from the hospital made the call."

"Then it must have been the police."

"No again. Aunt Marie checked with them, too. So whom does that leave?"

Paul smiled. "I see what you mean. You Buchanan women are very lucky."

"So lucky, it's almost spooky," Julie replied. "Let me tell you something else, something we don't generally mention outside the family. From the time of Manon de LaVillette to the last time the eldest Buchanan girl of her generation got married, a stranger appears with a wedding gift from an unknown friend."

"That's charming."

"Wait, it gets better. It always comes before the wedding, delivered by a polite messenger who won't give any details. When they open the present, they find a pouch, and inside the pouch are thirteen gold Louis *d'or* coins marked 1789. Always the same date, from the first coins mentioned in Manon's diary down through the coins my aunt Marie received back in the 1970s. How's that for spooky?"

Paul glanced at Julie in astonishment. "That's the *treizaine*, the thirteen gold coins given to the bride in traditional wedding ceremonies. Or at least in traditional aristocratic weddings. It costs so much that it has passed out of fashion these days, except for families like Catherine's." He smiled. "But what a coincidence, for them all to bear the same date. Do the ladies keep the coins to be handed down to the next bride?"

"No. They do with them as they wish. The eldest daughter of each generation receives her own *treizaine*. Tradition says Manon bought much of her household furniture with hers, from the very finest ateliers in England of the 1790s. The pieces became family heirlooms."

"And your aunt Marie?"

Julie smiled. "Marie was so lucky. The price of gold was really high in the seventies, so she and my uncle were able to put it into a big down payment for their house. It equaled half the value of the house at the time."

"Remarkable. All those coins bearing the same date," Paul mused. "Extraordinary."

"Every time. It's always a cliff-hanger, you know, waiting for the messenger to show up and keep the tradition alive. And, of course, it's always about twenty years between gifts, so when the next daughter is ready, the entire family wonders if it's actually going to happen again or if it stops with her."

"Perhaps I'm cynical, but could it be the father of the bride who sends the coins?"

Julie burst out laughing. "Paul," she said with a grin,

"we have Scots blood. Do you think any Buchanan father is going to go spend a fortune on thirteen eighteenth-century French gold coins just to make a show of it? No way. Our guys give practical gifts. We're not millionaires. Besides, where could you find thirteen Louis *d'or* so easily? And almost in mint condition. No way."

"And when you marry, you expect to see the messenger, too."

At that, Julie gave a shrug and a smile. "I don't know. Like everybody else, I think it won't happen to me because it just seems so improbable. And of course"—she laughed—"it may be quite a while before I get to see my *treizaine*." She remembered her recent dream and hoped in spite of herself.

Paul smiled warmly. He made no comment, but when Julie saw the look in his eyes, she smiled back as he took her hand in his and slipped his fingers through hers as they continued on their way.

He thought of that night a few months back when he and Julie had made love. He knew she must be thinking of it, too. No promises had been made, but that didn't mean he had dismissed it from his mind as something casual or capricious. On the contrary, he wanted to repeat it. Often. But first, they had to deal with the werewolf.

# Chapter Seven

Catherine felt a thrill of excitement as she prepared for her visit to Ian's home, an elegant prewar town house in the east Eighties. With Paul visiting old friends across the Hudson, she accepted Ian's invitation and dressed as carefully as if she were about to accompany her mother to the estate of some friend, for Ian was quite conservative about those things, and Catherine enjoyed pleasing when she could.

What a delight to indulge him, to show up in elegant ensembles from the couture houses and be admired. Her usual working outfits ran to jeans, boots, and sneakers. Sleek, unfussy, and expensive defined Catherine's style; family heirlooms comprised her favorite jewelry; her keynote fragrance came from a small *parfumerie* near Vence, and it carried the spicy scent of carnations, a favorite flower.

Ian's presence carried her back to a time in the history of her family when things followed a certain protocol, servants waited patiently to indulge a whim, however odd, and gentlemen divided their time between wives and mistresses. Very ancien régime, and fortunately long past. She had a degree from the University of Aix-en-Provence, her brother possessed an MBA from Wharton, and her mother served as honorary chairwoman of a non-profit agency that focused on helping Third World women adjust to life in France. Very modern.

Yet for all the accoutrements of modernity, Catherine felt inexplicably attracted to the lure of the past, of ancient histories, of legendary stories of werewolves, vampires, and weird creatures of the night. The Institut considered her one of their best. She considered it her passion.

Once inside the entrance foyer of Ian Morgan's Beaux Arts–style town house, designed in 1904 for a millionaire of the Gilded Age, Catherine paused to greet Vladimir, Ian's blond houseman, who ceremoniously opened the wrought-iron door for her, wished her *"Bon soir,"* and then led her upstairs to where her host awaited her in the salon.

"Ian, how nice to see you again," she exclaimed as he greeted her with a kiss on both cheeks. "It's been too long."

"Yes, but now here you are and looking so beautiful, that it was well worth the wait."

Dressed by Valentino, Catherine radiated femininity and chic, her simply cut black silk dress created to enhance her slim form and convey the image of superb style. A sixteenth-century pendant converted to a gorgeous pin added a touch of whimsy.

"That pin takes me back so many years," Ian confessed as he admired it. "I remember seeing it in a portrait of your great-grandmother, the painting that now hangs in the Louvre."

"Yes. She loved this pin. I was thrilled when I inherited it several generations after her. It could have gone to one of my cousins, you know."

"No," Ian said with a smile. "This one is yours. Diana the Huntress is a very suitable theme."

After that, Vladimir served a light dinner, with Catherine enjoying a delicious poached salmon with spring vegetables, beautifully presented on antique Limoges china. Ian merely drank a light wine as he conversed with her, appreciating her dark beauty in the soft glow of candlelight. He had known other members of her family long ago who shared that beauty; it appeared to be a legacy.

Once dinner was finished, they withdrew to the salon and stood watching the lights of New York while Vladimir busied himself with arranging for coffee and dessert on a side table.

"So," Catherine said as she felt Ian's protective arm on her shoulder, "I think you have something to tell me about our boy."

He nodded. "I've been in contact with Herr Doktor von Hoffman. He believes me, so it's now official, except for the DNA test. The last Montfort werewolf lives in Manhattan."

"Hoffman is very precise," Catherine reflected. "He's not one to tolerate false claims."

"I used his methods, as well as my own. There's no doubt about their accuracy. The force field is disturbed in the way a werewolf's presence would do it. This confirms my statement that this is not only a werewolf, but a powerful predator, one who has been latent for a long time. He's about to mature. You know what that means for the city."

"New York could be a gathering ground for were-wolves. I know that Hoffman considers it a prime location for various were-creatures."

"The biggest cluster of werewolves in the United States is actually in Texas," Ian offered. "New York is home to families of smaller species. Surprising, isn't it?"

"Many werecats," Vladimir added as Catherine sat down for coffee.

"Why werecats?" she asked in surprise. She hadn't thought of them before.

"Space, mademoiselle. Wolves need more room. Not too many like to roam the five boroughs. Not enough places for a wolf to hide. Cats, on the other hand . . ."

Then, after lighting beautiful beeswax candles in a silver candelabra, like a good servant, Vladimir disappeared to allow them privacy.

"It will be interesting to see the prey surface during the book signing," Catherine said quietly. "That is, if he has the nerve when we provoke him."

"Yes. Then you and Paul can see what we have to deal with. At least in his human form."

"And then?"

"We wait to observe the Institut's protocols about the results of the DNA test; then we go after him with everything at our disposal. I want it all to end with him, Catherine. All the horror that cursed breed has caused over the centuries will be terminated with his death."

"Nearly eight hundred years of Montfort werewolves," Catherine murmured. "What a record."

"And it all began when one poor fool named Albert abducted a Syrian princess during the Crusades and brought her back to France. The princess Sulame introduced the werewolf gene into the family so many centuries ago, and the Montforts are still paying the price."

Catherine looked into Ian's dark eyes and smiled ruefully. "Men are such poor, desperate creatures when it comes to women. They leave their minds at the door of the bedroom, I think."

After she finished her coffee and the conversation turned to this and that, Ian said lightly, "Shall we test your theory about men and their minds?"

Those gorgeous dark eyes glowed like coals in the soft candlelight as they caressed every curve of her body. He reached out to her and drew her to him, meeting no resistance at all.

"I can feel the blood racing through your veins," he whispered as he brushed aside her long, thick hair and gently kissed the pulse of her neck.

"It's the ultimate aphrodisiac for you, isn't it?" she murmured as she wrapped her arms around Ian, signaling her acceptance.

"You know my weakness," he whispered as he lowered his mouth to her neck once more. "Give me what I want. Let me leave my sanity and indulge my senses once more. You were made for this, you know. . . ."

"Ah, darling, if I really believed that, I'd be terrified," she breathed in his ear, giving him a soft kiss. "But tonight I'm yours. Let's make each other very happy while we can."

Catherine really didn't remember how she and Ian arrived at his bedroom door, but she did remember being

carried across the threshold and entering a world of pleasure, where sensual passion ruled and nothing prevented
her from indulging her most forbidden fantasies.

When Catherine awakened just before dawn, she
smiled as she saw her lover lying still beside her, exhausted from that night. Then her smile faded as her hand
rested on her breast, sensing the two small marks he had
left there, just beside the nipple. They had disappeared,
but she shuddered with pleasure, as she recalled how he
had made them.

Catherine closed her eyes and bit her lip as she remembered the intense shock that had roiled through her body
as Ian moved deep inside her, sinking his fangs lightly
into her breast as he did. The pleasure was sinful, wicked,
so primitive that it nearly made her explode with lust, a
shocking abandonment of all decency, for there was a
rule among those who worked for the Institut Scientifique
that there was to be no consorting with the denizens of
the night, Herr Doktor von Hoffman's old-fashioned way
of forbidding sex with were-creatures, paranormals, or
vampires.

Closing her eyes with a sigh, Catherine reached out to
clasp Ian's hand, the hand of Count Jean de Montfort, former landowner of vineyards in Touraine and a vampire
since the French Revolution.

*"Mon dieu,"* Catherine whispered to the painted ceiling. If he could rock her to her depths as a two-hundred-
year-old, what must he have been like back in the
eighteenth century?

As if to answer that question, the words slipped into
her mind as though Ian had murmured them. "He would

have driven you out of your mind with pleasure and made you think you had gone to heaven, *ma chère.*"

"You read my thoughts!" she exclaimed as Ian turned to her and gave her a wicked smile.

"Dirty vampire trick." He chuckled. "And by the way, it's not yet dawn. There's still time to sample my skills."

"I don't know if I can survive any more," she said as she caressed him.

"But you will, darling, and then we'll have a new record to surpass," he whispered as he buried his face in her neck and made her tremble with the anticipated pleasure.

# Chapter Eight

A few hours later, in the back office of Beau Bijou, a trendy jewelry shop just off Madison Avenue, the owner sat at his desk with a tall latte as he scanned the *New York Post*. He had arrived early, as usual, to go over the accounts, peruse trade publications, leaf through competitors' catalogs, and flip through European fashion magazines to see what kind of jewelry the fashionistas overseas sported at the moment. When he turned to Page Six of the *Post*, he read something that made him feel as if someone had just put a target on his forehead.

"Shit! I can't believe this!"

There, for all the world to see, a blurb stated breathlessly that Paul DuJardin, the French author of a series about the paranormal, had recently brought out a new book in France entitled *L'Affaire Montfort*, the story of the famed werewolf of western France and its cursed family. American fans could purchase the English translation starting this week, since the internationally acclaimed author would be signing copies at a bookstore in the city. Already well-known for his previous work, *The*

*Enchantress of Chamonix*, he had just sold the movie rights to that one.

"What a fucking asshole!"

Pierre de Montfort, jeweler to the trendy and impossibly rich, nearly choked on his latte. This was bad luck. Why couldn't this hack have stayed home in France and written about Hungarian werewolves? Or Russian werewolves? Or even French werewolves from Alsace? Why did he have to write about the Montfort werewolf? Shit!

Pierre struggled to remain calm. He'd never heard of this DuJardin guy. Maybe none of his friends had, either. Sure, they all read Stephen King, but Paul DuJardin wasn't Stephen King. And he *was* French. If any of his friends spoke or read anything besides English, Spanish was the choice. French wasn't trendy anymore. It was gone, outdated, as useless as Latin, thank God. One of the things John Kerry's detractors in the last election used to mention was the fact that he spoke excellent French. To Americans, this was the kiss of death.

Suddenly Pierre had a horrible revelation. Marianne McGill, his beloved, his blond, blue-eyed WASP girlfriend, whom he wanted to marry, spoke, read, and wrote French, the result of two years spent bumming around ski resorts in the Haute-Savoie. Shit.

Pierre tried to recall if he had ever seen Marianne reading the *Post*. Nah. She had a subscription to the *New York Times*. She even plowed through all the sections of the Sunday *Times*, with special attention to the business and society pages. He could not remember if he had ever, in all the months he had known her, spotted her with a copy of the *Post*. Or a copy of anything by this Paul DuJardin.

Maybe he was safe.

Pierre, born in America and educated in Europe, never felt entirely safe, not from snoops like this DuJardin guy, not even from his own DNA. He was one of them. Oh, yeah. Mr. Franco-American werewolf himself. He had heard all the stories about earlier Montforts, read about them till he knew every legend, absorbed every bit of information, and checked every possible sign. Marked from birth with a tiny red paw print on his thigh, he bore the telltale characteristic of his breed.

To demonstrate werewolf capability, you had to have the sign. Some Montforts like him concealed it beneath their clothing. Fate cursed others with a nice clear paw print on their hands or arms. Some, like a remote ancestor, were lucky enough to have it on their scalps, buried beneath a good head of hair. Pierre had contemplated laser surgery to get rid of his. Unsure if that would really work, he still figured nothing ventured, nothing gained. He lived in the twenty-first century, so why not be modern about it?

In his teens, he had undergone the first stirrings of his fate, the limbs that twisted into bizarre shapes, the hair that covered his body like a badly cut rug, growing all over his torso until he looked like somebody's sick joke of a stuffed animal. Fangs started to grow until they looked like a set of those wax Halloween teeth. Grotesque, Pierre thought with disgust.

This happened twice on its own before he found a way to control it. Then, mercifully, it all returned to normal. Pierre knew it would happen again.

Werewolves of the Montfort species possessed an ancient gene that delayed their full development until they were in their thirties as humans. Pierre knew this because his tutor in things werewolf, his late grandfather, made sure he learned it as a boy. Pierre's father, who might have helped him, could not because he lacked the gene. What a sorry excuse for a Montfort he was.

Pierre had adored his grandfather—his mentor, his idol. He despised his father, a successful banker, because he hadn't been chosen to carry on the family legacy, while Pierre had. Pride inflated Pierre's ego; knowing he possessed the ability to shape-shift made him arrogant. People who knew him found him either very self-confident or thought him an insufferable prick.

Behind the conceit, however, there lurked a tiny fear that somehow Grandpa hadn't taught him all the things he needed to know as a mature werewolf. Sure, he had inherited a magnificent gift, but he was still testing his capabilities, and didn't feel totally in control of his powers.

Stress exacerbated this problem, and chillingly, the fact that his grandfather had been shot and killed one night under suspicious circumstances made Pierre realize that this gift carried a price. Reading about this French werewolf tracker made his hormones go nuts.

There was one thing he'd found out that ran counter to all the werewolf lore in the movies—his changes had nothing to do with the full moon. It all depended on him and his skill, and stress was his Achilles' heel. Tension and anxiety made it hard to keep the wolf in check.

He lived in Manhattan, which meant he didn't have a traditional countryside to roam like his ancestors, but he still wanted to claim his turf. He did a practice run the second time he felt his limbs twist into odd shapes, stalking Central Park once after midnight, lurching into the dark like a drunk.

Still capable of wearing clothing at the time of his first excursion as a werewolf, Pierre staggered around, waiting for his instincts to kick in while attracting odd glances from people up to no-good of their own. Nobody bothered him except for some kid who had probably taken too many karate lessons. The guy saw him coming, leaped into defense mode with an earsplitting shriek, and stood there watching him until Pierre managed a growl and made a wide path around him. How lame was that?

After this shaky start, Pierre's transformations became more and more complete, with real lupine features developing and the taste for blood more pronounced. Then it all came together one night in the park, when he zeroed in on a stray drunk, pounced on him like a wolf, and left him dead from a broken neck and severed artery. His first kill.

He quite enjoyed it.

He didn't want some foreigner ruining his blossoming love affair with Marianne or his successful business with a sleazy exposé of his background.

Even if every word were true.

# Chapter Nine

When Paul met Catherine for breakfast the night after her stay at Ian's, he noted the circles under her eyes and her languor. He said nothing, but he remembered the energy-draining powers of vampires, and he worried about Catherine.

"You look as if you're planning to lecture me," she said lightly, almost anticipating his reproaches as they moved along the buffet of their hotel's breakfast room.

When they sat down at a small table near the windows, Paul found himself compulsively scanning his partner's neck for bite marks, even though he knew vampires healed them for their lovers when they fed from them. That thought nearly killed his desire for food.

"So, Paul, did you have a nice visit with your friends?"

"Yes," he said with a nod. "And what did you do last night?"

Embarrassed at how crass that probably sounded, Paul looked down at his plate. It was none of his business what the Countess du Vallon did with the former Count Jean de Montfort, as she would probably point out to him. They were partners and friends, not lovers. He had no right to try to monitor her affairs.

Catherine darted him a glance as she picked up her coffee cup. "I had dinner with Ian Morgan."

"Ah."

"Don't look at me like that. You know Ian and I have been close for a while. We have things in common."

"Yes. An aristocratic background and a love of antiques," Paul said drily.

"And a hatred of werewolves," she reminded him with a smile. "Ian is as determined to get rid of the Montfort werewolf as we are, probably more. Remember, with him it's personal."

"I know that," Paul agreed. "I empathize with him. He's had two hundred years to build up a hatred of the creatures that slaughtered his wife."

"But he's a vampire and it doesn't sit well with you that I find him so *sympathique*."

Paul shook his head. "In our line of work we've often had, well, unusual partners. I'm used to that. But let's be honest, there's an attraction between the two of you that worries me."

Catherine's dark eyes seemed pensive. "You shouldn't let it bother you," she said. "I have great respect for you. We've been through so much together. We're allies."

The guilty smile Catherine gave Paul did nothing to reassure him. Vampires were clever and manipulative, even the best of them.

"The Count Jean de Montfort had quite a reputation as a ladies' man back in his day," Paul persisted. "I wonder how many women he's had since then."

"Don't be vicious," she said mildly. "Love takes you where it will. One can't help it."

"Catherine . . ."

"I'm a big girl," she replied. "If I find him beguiling, I will see him."

"If you find him beguiling enough, he may draw you into his world, and you know where that may lead."

Her silence evoked centuries of aristocratic hauteur.

"Catherine, you know the admiration I have for you," he said quietly. "It would tear my heart out if you became his . . . consort. It would be like watching your favorite sister ruin her life."

That provoked laughter. "Consort isn't exactly what I had in mind," she said. "Believe me, I love sunlight too much. And besides, you have had several little flings that never brought a reproach from *me*."

"But they were with humans!"

"To each his own," she replied with a shrug. "But one thing I promise. I will never exchange blood with Ian."

"Or give him your own?"

"Oh, Paul," Catherine murmured as she turned her face away.

"Very well," he said. "It's your business, not mine."

"Karl von Hoffman left me a message last night," Catherine said, trying hard to shift the conversation.

That grabbed his attention. "Yes?"

"He would like us to get a sample of the Montfort werewolf's DNA if we can. Years ago, right after World War II, Hoffman's group managed to trap a German werewolf and run some tests on him. The subject broke free and killed two of the Institut's best scientists in his escape, but they succeeded in taking enough samples to further their studies. They're very interested in running tests on this one."

Paul shook his head. "I don't think we're going to be able to crate this one, pack him in a box, and ship him to Geneva as if he were a zoo animal."

"Well, to be perfectly truthful, I don't think so either, but we might still be able to get some DNA."

"Sure. When we kill him we can take samples and make the old man happy."

Catherine nodded. "Or if we're clever enough, we might be able to get a sample while he's still alive."

"That would be a plus. It might give us a better overview of what makes them tick."

"Something to think about, eh?" she murmured. "You know, when my ancestors first began to stalk these creatures in the fifteenth century, they would have been so grateful for the technology we use today."

"Sure. If they'd had cell phones, computers, and BlackBerrys, perhaps Count Henri du Vallon could have wiped out all the werewolves in his part of France. With a network of hunters constantly in touch with one another throughout the region, we could have been werewolf free long ago."

"Of course the werewolves would have had them, too," Catherine said with a shrug.

"Not necessarily. Few of the werewolves Count Henri brought down were men of means. Most of them were poor, uneducated peasants."

"Except for the Marquis de Fortbras," Catherine countered. "He would surely have had the best technology of his time at his disposal. Thank God he didn't have ours."

Both hunters reflected on that. The Marquis Gilles de

Fortbras, one of the wealthiest men in the southwest of France, launched a reign of terror that raged for fifteen years, killing relentlessly as a wolf in between stints as a royal counselor. Catherine's ancestor slew him after luring him to a deserted spot, surrounding him with his trusted men, and shooting him full of arrows. As a final touch, Count Henri cut off his head and hacked the body into a dozen pieces, burying it in as many places. After that, no peasant was killed by "wolves" in the area for the next ten years.

Fortunately for Count Henri and his men, the marquis had fallen out of favor with the king, and his neighbors were so glad to be rid of him, they didn't spend much time investigating his disappearance. His joyful heir came back from exile and claimed his inheritance, his wife remarried, and his peasants celebrated for three days at the news.

"My ancestors had more latitude in their pursuit of werewolves than we do," Catherine said with a sigh. "Count Henri was able to kill the marquis without facing the civil authorities. These days there would be an investigation."

"That's why we have to be very careful with this one," Paul said quietly. "If our information is correct, this one is a man of means with a growing reputation in his field."

"I want him to become the subject of gossip," his partner said. "You have contacts in the publishing world. Use them. Get a few magazine articles going on the legendary Montfort werewolf. Rub his nose in it. Werewolves are famously paranoid. Work it."

"In other words, make the poor bastard so jumpy he'll get all nervous and jerky."

"We'll make him so agitated, he'll make mistakes so we can take him down," Catherine said. "When they're rattled, they do stupid things and don't think straight."

"We're not back in the fifteenth century. This werewolf will have access to a whole range of weapons, including high-priced lawyers."

"If he reverts to werewolf, they won't be able to help him. We have to destabilize him, play with his mind, and goad him into shape-shifting, for we must kill him in his lupine form. If not, he'll come back stronger than ever."

"And we have to protect Julie," Paul said quietly. "She's a civilian."

"She's already involved. She translated the book because she wished to help us. She did this of her own free will," Catherine pointed out. "Julie has her own reasons for wanting this one neutralized. It's payback for the crime committed against Marie-Jeanne, a crime her family has never forgotten. She wants to help avenge her."

Paul nodded. "I understand that. But she has no training. She has no idea of what may happen with these creatures."

Paul's concern was so vehement, Catherine felt surprised. Then she looked at him carefully. "Are you speaking as a scientist or as a man enamored of a pretty girl?"

"Catherine!"

"Well, *mon cher*," she purred, "you felt quite free to question me about my friendship with Ian."

"That's different."

"Because he's not human?"

"Because he's dangerous."

Catherine drank the last of her tomato juice and smiled deep into his eyes. "So are pretty girls," she said softly.

# Chapter Ten

When the mail arrived at the Beau Bijou, the usual routine was a quick greeting by the mailman, a reply by Keri, the assistant, and immediate delivery to Pierre in the back room. Today things were somewhat different. A bombshell had landed among the bills, the catalogs, and the appeals for charity. A postcard bearing the flashy cover of Paul DuJardin's book had mysteriously arrived, sent by its publisher. How the fuck had they gotten *him* on their mailing list? Pierre wondered angrily. Was this somebody's idea of a joke?

He sat down and read the blurb that went with it:

*For centuries the feared Montfort werewolves ravaged the beautiful province of Touraine, killing without pity, striking without warning, enjoying an uninterrupted reign of terror. Here, for the first time, is the true account of the accursed family and their destructive gene from hell.*

Pierre felt a faint stirring. He fought it. Gene from hell didn't cover half of it, he thought. Shit, he had to keep control. This kind of thing was bad for him.

He took a deep breath. That helped. Restraint returning, he took another look at the postcard and noted the listing of the time and place for the book signing it announced.

This was a direct challenge, and it had to be answered. If he allowed this guy to cash in on his family history without some kind of response, people who knew him would think he was a pussy. He had to go to that book-store and tell the world this DuJardin was just some hack who was out to make a fast buck. Stop this crap in its tracks. That's what his grandfather would have done.

No way in hell was he going to allow some foreign asshole to diss him in public and get away with it. He had his reputation to think about. And he had Marianne to consider. He hadn't intended to reveal his secret until after they were married, and even then he'd wait until she had given birth to his child. She was an incredible woman, sexy and strong, and he wanted her as his mate. But she was also conservative and blue-blooded—she'd never marry him if she knew.

He looked at the postcard again, sneered, and tucked it away in his pocket. He felt the urge to attack, stirred up by this provocation. He could feel the desire to bite, to wound, to tear and shred. *All right,* he thought, *get a grip.* He could control it. He wouldn't allow it to control him. For now.

Pierre felt the vibration on his cell phone and ignored it. Keyed up for the transformation he felt coming, he could only concentrate on one thing at a time, and right now that meant prey. Stress and tension required an out-let, and tonight the wolf demanded to emerge.

Cruising the dark streets near the Brooklyn Bridge,

Pierre drove carefully, taking in the narrow streets, the alleys, the few pedestrians who walked purposefully toward homes or subway stops. At one in the morning, not too many people strolled by, and those who did weren't inclined to linger.

Genes of a distant past, a fiendish legacy from the family's Crusade history, began to cruelly assert themselves once more. As Pierre drove his fancy Jaguar through the deserted streets of Brooklyn, he could feel the distortions in his limbs, the warping of muscle and bone; he could even feel the fur beginning to grow on his body, enveloping him in silver-gray shagginess. He could have been the floor cover on a minibus from the seventies, he thought bitterly. Yeah, the Werewolf Express.

Shit, he hated this. He couldn't escape it, put it on hold, or ask it to call back in two weeks. He felt oppressed by his heritage sometimes, condemned by it, ruined by it, in fact.

Okay, he was proud to be a Montfort werewolf, but not when the change sneaked up on him. It made him feel like a teenager in the worst possible sense. Here he was, an artist, a designer of·over-the-top, high-priced jewelry, a man whose work had just been featured in all the top American and European fashion magazines—and nature does this to him! What a cruel, perverse joke. And all because some ancestor back in the Crusades couldn't keep his paws off a princess from some raggedy-ass backwater place in the Mideast. If Grandpa were still alive, he'd help him over the rough spots, but Pierre was on his own, still seething from reading that postcard.

Pierre's pain escalated; he found himself unable to drive in his condition. He pulled over to the side near deep shadows and struggled out of his clothing, tossing everything into the backseat of the Jaguar. There was so much fur now that he had almost completed the transformation. Managing to take out the key before his hands became paws, Pierre hid it underneath the floor mat and pushed open the door, leaping out like the wolf he was, greedy for prey.

Trotting down the street toward the bridge, the eager wolf sniffed the air, catching the scent of humans, alcohol, perfume, and sex. Promising stuff, it thought. In the pale light of the streetlight, it saw its prey, a thin young man in a Brooks Brothers suit who obviously had been out celebrating at the nearby Water Club. The guy moved like a puppet with twisted strings, lurching drunkenly down the sidewalk, pausing to stare at the surroundings, unsteadily going ahead, and then stopping again to get his bearings. The human seemed lost, drunk, and helpless— prime werewolf bait.

The wolf felt its fur bristle with the desire for the chase; its whole being lived for this moment, tracking the quarry, sighting him, and bringing him down. Deep in its throat came a growl, low and primitive; it narrowed its blazing yellow eyes as it zeroed in on the target.

Without warning, the great silver wolf began to race down the street, lunging at the man from behind and knocking him to the ground. As the drunk man screamed and flailed helplessly against the superior strength of the animal, the wolf wrapped its fearsome jaws around his neck and hung on, biting two or three times for good measure until it cracked the man's spine and made blood spurt from the carotid artery. Finally, wearily, the man stopped fighting, went very still, and pulled the wolf down from the sheer force of his dead weight as he sank to the sidewalk, lifeless.

Licking its chops, the wolf prodded its victim with its front paw, found no response, and began to feast, ripping away the clothing to gorge on the soft flesh beneath. When it was done, it felt sated, even slightly ill from its indulgence.

A little bloated after its hurried meal, the animal stared at what was left of its victim and felt no remorse. Nature didn't care about losers.

With one victim dispatched, the fearsome predator proudly surveyed its work, turned, and trotted off in search of another, its appetite for blood whetted and almost insatiable tonight. It was so pleased with itself, it even paused to raise its head and let out a series of howls, alerting the world to take note of it, out and about in its territory, the newest Montfort werewolf on the prowl.

The next morning, as Julie Buchanan woke up, headed to the kitchen, and put a cup of water in the microwave, she heard the radio blaring the latest local news: "mayor announces layoffs", "fire in the Bronx"; "dead bodies savaged by animals in Brooklyn." The usual.

As the beep of the microwave announced that her water had boiled, Julie got out a box of Lapsang Souchong tea, measured a teaspoon of it, and placed it in a paper filter. As she dunked the tea in the mug, something told her to pay attention to the broadcast. That last item seemed odd.

At first she thought somebody had gotten chewed up in the Prospect Park Zoo. Maybe some jerk forced himself into a cage. It wasn't the first time. Years ago, some kid was actually eaten by a polar bear.

"Apparently the first victim, as of yet still unidentified, had been out drinking, was heading for the subway, and found himself overtaken by a pack of feral dogs. Sources from the community have alluded to a second victim, several blocks from where the first was discovered. Police have not yet confirmed this. Mothers are advised to keep small children close to home in the event there is a dog pack out there. In other news . . ."

Wild dog packs in Brooklyn? Well, New York had everything, but Julie found it a little far-fetched. Still, stranger things had happened.

The following day all the local papers carried the story of the animal attacks, with the *Times* enlisting the opinion of a zoologist with an advanced degree in all things canine.

According to the expert, this kind of attack was too vicious for the average dog to carry out alone, and would of course be consistent with the pack behavior of dogs driven wild by abuse, abandonment, or both. However, in his opinion, the kinds of wounds described by the authorities would point to exceptionally ferocious dogs such as pit bulls or Rottweilers, not your average pooch gone bad. From his experience with animal attacks, it appeared to be the work of a crazed carnivore, given the types of wounds inflicted on the victims.

BAD DOG NIGHT greeted the readers of the *Post*. Offering grisly details of the wounds, the reporter added a photo of grim-faced cops surveying the death scenes, the first near the bridge, the second a few blocks away.

"He was such a nice guy. He could never pass a stray dog without wanting to take it home," said one tearful friend of the deceased, a young stockbroker. "I can't see a mutt doing this to him."

The second victim was a young woman who worked for the Department of Social Services, whose friends described her as a cat person. "The dogs probably smelled the cats on her clothes and went after her," one woman speculated. "My dog hates them, too. Always gets upset when I come home from a cat lover's house. Makes them real wild, you know. That's probably what happened to her. And now I'm going to be stuck with her caseload."

The police alerted the neighborhood to be careful and announced they were also working with the animal control squad. At his weekly press conference, reporters repeatedly asked the mayor if he was going to assign more police to Brooklyn, and if they would be shooting strays on sight. "Yes, and no," said His Honor.

# Chapter Eleven

In the chic SoHo hotel where he was staying, Paul scanned the newspapers over breakfast, and he felt a chill as he read and reread the details of the attacks. In each case, the victims were out late at night following an evening of drinking with friends and were heading home alone. Somewhere on their path to the subway station, a pack of wild dogs overtook them and ravaged them. He didn't believe it for a minute.

Wild dogs were more likely to attack another animal than a human, especially if they had once been pets. Some inborn instinct made them wary of humans, unless they were in such a state of hunger that nothing could hold them back, but this was Manhattan. Any *toutou* with half a brain could find barrels of food scraps behind restaurants throughout the city. Just follow the rats.

He didn't believe the dog theory for one minute. No, this was a classic werewolf attack, with the victims struck from behind, thrown to the ground, and covered with bite marks around their necks, with bones broken and arteries severed.

It was the way they operated, all strong teeth and muscle, against which no human could hold his own. Two or three chomps on the throat and the victim expired, choking on his own blood. Then the werewolf would feast on his flesh, gorging itself until it was sick of the taste. The pattern hadn't changed in centuries.

Julie felt like a child waiting for Christmas. The book signing was Paul's moment, but she shared in it, too, since she had translated his work. Apart from her professional interest, she adored the man.

She hadn't worked on more than five translations in her career, but a few had been torture, with the authors bickering over choice of vocabulary, style, even font, for heaven's sake. Paul hadn't been like that at all.

The book interested Julie on a level that startled her. Professor Buchanan, a specialist in eighteenth-century European history, enjoyed learning about a subject that her rational side would never acknowledge. At the heart of this interest lay the family history—the family legend, one might say. To accept a belief in werewolves on face value took an immense leap of faith; Julie didn't know if she could quite manage that, but from what Paul's writing showed her, she wasn't so dismissive of them any longer. There *were* scary things that went bump in the night, and some of them had big teeth.

Paul, on the other hand, had a charming panache that made Julie think of heroes of 1940s films, resourceful and daring. All he needed was the trench coat, fedora, and Gauloise cigarette.

Julie smiled at the thought of Paul as the lead in, say, *Casablanca*. Yeah, he could have given Bogart a run for the money. And she wouldn't have gotten on that plane. Not for anything.

Just as Julie sat looking over a pile of undergraduate papers, thinking of Paul and his many attractions, the phone rang and she picked it up, expecting to hear someone from work.

"Julie, it's Paul. How are you? Am I interrupting something, or are you free to talk?"

"Hello," she said with delight. "I'm working on some extremely boring term papers, and I am definitely free to talk. It's nice to hear from you. How are the plans coming for the book signing?"

"Everything's in place. I stopped by the shop to sign a few copies beforehand, and all is ready. They have plenty of books on hand."

"Good. I hope we get quite a crowd."

"So do I," he said with a smile in his voice. "Especially one particular customer."

"Yes. I can't wait to get a good look at him," she admitted.

Paul paused and said casually, "Julie, I know it's a weekday tomorrow, but would you be free to go with me across the Hudson?"

She blinked. "You mean to New Jersey?"

"Yes."

"Sure. Where?"

She didn't know why, but the idea of going on a trip to New Jersey with Paul struck her as hilarious. Sure, she had grown up there, but she couldn't imagine why a sophisticated globe-trotter like Paul would care to visit. Not that the Garden State didn't have its charms, but what was there for a French werewolf hunter?

"Wait," Julie said with suspicion. "You don't want me to take you to the spots they use as backdrops for the *Sopranos*, do you?"

"Oh, no," he admitted. "I've seen those."

"Don't tell me you and Catherine located a werewolf in Hoboken."

"Nothing like that. It's much more mundane. I'd simply like to spend a pleasant afternoon in the sunshine with a pretty girl. I'll pick you up after your last class tomorrow and we'll cross the bridge, find an agreeable spot overlooking the Palisades, and have a picnic. Would you like that?"

Julie burst out laughing. "I'd love it," she replied. "What shall I bring?"

"Just yourself. Leave the rest to me. *D'accord?*"

*"D'accord,"* she answered. "Sounds lovely. I'll be waiting for you at one o'clock near the main gate."

"Wonderful. Until tomorrow."

"See you then."

When she hung up the phone, Julie grinned like a teenager. She wasn't kidding herself. There was something going on when Paul wanted to take her on a picnic in the middle of the week while he was in New York to plug his latest book. That had to mean he couldn't wait for the book signing. She hoped it meant he really wanted to keep her in his life. Julie smiled as she returned to her students' boring work. Things had just gotten a lot more exciting.

"How did you ever find this place?" Julie demanded as Paul's rented car crossed the George Washington Bridge and navigated a narrow road that took them to a delightful riverside area near a marina, just across the Hudson from Manhattan.

"Some friends brought me here a few years back. I've always loved it. You can relax and watch the river traffic go by and enjoy the best view of New York. I come here to unwind."

"It's nice you thought to bring me," she said with a smile.

"Well, I wanted to see you again and prepare you for the possibility of meeting one of the Montforts."

"All right. Any special instructions?"

Paul took a picnic basket from the backseat of the car and found a table nearby, where he spread out a respectable lunch of roast chicken, green salad, a crusty baguette, pears, and a really nice Brie, accompanied by a bottle of wine and another bottle of Perrier.

"This is wonderful," Julie exclaimed. "Where did you get it?"

"From a deli near my hotel. They have everything."

When they had consumed the meal, Paul and Julie took a walk along the river, enjoying the pleasures of a warm September afternoon and a spectacular view.

"We expect Pierre de Montfort to show up," he said. "My friend Ian made sure he knows about it. He sent him a postcard from my publisher."

"Will he do anything crazy?"

"I don't expect him to shape-shift in the middle of the store," he said with a smile. "But he's been provoked. He won't let that pass."

"Should we be afraid of him?"

"Yes," he said seriously, "but not at that moment. It's

important for you to encounter him and know what he looks like."

"So I can go in the opposite direction if I see him again?"

Paul gave her a slow smile. "Precisely," he said.

When Ian Morgan met with Paul and Catherine that evening, they discussed the alleged animal attacks. None of them believed animals had committed them.

They stood talking on the balcony of Ian's town house and surveyed the city lights, with the sounds of New York filtering up from below like a musical backdrop of horns and sirens.

"He's reverted to type," Ian said. "Or there's another werewolf out there. Maybe it's the first time he's done it, but he's killed two people, both fairly helpless. The young man was drunk and the woman was small. Not much of a challenge, but predators don't look for that. They want an easy kill."

"I would think that this one is fairly new to the werewolf life," Paul speculated. "Otherwise we would have heard about more of these killings. Remember, the Montfort is a late bloomer."

Ian shrugged. "Perhaps there were earlier killings that were passed off as dog attacks."

Paul shook his head. "No, these are sensational murders. The papers would certainly have devoted space to such deaths. If they haven't mentioned them before now, it's because they didn't occur. Or they didn't fit the pattern," he added.

"Then the newest Montfort werewolf has begun his

reign of terror in the city, and we will have to neutralize him and put an end to his career."

"And we have to make sure he doesn't kill again."

At that, Ian Morgan gave his friend a grim look. "That may be easier said than done," he said quietly.

Paul appeared to be preoccupied as he stared out into the night. "There's one other thing that bothers me," he said.

"What is that?" Ian asked as he glanced at Catherine.

Paul surprised him when he said quietly, "I am worried about Julie Buchanan's involvement in this. We're hunters; we know the risks. She is a civilian. All she's done is translate the book. If any harm came to her, I wouldn't be able to live with myself."

Ian nodded. "Don't worry," he assured Paul. "I have some resources. I will assign someone reputable to keep an eye on this young woman."

"Thank you," Paul said.

Catherine ventured a guess. "The Russian?"

"Yes. He's always happy to help out in an emergency," Ian said with a grim smile. "He hates werewolves. Remembers them from the motherland."

"Ah, yes. Our Slavic brethren have had their own troubles with the breed."

"But not as much trouble as the Montforts cause," Ian reminded him.

"With luck and skill, the present one will be the last of his line," said Catherine. She raised a glass of wine and clinked it against Paul's. "Death to the *loup-garou*."

"Amen," he said softly.

In the Beau Bijou, the day after the attacks, Pierre de Montfort appeared to be in top form, bantering with favorite customers, teasing them with hints of new creations especially for them, and telling all the over-forties how young they looked in his latest creation, a diamond-studded necklace of interlocking circles, representing timelessness. They loved it.

Reports came in from Palm Beach that trendsetters had made them *the* summer accessory for lunch on Worth Avenue or dinner at the oceanfront mansions on A1A. In the Hamptons, they wore them everywhere, with fashion-istas comparing the tiny telltale tags to make sure they were Pierre's and not some knockoffs. His assistant made him smile when she brought in a French magazine devoted to royalty and celebrities and pointed out three European princesses wearing Pierre's design at various summer weddings in Scandinavia.

"You're everywhere that counts," the girl gushed. "You'll go global soon."

*Yes,* he thought. *A Montfort boutique in every capital city from London to Tokyo. I'll be like Armani. Or Gucci. What a glorious idea.* He could picture himself with first ladies, countesses, starlets, all preening in his designs. From jewelry he could branch out into clothing, furs, and sportswear. *The sky's the limit.*

Pierre thought of the possibilities and smiled a beatific smile, the sort a man might if he had just been given his heart's desire.

"If we go overseas, I want to work in the Paris branch," his assistant, Keri said. "It'll give me a chance to use my French."

Instantly Pierre seemed to deflate. "You speak French?" he asked as if she had just told him she had a disgusting disease.

"Oh, yeah. Studied it for five years in school."

"How nice," he said, through clenched teeth. "Of course we could use you in Paris." He paused and said, "Do you read much in the language? Like novels, maybe?"

"Only fashion magazines and gossip. The important stuff."

"Ah, that's good," he said. "You can keep me posted."

# Chapter Twelve

Catherine was worried. Their visit and Paul's book had spooked the Montfort werewolf just as he was reaching maturity, and he had reacted as his ancestors would. She only hoped this would make him easier to confront and kill. Until then, the city was in danger.

That she would exterminate this evil creature was a given for Catherine; she had failed only once before, and that was because of some backstabbing behind the scenes in Geneva.

On the trail of a particularly vicious specimen, Catherine had confided in a colleague, who had decided to steal the glory for himself by taking on the werewolf alone. The move proved fatal for him and infuriating for Catherine, for the werewolf decamped shortly after killing its foolish pursuer and never returned to the scene.

That sad episode taught Catherine the value of secrecy, and except for Paul, whom she trusted with her very life, she never again revealed her plans to another member of the Institut.

She considered calling Julie to warn her of their

suspicions about the so-called dog attacks, and in fact had her hand on the telephone twice, but the memory of that betrayal made her refrain. If she truly believed the girl to be in danger, she would have arranged to have her removed from the area, but she saw no point in sharing information that might cause Julie to start talking about it with friends, relatives, or colleagues.

No. Paul had called up a friend who wrote for the *Observer* to share carefully planted tidbits with him in order to rattle the prospective werewolf, but that was business, a calculated bit of provocation designed to shake him up and goad him into doing something stupid, making himself vulnerable to his hunters. Office chitchat in the halls of James Miller College, on the other hand, was out of the question.

Catherine Marais never let friendship make her relax her guard.

Ian had entertained Catherine and Paul earlier in the evening, reviewed notes, flirted playfully with Catherine, and had to remind himself not to mix business with pleasure. Paul preferred to stay focused, and Ian was aware of that. He appreciated the talent and the dedication of the young Provençal, and he really had no desire to, as the Americans were so fond of saying, "push his buttons." Being a man of the eighteenth century, he simply found it difficult to ignore feminine charms.

Ian sometimes wondered if his fate to go on living endlessly wasn't a punishment for the sins of his youth. No, in his new incarnation as Ian Morgan, Count Jean de Montfort was capable of exercising more restraint. Still, he could sample the affection of a beautiful woman and take much pleasure in it, as he had done with a variety of ladies from the eighteenth century to the present.

Strange how fashion changed but female psychology never did. Whether his ladies wore crinolines, bustles, high waists, or low waists, they all wanted to be loved forever and would generally forgive his transgressions if he swore that he would do just that. Of course, having a personal fortune that increased from century to century proved useful as well, but it was the sincere words of love that produced the best results. That and really fine jewelry.

Oh, yes, he would love them forever; it was no lie. He would love them and outlast them, the women growing old and passing on while he remained the age he was when he first entered immortality, a handsome and healthy thirty-eight. Unjust, yes, but impossible to escape.

Ian had affection for Catherine; he might even say he loved her. He certainly loved her beautiful face, her lovely body, the way she managed to ignite his desire with a look or a caress. He wished he could persuade her to undergo the transformation to vampire and remain with him forever, but she had always refused. She was maddeningly independent, a trait that served to only excite him more.

In spite of a strong attraction for Catherine, Ian knew she had the possibility of a future with a human, and he really didn't want to interfere with that. At heart, he believed humans ought to mate with humans. A fling with his kind was a mere divertissement, a sort of promise that "what we do on the dark side remains on the dark side." It wasn't meant to see the light of day.

When all was said and done, Ian and Catherine were

separated by an abyss that could be crossed only with her willing consent, and despite their sexual connection, he doubted she would ever take that step.

Ian felt bound to respect that. He would have to be content with the emotional fireworks in his affair with Catherine, he thought with a smile. Just like back in the old days when one could do whatever one pleased as long as it was consensual.

For all her self-sufficiency, Catherine knew how to spark his passion and singe him with her own. It was what made him love her. She was *un grand amour*, not a passing fancy, and he wished she would give in and take that step into the unknown so that they would be together forever.

What he might do with lovely Julie Buchanan, however, bore no resemblance to the mores of the profligate vampire. She merited the greatest tenderness and care.

# Chapter Thirteen

"You were very restrained tonight, almost as if you were on your best behavior. Very commendable."

"You sound like my mother," Catherine replied as she sighed and stretched in her bed.

"Obviously your dear *maman* has exacting standards," Ian responded. "I would love to meet her someday. I wonder if she inherited the dry wit of your ancestors."

"*Maman* can be pretty ironic when it pleases her. Nothing much takes her by surprise, either, although I doubt I could explain *you* to her."

"Ah, the natural tendency of the uninitiated to dismiss creatures like myself. I understand completely."

"Thank you for being so nice to Paul," she said quickly. "He tries hard to understand you. . . ."

"But he distrusts me for being so fond of you—even though I consider him a friend. I feel the pain of separation when I must watch but not touch, *ma chère* Catherine. Really, it is such a torment."

Ian said that with just the merest hint of a sigh, but the

implication made Catherine feel as if she wanted to take him in her arms and caress him, hold him against her body all night long, and make passionate, blissful love until dawn.

"Yes, I feel it, too," Catherine murmured. "I much prefer a physical expression of my feelings."

"We can easily arrange that," Ian said cheerfully as he gazed down upon her supple form arranged so tantalizingly before him. "Would you like me in your arms all night long? Nothing would please me more."

Catherine turned her face to the pillow and smothered her naughty laughter. "Yes! Come to me right now," she commanded. "Exercise your *droit de seigneur* with me as if I were a nubile peasant girl, virginal and secretly delighted to let her feudal lord have his wicked way with her."

She turned to watch him undress. She had never wanted anyone more. Her whole body ached with desire for Ian, his strong arms, his beautifully muscled legs, his chest . . . and other, even more interesting parts that worked so superbly well and never seemed to tire.

Ian undressed casually, unembarrassed to have an audience. He knew the effect of his lean, well-muscled body on women; he'd had two hundred years of compliments, but never tired of seeing the expressions on their faces. It almost made the eternal separation from food worth it. Thirst, on the other hand, could be sated from many sources.

"Catherine," he said as she slid over to make a place for him in her bed, "you make my heart race each time I look at you."

"You have no idea of the effect you have on me," she

purred. "I love to watch you. I love the way you move, the way you never seem to be in a hurry. You take your pleasures with such delightful ease."

Ian reached over and turned off the light on the night table. "We have until dawn," he reminded her. "In over two hundred years I've never been able to watch a sunrise with someone I loved. You have no idea how hard it is to give up such things."

"Then, my darling, I'll try very hard to make you savor the pleasures of the night," Catherine whispered as she wrapped her•arms around him and kissed him passionately on the mouth, flicking her tongue in and out as they moved in a tangle of expensive sheets, entwined like snakes, embracing, touching, exploring, consumed by their desire to possess each other.

Catherine pressed her body against his as Ian brushed her neck with his fangs, the sensation hot and fiery on her skin. She gave a little gasp, torn between delight and frustration as he pushed her legs apart and pressed his hardness against her, teasing her.

He kissed her again, leaving a trail of kisses down her neck, down her breasts, taking a hard pink nipple in his mouth and sucking on it playfully as she moaned with pleasure.

Ian caressed Catherine's thighs, gently moving his hand between them, exploring the wetness, driving her mad with his rhythm.

"Now!" she whispered as he kissed her hair, her breasts, her face. Catherine arched her back and dug her fingers into Ian's back as she caught her breath.

"You're so demanding," he murmured. "You would make me your boy toy."

"Now is *not* the time to go modern on me," Catherine murmured as Ian entered her and left her breathless as she raised her hips to accommodate him, all of him. "Oh, God," she exclaimed as he thrust inside her. The hot, steady rhythm enslaved her senses, seared her, possessed her, brought her to a height she could never have imagined. She was on fire with lust.

When he knew he had satisfied her so thoroughly that she was incapable of even taking her fingers out of his hair, Ian looked down into her dark, sleepy eyes and smiled the smile of the eternal charmer that he was.

"Catherine," he whispered tenderly, "give me what I want so badly."

"Take anything, make me go out of my mind," she murmured, barely stirring. "I'm yours."

Ian nodded, smiling at her voluptuous state of exhaustion, her tangled hair splayed out over the soft pillow, her breasts overflowing the soft confines of the silky peach-colored nightgown, her legs wrapped around him in sweet possession of her lover.

"Turn your lovely head, *ma chère*, so that I may get a good taste of you," he commanded as he left a trail of kisses across her breasts and down to her belly, making her quiver with desire.

Catherine gave a soft, tremulous sigh and did as he asked, closing her eyes as Ian enveloped her in his strong arms and gently brushed her skin with his fangs. She shuddered with pleasure as he sank them into her neck, gently, delicately, as if he were trying intensely to give the maximum bliss while he extracted the dark red life-blood that sustained him.

"How do you do that?" she whispered convulsively as

she felt the shock that accompanied the act. "Oh my God, Ian, this gives me twenty orgasms all at once," Catherine breathed as she let the waves of astonishment wash over her limp body. "It's better than the sex! And that was fantastic."

She cried out as he delicately withdrew his fangs and kissed the spot from where he had fed, healing the little cuts with a brush of his tongue, sealing the skin once more and leaving no trace of the vampire's kiss.

As he lay quietly beside Catherine now, both of them exhausted by the lovemaking, Ian savored the essence of his lover's blood, still tasting it on his lips and in his memory. It was good blood, not surprising in a woman with such a noble lineage, he thought with a wan smile, but it had piquancy, a zest that very few women possessed nowadays, a rare vintage.

That word made Ian remember the days when he owned one of the finest vineyards in Touraine, long ago before the damned Revolution that destroyed his life, his family, his prospects for a happy future with Marie-Jeanne and their son.

As he turned his head to watch his drowsy lover, Ian gently kissed her cheek and bade her go to sleep. They were both exhausted; there was nothing left to achieve tonight. They had done it all.

When Catherine awakened the next morning, with Ian's scent still imprinted on her skin and traces of their lovemaking on the sheets, she smiled like a naughty child and glanced toward the window, where she could see the sun rising over Manhattan. Ian was long gone, back home in his town house and deep in the vampire's daily repose, hidden in some secret place where no one could disturb him.

And she was alone in her bed with a body that ached from their lovemaking and a terrible thirst for more.

# Chapter Fourteen

As Ian lay in the bed he used downstairs in the basement of his town house, secluded and secure for his daytime slumber, his mind returned to the pleasures of the night. How seductive that woman was, how greedy she was for his body, how she understood what he wanted most.

It was the taste of Catherine that kept him enthralled, the subtle essence that left him weak with desire and desperate to savor her. In his youth, Ian had sampled many a willing lover, but since his transformation into a vampire, the one outstanding attraction, the thing that took precedence over all other forms of beauty, remained the blood. If a woman was lovely but lacking in flavor, he refrained from touching her. If she had the right essence, she captivated him. Catherine had it all, beauty, brains, style, background, and blood that could make him risk a walk in the sunlight to sample it. He adored the woman.

Stirred with memories of Catherine, Ian's sleeping mind drifted to other things, other necessities. Julie Buchanan, for instance.

Julie had to be protected. This thought managed to

penetrate his sleep and even his lust for Catherine. If a vampire could be altruistic, Julie awakened that side of him. Ian had promised Paul to safeguard her, and he was about to do just that.

It was he who had entered her dreams, planting the desire to go to France and visiting her subconscious afterward. Ian viewed her as a fitting spouse for Paul, even though he never consciously met her. In the vampire world of dreams and shadows, he had already observed her without her ever being the wiser, just as he had once rescued her female relatives before her. Mysterious and faithful, he watched over the Buchanan women.

At eight that evening, Ian stood at his balcony, looking down on the lights of Manhattan. They swirled below him in ever-changing patterns, making an electric tapestry of color. This delighted him; he had enjoyed watching the picture transform itself over the years, from the gaslight haze of the nineteenth century to the advent of electricity, from the carriage lamps of the past to the constantly growing stream of light from automobiles too numerous to count. Progress. He had once driven a smart phaeton with a superb pair of black horses; now he drove a Porsche, a Mercedes, or a Lexus.

"Monsieur, your guest has arrived."

Vladimir entered the salon and bowed slightly to his employer. A dark-haired young man in a charcoal gray turtleneck and slacks followed, standing respectfully before the mysterious Ian Morgan, waiting for him to speak first.

"Welcome, Pavel," he said politely, extending his hand. "I'm glad you could join us this evening. Would you care for a drink? Perhaps vodka."

"Thank you, sir," he said.

"Sit down. Vladimir, please get the vodka for my guest. Would you enjoy a Stoli?"

"That would be excellent, sir," Pavel replied as he seated himself on an antique chair and waited for his host to explain the reason for his summons. It had to be important; otherwise Vladimir would never have requested his help.

A few minutes later, Pavel had a drink in hand and Ian got down to business.

"You have a certain reputation in the émigré and werecat communities," he said. "You enjoy the trust of many prominent people. In human and werecat circles," Ian added.

"I work discreetly," Pavel said. "I was well trained by the Russian Special Services."

"You earned a medal for your work in Chechnya. Undercover surveillance."

"Yes," he admitted without further elaboration. "That's what led to my work in surveillance here. I've also done jobs that involved safeguarding diplomats and people of means."

Pavel had indeed worked for the Special Forces, had grown disgusted with the carnage on both sides of the Chechen war, and had tendered his resignation after the infamous Moscow theater incident where Chechens took over a theater and held the audience captive while the Special Forces planned a daring rescue. The army bungled it so badly that more hostages died during their liberation than during their captivity surrounded by armed guerrillas. After that night, when he lost a beloved girlfriend at the theater, Pavel wanted no part of Special Ops.

He withdrew, spent six months in a monastery in Suzdal, then decided to immigrate to the United States and start a new life, encouraged by Vladimir, another werecat, a cousin of his mother.

The surveillance business became a natural extension of his talents. In his leisure time, Pavel enjoyed the music of Tchaikovsky and Scriabin, the novels of Tolstoy and Pasternak, and nights out in Brighton Beach among other Russian expats. He could consume vodka by the hour and keep a clear head, a useful skill for a man who had to keep a constant lookout for trouble.

Vladimir remained in the background, quietly observing the exchange. Pavel was a distant relative, and Vladimir was one who looked after his family.

"The person I would like you to guard is a young woman, a college professor named Julie Buchanan. She must not know she's being watched, but she must be protected."

"Is she being menaced by anyone in particular?" Pavel asked. "Has she received hate mail, threatening phone calls, obscene e-mails?"

"No. This is strictly preventive. She recently translated a book about the Montfort werewolf, and there is the possibility of an attack by a descendant. Nothing certain, but one doesn't want to take unnecessary risks, either."

Pavel nodded. Usually his clients were in more obvious and definite danger, but he wasn't one to discount prevention. If the client believed the lady to be at risk, Pavel would do all he could to safeguard her.

"The Montfort werewolf," he murmured. "That breed is legendary. There hasn't been a killing attributed to one of them in ages. Among our kind, we believe they had become extinct."

"Most people thought so. However, some of us are not convinced. Do you recall the recent killings in Brooklyn, where a young man and woman were supposed to have been savaged by a dog pack?"

Pavel raised dark eyebrows. "You think it was the work of a Montfort?"

Ian nodded. "It's a real possibility," he said.

Pavel thought about it. The Montfort werewolf was a creature of renown among the werefolk. They were infamous in France, of course, but also in lands known for their were-creatures—Russia, Hungary, and Romania, among others. Pavel had fought Chechen terrorists, Georgian Mafiosi, and a few werewolves in the Moscow suburbs, but to deal with a Montfort was to enter the big leagues. His green eyes nearly sparkled as he smiled with anticipation.

Some of the older werecats had muttered about a rogue operator on the loose in Manhattan, stirring up trouble for them all with its vicious attacks. None of them wanted the spotlight on any of their clans.

"When do I start?" he asked as Vladimir exchanged pleased glances with Ian. "I'll cut his heart out if I have to."

# Chapter Fifteen

"Pierre, are you there? Answer, if you are. It's Marianne."

Pierre heard the familiar voice on his answering machine and picked up. He sat in his office among pages of new jewelry designs, planning next season's offerings. This offered a pleasant distraction.

"Hello. What's doing at the auction house?"

"Oh, the usual," she replied. "It's not that. Did you read the latest copy of the *New York Observer*? Do you know anything about it?"

"No," he said. "What's in it? Something about me?"

Pierre intended that as a joke, but to his surprise, Marianne replied, "Yes. Well, sort of. It's beyond bizarre."

"What are you talking about? Nobody's come to interview me. Are they writing about the new designs?"

"Designs? No. They interviewed some Frenchman about a new book he's bringing out here, and according to him, the Montforts have a curse hanging over them. Some of them turn into werewolves. Can you believe it?"

Pierre's first reaction was to let out a howl and smash

the telephone, but he manfully restrained himself. "Oh, what a crock," he said with a dismissive laugh. "How can these people write this stuff? Did he encounter aliens, too?" *Shit,* he thought. *So now she's heard about it, too.* He felt the familiar prickling of hair on the back of his neck.

"No aliens, just werewolf lore. According to this Paul DuJardin, the Montforts were infamous for their ability to produce werewolves. They terrorized their part of France for generations. They were from Touraine, the area where your family lived. Are they some kind of cousins?"

"Oh, I doubt it. The Montforts I'm descended from had an unblemished record. They were warriors, royal counselors, diplomats. None of my ancestors ever went running around the countryside howling at the moon."

"Oh, yeah? Well, get ready for a shock. The Frenchman lists you as a member of the family in the United States."

Pierre felt as if someone had turned up the heat in the room and put a stranglehold on his throat. He tried to speak and only succeeded in making angry, croaking sounds.

"Sweetie, are you okay?" Marianne demanded, sounding concerned.

"Yes. Fine. Just lost my voice for a moment," he lied.

His heart pounded. His hormones went into overdrive. More of this werewolf crap. People would read this and start to make stupid comments. All the anger that surfaced when he received the postcard came flooding back. It teased his control, urging the hormones to let loose. Fuck!

"This might be good for business," Marianne opined.

"I'd like to know how," he said with forced calm. "Come to the Beau Bijou and meet the wolfman?"

"No," she said with a laugh. "But people are curious. You'll get your fifteen minutes of fame, maybe end up giving interviews on talk shows, and sell more jewelry. It can't be anything but helpful."

"Helpful? For people to think I'm some kind of weirdo? Yeah, that would do it. I've spent years building up the business as the place to go to for that special jewel for that special someone, and now I'm going to do a sideline as a circus freak. Great fucking reward for all my hard work," he said sarcastically.

"Don't be so negative. Have you ever watched those reality shows? Some of the oddest people end up as celebrities. The public likes weird."

"Well, I already have a reputation," he replied, "and it's for class and chic."

"Oh, for goodness sake, Pierre, lighten up. We have a reputation at Durand et Frères for class, too, but if we can make money on something *louche* that people want, we hold our noses and go for the money. It's called business."

"No, it's called libel," he replied.

"He didn't come right out and say you're a werewolf, so it's not. He's only citing historical cases. Besides," Marianne said with a laugh, "why are you getting so upset? Werewolves are only figments of the imagination. It's not like he said you robbed a bank or something real."

"He's trashing my family, and we don't deserve it. I'm proud of my ancestors; they helped write the history of France."

"And it sounds as if they took a bite out of it, too," Marianne said with an inane Groucho Marx tone of voice, which she seemed to find hilarious since she couldn't stop laughing like a loon at her own feeble joke.

Pierre felt wounded, as if the woman he loved had just betrayed him and gloated over it.

"I really can't appreciate your humor right now," he said coldly. "And I have to work on a design for a client, so I'll call you later. Okay?"

"Okay, wolfie," Marianne said, still snickering.

"Good-bye," he replied.

*Son of a bitch! This little shit writes a trashy exposé of the Montforts, comes to New York to pitch it, and gets himself into a magazine Marianne reads.*

*And she thinks it's a scream. Sure, she doesn't know the half of it. She's never seen me struggle to stop the transformation process, never seen me change into a wolf and roam Central Park, searching for prey. "Wolfie!"*

*She doesn't know who she's talking to,* he reflected. *If she did, she wouldn't dare make jokes, wouldn't dare to tease me. She'd walk on eggshells around her werewolf.*

Humans could be so stupid when they laugh at things they don't understand, Pierre thought. And this was Marianne, the woman he loved and wanted to marry. The woman he had chosen to bear his children.

As he stared at the design he had been working on when the phone rang, he could feel the hormones raging within. The wolf was calling. And he was furious enough to let him in.

The Russian Blue cat moved steadily across the lawn of James Miller College as if on a mission. Keeping to the grass, he made his way into the administrative building in the wake of a group of careless students who opened the door and failed to notice him until he was already inside and walking up the stairs toward the offices housing the history department. Once there, he appeared to know where he was going as he walked the corridors, glancing into open doorways until he found what he sought. Perfect.

Professor Julie Buchanan sat at her desk grading papers, absorbed in her work. Pavel noted her room number, the fact that it was actually a two-room suite, and he observed a second person sitting at another desk in the back room. This had to be Chuck Dailey, according to the official listing.

The werecat paused just briefly enough to take in what he needed to see, and kept going, relying on the human fondness for felines to prevent anyone from throwing him out. Later that night, when the building was deserted, he would slip back in human form, install high-tech surveillance cameras and recorders and ensure the subject's safety at work. He could then monitor her with an ingenious hand-held device no larger than an iPod.

To assure Professor Buchanan's security at home, Pavel's assistant had replicated this kind of installation inside and outside her apartment earlier in the day, soon after the professor had left for work. Posing as a ConEd worker, he had gained access to the premises and even managed to plant a device on the door frame. Pavel left nothing to chance.

# Chapter Sixteen

Preparing for his book signing, Paul had visited the manager of the Fifth Avenue store who had arranged the signing, chatted with the sales staff, had coffee with two pretty young women who insisted on having him autograph their copies, and thought endlessly about Julie Buchanan.

Frustration with Catherine's infatuation with the vampire occupied some space in his mind, but it receded now as he found himself thinking more and more about lovely, intelligent, charming Julie Buchanan. Julie was special. He hadn't found himself so taken with a woman since he was a university student. If she ever realized how she affected him . . . Oh, hell, she knew. She had to. What man with a busy schedule calls up to take a woman on a picnic in midweek? He grinned as he recalled it—pure pleasure. He would have been happy in the middle of a hurricane, alone with her.

Used to feminine wiles and a variety of strategies women—and were-creatures—employed, Paul thought he had seen it all. But the day he met Julie in that patch of sunlight at Marie-Jeanne's memorial in the gardens of the Château Montfort, he thought he had been put there by fate.

She wasn't just sexy, beautiful, and absolutely down to earth, but smart. The beauty had a brain, and no apparent complexes. *Mon dieu*, they all had complexes, issues, whatever you wanted to call them these days. He was tired of pretty girls with long, convoluted stories involving drugs, alcohol, and self-destructive tendencies. He didn't want a woman who represented the dark side; he had enough of that in his work. Julie was sunlight and rationality, with just a touch of the young Brigitte Bardot to keep a man on his toes. A hottie with brains.

Paul grinned. He wanted her. He also didn't want her to think he was some stereotypical Frenchman who planned to use her and forget her once he was back home. Hell, he wanted to take her back home *with* him. The only problem was he spent most of his time living in hotels on assignments all over the globe. He could hardly ask her to give up her job and go werewolf hunting with him and Catherine. He had to work something out if he wanted to have a future with this woman. That was why he was so concerned about her safety. And Paul didn't want her to feel pressured or used. He didn't want a fling; he wanted something long-term.

His life offered ample opportunities for adventure, travel, even public service—if one considered exterminating werewolves a public service, and most people probably would if they ever got to know a werewolf. But it was also a life of secrets, of hurried meetings in dark places, of warfare against an evil that had threatened mankind since earliest history—not the kind of thing you left at the office at five o'clock. It took its toll. It wasn't the kind of life most women would accept, waiting for your man to come back from the battle, not knowing if you were going to be a widow at any given moment. Soldiers' wives learned painfully how to deal with it. Paul admired their stoicism, their grit. Would Julie be able to cope with it? He passionately hoped so.

"Pierre, this is Marianne. If you're around, pick up the phone." She waited, listened attentively, then sighed and put the phone back in her Fendi bag.

This was really so annoying; here she was, the darling of Durand et Frères for the moment, the woman of the hour, and she can't get her own boyfriend on the phone so she can brag about her coup. What a letdown.

When Marianne finally gave up trying to get in touch with Pierre, Jim Perkins, an expert in eighteenth-century furniture who worked down the hall, stopped by to see if he might interest her in drinks after work.

He was a rising star, with socialites from Bal Harbor to Miami mentioning him by name when they wanted to unload eighteenth-century chairs or tables with Limoges inlays, rococo candelabra, or ormolu clocks. He had the power.

"Sure," said Marianne. "Is six thirty good?"

"Works for me."

"Well, I'll see you right here at six thirty, then."

"Great."

He actually looked pretty good, Marianne thought. Nice suit, nice tie, no visible tattoos. That was the one thing she disliked about Pierre—that tattoo that looked like a paw print. He claimed it was a birthmark, but it was so precise, she knew it was a tattoo. When he was young and drunk, he probably went out carousing with a bunch of guys who all decided to do something macho and get their hides worked on. So stupid. Fortunately Pierre's tattoo appeared only when he was naked, so it wasn't that bad. It decorated his upper thigh and remained undercover most of the time. Still, just knowing it was there irritated Marianne. It seemed so tacky.

Annoyed at the thought of Pierre being out of touch at precisely the moment she wanted to talk to him about her success with the sale she had just concluded, Marianne spitefully pulled her phone out of her bag and turned it off.

Let him wonder about her for a change.


Pierre waited impatiently for evening. When his young assistant finally wrapped things up, he wished her a polite "Good night," and left through the back door, where his Jaguar awaited him, tucked away behind the building in New York's best hidden parking spot.

.When Pierre eased out into traffic, he hit the button on his XM satellite radio and cruised to the beat of his favorite eighties bands, his inner wolf eagerly waiting for the release that followed a kill, anxious to be on the hunt.

Manhattan had Central Park and lots of joggers, even at night; Pierre considered a visit but knew he had to be careful following his foray into Brooklyn.

He needed someplace dark, deserted and out of the way, he decided as he turned up the volume. Then he headed for the docks along the Hudson River.

As soon as he pulled onto a desolate stretch of gravel, parked, and flicked off his lights, he saw what he wanted: a young couple seated on a makeshift bench, too en-

grossed in each other to pay more than casual attention to
him.

The wolf in him struggled to break free as he stared at
his prey. Pierre forced himself to hold back, to control the
change more skillfully than he had before, to master himself and his lupine nature. He had to be in charge, not the
wolf.

When he felt capable of dominance, he allowed the
wolf to arrive. Grunting, he struggled out of his clothes,
throwing his jacket and pants onto the passenger seat, and
opened the door as his limbs began to contort and grow
furry.

Barely making it out of the car before he fully transformed into a wolf, Pierre found himself on all fours on
the gravel, his form that of a large gray wolf. With all its
senses on fire, the wolf headed toward the couple, intent
on its kill.

Sounds of paws hitting gravel brought the humans out
of their romantic haze. The woman's voice rose in a
shocked yelp as her partner was struck from behind by
the beast and both were sent sprawling to the ground, his
screams of pain piercing the night as the animal's jaws
clamped mercilessly around his neck, his shoulder, his
arm. Soon the shrieks of pain ceased and the man lay still,
his mutilated body thrown on the ground like roadkill.

"Oh God, no!" sobbed the young woman. She rose unsteadily from where she had been flung by the attack and
stared in horror at her boyfriend's dead body, then into
the yellow eyes of the creature that had killed him. She
was doomed.

The wolf sized her up. She was smaller than the other
human and throwing off the rancid scent of terror. She

wasn't even a challenge to his skills. In an instant he was on her, knocking her to the ground, tearing at her throat, shaking her savagely as she tried feebly to defend herself. Within minutes she was dead, her throat torn open, her flesh a feast for the predator.

Raising his head to the starry sky, the wolf stood proudly over his victims, inhaling the scent of blood, then let loose a howl of triumph that floated above the dark river and into the sky over Manhattan. Let his enemies beware and hunters stay away. He was big. He was powerful. And he was now king of the night.

# Chapter Seventeen

On the afternoon of the book signing, Julie refreshed her makeup and had an animated conversation with Chuck Dailey, her office mate, who ribbed her unmercifully about the subject of Paul's work. He winked at her as she left and told her to watch out for the Big Bad Wolf. Wearing a simple black dress and exotic silver jewelry, she looked splendid as she headed out the door, bound for the bookstore.

"Yo, Professor, lookin' good," commented a student as he gave her the thumbs-up sign. "You got a date?"

"Sort of," Julie replied with a smile.

"Well, have fun."

She grinned. She didn't want to tell the kid her date was with a roomful of people who wanted to meet Paul DuJardin, specialist in the paranormal of the furry kind.

The subway arrived at the station on time, picked her up and dropped her off a block away from the bookstore, all without incident. She didn't notice a sleek Russian Blue cat with green eyes walking about a block behind her, casually keeping her in his sight, just one more anonymous detail on the sidewalks of New York.

Running a bit early, Julie stopped for a Mocha Mint Frappacino at the nearest Starbucks, leafed through the *Times*, and arrived at the bookstore just in time to see Catherine and Paul walk in, accompanied by a very good-looking, tall, dark-haired man.

This must be the friend Catherine had told her about; he seemed to be a good match for her, both of them striking brunets with a certain style about them. She smiled happily at the sight of Paul, and like an excited child, raised herself on her tiptoes to wave to him, focusing on him in the crowd of people.

"Julie!"

Smiling, Julie walked quickly toward Paul and greeted him and Catherine with a kiss. Then they introduced her to their friend.

Up close, he was a lot paler than most people at the tail end of summer, but it became him. He was tall and trim, elegant without being effeminate, and dressed in Ralph Lauren.

"Julie Buchanan," he said in a voice that could have melted the polar cap, "you have no idea how delighted I am to meet you. Paul and Catherine have told me so much about you. I'm Ian Morgan, by the way."

"I'm so happy to meet you," she replied with a smile that lit up her beautiful blue eyes. "Catherine said you were coming."

"I've known Paul and Catherine a while now. We go back a very long time."

"Years," said Catherine with a sly smile. "He's known scads of my relatives."

For a moment, Julie thought she was imagining it, but she saw a gleam in Ian Morgan's eye that had nothing to do with books. He was devouring her with his eyes in a way that was subtle but interested, a very gentlemanly expression on his face—a mixture of charm and bemusement—almost as if he were looking at someone he used to know from a long time ago, someone very dear to him. It startled her.

Catherine noticed it, too, and she slipped her arm through his as she motioned to the display of books arrayed on a table in the back of the room. "That's where Paul's going to be holding court," she said. "Shall we see how many books they have for starters?"

"By all means," he replied. "Let's hope they have a good supply."

Julie caught Paul's eye as Ian and Catherine turned to move to the table; she smiled. Both noticed Catherine's gesture of staking her claim to Ian.

*Somebody's in love,* she thought.

"Paul told me he met you at the Château Montfort," Ian said to Julie. "What do you think of the place?"

"Oh, it's magnificent," she replied. "It was such a thrill for me to see. My family has a weird connection to it, but it's a long story. . . ."

"Ah," he said. "For me it's the prettiest château in Touraine. I spent many happy days there at one time, a long time ago."

"Perhaps you'll have a chance to revisit it someday. It's one of those châteaux-relais where you can stay overnight. They even have a nice golf course," Julie added.

To her surprise she saw the merest flicker of a wince.

"They tore up several hectares of the vineyards to create the course," he said. "Dreadful waste."

"A Scottish game for wealthy American tourists," Paul said with a smile. "That's life in modern France."

Ian was about to make a comment, but stopped when two ladies nearly pushed him aside as they headed for Paul, clutching copies of his book.

Ready to greet his fans, Paul turned to the ladies and gave them some background on the Montforts while he signed copies and answered questions about his research.

Julie had the oddest feeling about Ian Morgan. In some part of her being, she felt she knew him. It was some trait, something indefinable and familiar that gave her the idea, as if they had met before and she couldn't remember where or when. Yet would any woman forget a man like this? Not very likely. He was so attractive, so charismatic, he compelled her as no one but Paul ever had. It was beyond bizarre.

More book buyers arrived and chatted with Paul, asking him to sign their copies. As customers impatiently lined up, a tall, athletic-looking man entered the bookstore, glanced around as if he were reconnoitering the enemy's position, stopped in his tracks, and then headed angrily for Paul, fury in his eyes.

Julie saw him and took a step back. Catherine stood her ground.

"Here comes our boy, locked and loaded," Paul muttered under his breath. "Get ready."

Julie watched the crowd part to allow the intruder. She knew that Paul and Catherine were hoping to draw the werewolf out tonight, but she honestly hadn't believed he truy existed, never mind that he might come to the signing, as the others had predicted.

"Are you Paul DuJardin?" the man demanded loudly.

"Guilty as charged," Paul said lightly.

"Well, I'm Pierre de Montfort, and I'm here to let you know I'm disgusted by your book."

"I'm so sorry, sir. How did I offend you?"

"Your book calls my family a pack of werewolves," Pierre said in a voice that carried across the room. "How would you like it if some hack slandered *your* family?"

After the first stunned silence, Julie noticed book buyers start to murmur, glancing at Pierre, then at Paul, pushing forward to get a better look at this person claiming to be a Montfort. She heard a man say, "This is incredible. That guy says he's a Montfort!" A woman reached for her cell phone to dial her sister, send her the Montfort's photo, and ask her if she wanted a copy of the book. She wanted the Montfort fellow to autograph it, too, right next to the author.

"You people are only encouraging this parasite if you buy this trash," Pierre said in exasperation, as he sent a pile of copies sprawling all over the table. "This is not the truth!"

Julie almost laughed as some young man in jeans and sneakers suggested that he wasn't a real Montfort, that this was some kind of publicity stunt, staged to sell books.

"Publicity stunt? Are you crazy?" Pierre demanded. "I'm telling you people to save your money, to boycott this crap. It's all a lie. The werewolf story is fiction, without a shred of evidence to back it up."

"If you really are a Montfort, you know it's true," said

Ian, looking him calmly in the eye. "There is actually quite a lot of evidence to substantiate it." He looked at Pierre without wavering, taking in his size, his anger, his frustration.

"It's all fiction, created to slander a noble family and cash in on stupid stories that have been around for centuries. These are fairy tales. This man does not tell the truth."

"Then why do people in the province still ask the local priest for a special blessing against werewolves and all things that go bump in the night?"

"Because they're a bunch of superstitious peasants," Pierre retorted, "and the church humors them."

"There is a lot of research being done these days," Paul said. "This is not fiction."

"Research? Some fool spreading stories about mythical creatures and calling it science? It's bullshit, pure and simple," he shouted in exasperation. "It belongs to the Dark Ages, not to the twenty-first century!"

Then he glanced around at the group surrounding Paul and said, "Are you all in this with him? Is this some kind of conspiracy?"

Julie felt a momentary chill, as if this angry man was suddenly dangerous and capable of anything. She drew closer to Paul.

"Now, I'm sure the gentleman's intention wasn't to slander your family," said a voice from behind Pierre de Montfort, a deep voice with a faintly Slavic accent. "It's simply an exciting story, no?"

Pierre turned to glare at the man.

"No need to get so exercised, my friend. It's all just a

fascinating read, for when you feel like having a good scary book to entertain you, nothing more."

Paul took advantage of Pierre's brief silence to chime in. "I'm sorry if I've caused any offense," he said quietly. "That was never my intention. But hearing the truth is sometimes painful to those involved in less than savory activities, and for that, I don't apologize."

"My ancestors were noblemen. There was nothing unsavory about them."

"Excuse me, sir. Do you mind if I get Mr. DuJardin's autograph?"

A large woman elbowed Pierre aside and sidled up to Paul, obviously unimpressed by Pierre's diatribe. Then, as an afterthought, she asked, "Would you mind signing the book, too?"

Julie nearly burst out laughing at the look on Montfort's face. He seemed beside himself. Not only was he not scaring anybody off, but the people wanted him to participate in this! Like he was an extra in some low-budget movie. Meet the Montfort. Get his picture. Step right up.

"Sign mine, too," somebody else said.

"Will you do mine?"

Half the people in line now wanted a double signing—Paul and the Montfort.

Pierre turned back to Paul and the line of customers waiting to have their books signed. He snarled and said, "You people are all deluded if you believe in these concoctions. It's not true. It's all crap."

"Whatever," said one young girl with multiple piercings, dressed in Goth black. "All I know is I liked his other books, so I'm buying this one. If you don't like it, go buy something else. Just get out of the way, will you?"

The crowd responded with a resounding "Yeah!"

Pierre turned around and flung at Paul, "You haven't heard the last of this from me."

Then he turned and headed out the door just before the police the manager had called could show up and escort him out of the store.

Julie watched his retreating back and she shuddered. She moved closer to Paul as he glanced at her.

"Welcome to our world," he said with a smile.

# Chapter Eighteen

Ian invited Catherine, Paul, and Julie to join him for dinner at his home after the signing, more to discuss Pierre de Montfort than for food. Julie was now deemed trustworthy enough to be part of the group.

"Aren't you afraid he might do something?" Julie asked.

"Like what?"

"Attack one of us."

"Well, yes. He could certainly do that," Paul said. "But I don't think he will just yet."

"Why?"

"For one thing, because so many people saw him there at the store. If he were going to hurt us, he'd wait for a bit, to let people forget."

"*Then* he'll attack us," Julie said glumly.

"Or we'll attack him," said Ian.

"Is he the latest Montfort werewolf?" Julie asked. "Can anybody prove it?"

"We have been keeping tabs on him," Catherine replied. "He's the one."

"You've all had experience with these things?" Julie asked in amazement.

"Yes," said Catherine. "Paul and I recently worked on a case in Alsace where we had to find an especially vicious werewolf. He doesn't bother anyone any longer."

"You mean you . . . ?"

"Solved the problem," Catherine said blandly. "The locals were quite pleased with the outcome."

"You really do this? Solve problems with werewolves?"

Julie could not believe this conversation. Sure, she had gone to France to study the Montfort werewolf legend, but to think that Catherine and Paul were real werewolf hunters was too much for her. They seemed so normal.

"You think, perhaps, that because the Montfort werewolves' most famous victim lived so long ago it makes them something out of the past?" Catherine continued. "No, unfortunately they exist to this day. The old ones die and are replaced by new ones. It will go on and on till somebody exterminates their line. Pierre is the last Montfort on the planet. If he were to be eliminated, the Montforts would die out and so would the evil gene."

"What if he has children?"

"So far we know he's single—a very eligible bachelor, according to our sources. He has a girlfriend but no offspring. We've checked out his past, too. No illegitimate children, either."

"Thank God for that," Paul added.

"Yes," said Catherine. "I've never had to, ah, eliminate a child. I wouldn't like to start."

Julie looked shocked. "You mean if you knew the child could turn into a werewolf, you might do that?"

The Frenchwoman gave a subtle shrug. "Who knows?" she replied. "If he already had the potential and showed signs of transforming, we would have to."

The stunned expression on Julie's face made Paul wince. "We've never done that," he explained. "This is merely a 'what if' kind of thing."

"Julie, these are the embodiment of evil," Ian said. "They present themselves as humans, live like humans, interact with humans, all the while stalking their victims and changing into wolves to hunt and kill them. You can't trust them. It's literally you or them."

"Can they prevent themselves from changing?" she asked. "What if they decide to live as humans and never make the transformation?"

"It's their nature," Catherine said. "It's bred into them, into their genes. When they're young they learn to control it, so that they can let the animal loose when they choose. Sometimes it's too strong for them and they find themselves turning before they want to."

"But they can develop enough self-discipline to stop, can't they?"

"Only a mature and very seasoned werewolf can really exercise total control over his lupine nature," Ian told her. "Like all other skills, this has to be learned and practiced."

"And they never want to eliminate the possibility of becoming a wolf," Paul said. "It's too deeply ingrained."

"So they live a lie, acting out a charade while those around them believe what they want them to believe, in some cases never knowing who they're dealing with until it's too late."

"What a pathetic life," Julie murmured. "Never telling the truth, never being an authentic human being . . ."

"Never being honest with those who care for you," Ian added, with a sad look in his eyes. "It takes its toll."

Catherine glanced at him with sympathy. She knew he wasn't speaking only of werewolves.

"Well," Paul said as he raised a glass, "let's drink to a successful hunt."

The group raised their glasses and nodded. "Death to the werewolf," they promised.

"Yes," said Ian. "And just how are we going to bring him down?"

"By making him so paranoid he'll change more frequently, giving us the opportunity to kill him. And we've already infuriated him at the signing. Let him stew over this. Meanwhile," Catherine added, "I'll ask a couple of operatives to try to get a DNA sample to make Professor von Hoffman happy. They can also add to his paranoia by showing him something that ought to make his heart race when he takes a look at it."

"Which is?"

"That's my secret," Catherine replied with a sly smile. "Something very old with lots of family history behind it. I can guarantee it will get a reaction from him."

"Will it make him go werewolf on them?" Julie asked nervously.

"No," she said. "But it will definitely shake him up."

"Good," said Ian. "That's what we want."

"How can I help?" Julie asked.

Catherine, Paul, and Ian looked at her, at one another, and they shook their heads.

"You stay out of this," Ian said firmly. "You're not involved. Don't put yourself at risk."

"But I am involved," she protested. "My family has been involved ever since that Montfort werewolf ate my great-great-aunt over two hundred years ago. For years opinion in the family has been divided over which Montfort actually did the job, but after reading Paul's book, I've come to believe it couldn't have been her husband. It must have been Raoul, the treacherous cousin."

"It was. He was a despicable creature, a cowardly little beast," Ian said firmly.

"You sound as though you knew him," she teased.

Ian Morgan gave her a slow, sly smile. "Paul's story brings the history to life," he said simply. "He's a marvelous writer."

She didn't notice the look Catherine slanted at Ian as he said that. Julie was looking proudly at Paul.

# Chapter Nineteen

Pierre was drumming his fingers impatiently when he finally got through to his girlfriend. He tightened his jaw when she told him she was at a bar having drinks with a colleague.

"Where were you yesterday?" Marianne asked as the waiter stopped by to ask if they wanted refills. She indicated she was fine. "I tried several times to reach you and you didn't answer your cell."

"Oh, I had to concentrate on something important," he said dismissively. "I turned it off for a while."

"Well, you missed the big news," she said acidly. "The Christine Bellerive auction I organized went two million over the expected total. It was a huge success."

"Congratulations. We'll have to celebrate."

"I did celebrate," she replied. "With Jim."

"Jim. Who the hell is that?"

"One of my friends from work. He invited me for drinks and since you couldn't be reached, I accepted."

On his end of the line, Pierre rolled his eyes. She was pissed off at him for something he didn't even know he did. That was female logic for you. So she went out with Jim Whoever-he-is. Pierre hoped he was gay or married or both. He didn't like to hear that somebody else asked her out. He liked it even less that Marianne had accepted.

"Well, this is obviously a very special coup for you, so we'll have to celebrate in proper style. What about dinner tomorrow? You pick the place. And," he added, trying to sound like the kind of man who respected his woman's achievements, "I'll create something to mark the event. Gold, silver, whatever you like."

Marianne didn't take long to reflect. "Gold," she said decisively. "A pendant."

"My pleasure," Pierre agreed, grateful he hadn't mentioned platinum. He had just designed a starburst pendant to try it out in his shop. He'd give it to Marianne and make her happy.

"For dinner let's go to that Italian place I always liked, the one on West Forty-eighth. Seven o'clock. Make reservations now."

"Fine," said Pierre. "Mario's at seven tomorrow night. Just you and me."

"Yes. And my present."

"Right.

After the latest killings, Pierre felt as if he radiated power. Nobody could challenge him. He had cojones. He roamed at will, tracking and killing as if he had done it all his life. He was the new master of the five boroughs, for heaven's sake. Who was this Jim person in comparison with him?

Looking into a mirror, Pierre exposed his teeth in a grimace, almost wishing he could see them grow before his eyes. These babies were made for chomping, chewing, tearing off chunks of flesh from poor, stupid, unwary humans. Could Jim make the same claim about his choppers?

Pierre didn't think so.

Shortly after lunch the next day, an attractive European couple took the subway to a station on Madison Avenue and spent half an hour scoping out the area before they rang the bell and were buzzed into the Beau Bijou by Keri, Pierre's assistant.

Pierre, in the back room, heard the sound, glanced up from a trade magazine to look at the video monitor on the wall, and smiled. He liked customers who looked like them—affluent and chic. The woman's expensive European clothing let him know she could afford to shop there.

"Hi, have you ever been here before?" Keri asked.

"No, this is my first time," said the woman, a well-coiffed blonde. "Somebody from home told me how beautiful your designs were, and I had to stop by and see for myself. Obviously she told the truth—didn't she, darling?" she said with a smile at her husband.

"Oh, what does she have?" asked Keri, warming to her new customer. "Something from last year's collection? Our little flowers?"

"Mmm, yes, it was definitely floral," the blonde said. "Very elegant."

"Those were really popular. All the twenty-year-olds had to have them."

"Does the designer create the jewelry here or does he have another place where he does the real work?" the man asked. "An artist I know in Munich has that arrangement."

"Oh, no, Pierre works in the back, except when special techniques are required. Mostly he works here."

The customer's eyes opened wide as she smiled at Keri. "Is he in today? Do you think he might come out to the showroom if I had a question about a commission?"

"Oh, yeah. Pierre's a cool guy like that. He likes to meet his clients, get feedback, find out what they like and don't like. He's always interested."

"That's wonderful. Then I'll actually be able to meet him and make my friend jealous," she said with a charming laugh as her husband gave Keri a smile.

"Well, just browse around, and I'll go call Pierre to come in and speak to you."

In the back, Pierre watched the clients and Keri on the screen. Now he was going to have to go out and schmooze them. He put down his magazine, got up, and met Keri just inside the door, but out of sight of the visitors.

"Does she look like she wants to buy?" he asked softly.

"Oh, yes. She loves your work. Come on out and talk to her."

With a glance at himself in the mirror he kept near the desk, Pierre walked into the showroom. He appraised the good-looking woman with blond hair, green eyes, and a certain something that only money can impart. The husband looked as if he could indulge her every whim.

"Hello, I'm Pierre de Montfort," he said graciously as he extended his hand. "Delighted to meet you. What can I help you with? I don't remember seeing you in the shop before. Are you from out of town?"

"Yes, way out of town. From Europe."

"Where in Europe?

The lady said, "From Berlin. My husband and I are here on vacation."

"Lovely city," Pierre noted.

"Yes. We like to travel," she said cheerfully. "It lets you meet so many interesting people."

*Including werewolves and others of indeterminate origin,* Pierre thought.

"We heard about your shop through friends, and since we were so taken with your designs, we decided to visit and ask if you still did special orders."

"Certainly," he assured them. "What is it you'd like to have?"

"Well, last year my husband and I visited the château country in France and came home in love with the art of the Renaissance."

"Ah, yes," said Pierre with a nod. "Beautiful workmanship in those places." He hoped the lady was looking for a necklace in sixteenth-century style with lots of gold and precious stones.

"Show the gentleman what you found, darling," said the husband with the look of a man who was used to humoring her.

The lady opened her bag and took out a piece of paper, which she spread on the counter. "This is a design I found in an old place in Touraine. Isn't it gorgeous? So exotic. It really doesn't even look French."

Expecting some sort of Renaissance piece, Pierre's face lost its pleasant expression as he leaned over to examine the sketch. In fact, he looked stunned. His hands began to tremble as he touched it.

"You're right. It isn't French. Where did you find it?"

he asked, looking bewildered, then suspicious. He couldn't believe what he was seeing. His heart raced as if the police were about to crash into the front door shouting, "Werewolf! Shoot to kill!" Where the hell had these people located this, of all things?

"Oh, in some old château. It was quite an attractive place that now takes in guests. I found this design on an arch, and there's something so appealing about it that I wanted to copy it. Do you think you could make me a pendant in gold with the same design?"

"Did anyone there tell you what it signifies?" he asked abruptly, glancing at the woman, then at the man.

"No," replied the blonde. "It was simply an escutcheon over a staircase. Is it something famous?" she inquired.

"No," Pierre replied with a shrug. "Not that I'm aware of. It's just a very old emblem, probably from a coat of arms, with non-European stylistic elements. Very unusual."

"Well, do you think you can transform it into a pendant, then?"

"Oh, yes," he said with a careful look at his customers. "But naturally, it will be expensive. I'll use eighteen-karat gold and precious stones. It will be one of a kind."

"But of course," the lady said with a delighted smile. "I knew this was a commission for an artist."

"It's difficult to put a price on it before I begin to assemble the materials," Pierre said, half wishing they would go away. This little surprise made him profoundly uneasy.

The husband smiled and said with the look of a man who loved to please his wife, "My darling wants this and

I want to make her happy." Pierre wondered what their limit might be.

"I'm going to estimate—and this is only a ballpark figure—about thirty thousand dollars." He glanced at the couple. "Is this acceptable?"

For a moment, the woman looked nonplussed. *Ah,* thought Pierre, *too much.*

"The thirty thousand I understand," she said, "but what does this expression 'ballpark figure' mean?"

He had to smile. "It means a rough estimate. It could be more. It could be less," he explained.

"Then please go ahead with the pendant," the husband said with a shrug. "It's fine."

"All right, then. I'll keep your sketch and begin to make preparations for the work."

"We're going to be in New York for only a few weeks at the most," the lady said. "How long do you think it will take to make?"

Pierre thought about the time frame and said thoughtfully, "If I begin almost immediately, I might be able to present it to you in ten days."

"Excellent," said the husband. "We'll give you a deposit now and call you in a week and a half to see if it's ready. Is that acceptable?"

"Perfect," Pierre replied with a smile he didn't feel. In fact it was the only time in his career that he felt both repelled and fascinated by a project. "It will be ready."

"Oh, and could I trouble you for a catalog to be sent to my home address?" the blonde asked.

"Of course. We have a Web site, too. You can place an order overseas by phone or Internet if you like. I have many European clients," he added. "We're international in scope."

The lady asked for a pen and wrote down an address in Berlin that was a drop box for the Institut. "I want to show it to some friends," she explained.

"Wonderful. Perhaps they can find something, too."

"I'm sure they will," she said with a smile and a handshake. "It ought to make their day."

When Pierre saw them out and returned to his back room to study the sketch, he sat staring at it for what seemed an eternity. Of all the motifs in the world, how did those two come to bring this to him, and right now when he was beginning to establish himself as the reigning werewolf in the territory, the last scion of the Montforts?

Just looking at it brought a frisson of emotion to Pierre, for before him on his worktable was a sketch from the coat of arms of the princess Sulame, a princess of Syria in the days of the Crusades, Countess de Montfort by marriage, the carrier of the werewolf gene that ran like a bloody thread through the fabric of his family.

This was an omen, he thought, although he wasn't sure if it was a harbinger of good or evil.

# Chapter Twenty

Pierre glanced at the photo of Marianne on his night table as he prepared to meet her at Mario's restaurant. He wondered if she would like his peace offering enough to forgive him for missing her damned phone call.

At dinner he listened attentively to the recap of Marianne's recent triumph with the Christine Bellerive auction because he himself had been a fan of the late actress. Marianne had arranged the auction and had established herself as a major player with its success.

His attention to the details of the auction placated Marianne. He showed her work the respect it deserved and that mollified her.

"Marianne," he swore, hand on heart, "the only reason I missed your call was forgetfulness. I was so wrapped up in what I was doing that I couldn't have any interruptions. I was in the zone and I was blocking out all distractions. Just a typical male thing."

After all that humility and breast-beating, Pierre then inquired about Jim.

"Oh," said Marianne, "he's a rising star at Durand et

Frères, the go-to guy for Chippendale or Sheraton. Rich
ladies up and down the East Coast and Texas want him to
show their antiques."

So he knew a Chippendale from a Sheraton, big deal.
Could he change shape and throw a scare into eight million people? No way. Could he hunt down and eat his
rival? Pierre didn't think so.

Pierre was a Montfort werewolf—cunning, merciless,
and vindictive to the Jims of this world. Nobody trifled
with them and came out on top. Nobody. Especially
where their women were concerned. Montforts were possessive, proud, and territorial, and Pierre was beginning
to feel that his territory now encompassed all of New
York.

What could some pathetic Jim do to counter that?

Marianne looked at him and smiled. "Jim is just a
friend from the office," she said as she linked her fingers
through his. "He's not in your league."

Pierre watched Marianne carefully as she sipped her
coffee. He liked the way the new pendant sparkled where
it rested over her heart. He could practically feel the beating of that heart as the blood coursed through her veins.

"There's one design I would like to give you above all
others," he said as he looked at her tenderly. "The most
beautiful engagement ring in the world."

"That's so wonderful, darling," Marianne said with a
smile. She paused before adding, "But I wonder if it's just
a little too soon. I'm having an exciting year, and I'm so
busy I don't even have the time to think about that right
now. There's no spot in my calendar for it."

Pierre couldn't believe his ears. She didn't have room
on her calendar to get engaged? Like getting engaged was

some kind of dentist's appointment? She was his mate, and werewolves were possessive of their mates. Didn't she want to be his after all these months? What was the matter with her?

"Marianne," he said with the hurt showing in his voice, "I thought we wanted this. Both of us."

"I do, Pierre. Just not so fast."

"You're sure there's no one else?" he asked with a grim expression.

"Pierre, you're my one and only," she said with a playful squeeze of his hand.

"You're sure?"

"Positive," she said. "I love you. I don't want anyone else."

"Me either."

When Pierre took Marianne home and made passionate love to her that night, he was sure of two things: that he loved her more than life, and that he had to get rid of Jim.

The wolf needed another meal. Soon.

"Julie, I hope we didn't frighten you when we told you about what we do. I know it's unusual."

Paul strolled down Fifth Avenue with her, past the Metropolitan Museum and along the borders of Central Park. He tried to read her expression as they walked, taking in the tourists, the trees that were just beginning to turn, and the folding tables covered with the wares of venders that lined the sidewalk.

"Well, I have to say that it was a shock when you told me about the work you and Catherine do. Even after all the time I spent on the translation, I didn't really think those, ah, creatures were running around today. I just couldn't take it in."

"And now do you believe me?"

She looked at him and nodded. "Yes, especially after reading about that last attack near the Hudson. I noticed the newspapers were talking about large carnivores like wolves or coyotes now. That's a step up from dogs."

"They didn't even try to pin the attacks on pit bulls," Paul said. "And they usually play up the pit bull menace whenever they can."

"Well, we had a coyote running around Central Park recently," Julie said. "So they know they're a possibility."

Paul smiled. "Yes, I read about that. Very odd."

"Pierre de Montfort seemed capable of violence," Julie said uneasily. "He's a scary guy. Imagine him in fur and big teeth. Not a pretty picture."

"If he ever crosses your path, even apparently by sheer accident, you must call me or Catherine. With them, nothing is an accident. But," Paul said with a smile, "I don't think he would do that. I'm the pest he hates for writing the book. If he has plans to attack anyone, it would be me. We have people watching him. Two of our operatives went to his shop yesterday and spoke with him."

"What did they think of him?"

"Pleasant enough. Prices were outrageous. He's charging them thirty thousand dollars to produce a pendant in gold and gems."

"Who is funding this, Paul? That's a lot of money."

"The Institut has funds for that kind of thing. Provocation can be expensive." He glanced at Julie and said quietly, "They paid him a visit to acquire his DNA and fill in the last blank before takedown. The methods are so advanced now they can get it from his touch."

"Maybe he'll be so agitated he'll eat the agents when they come back to pick up the finished product."

"We've thought of that, although I doubt he'd do it on his own premises in the middle of Madison Avenue. When they return, there will be a whole security operation in place."

"Guys from the Institut?"

"Yes. Our people will never allow them to be alone with Pierre, just in case he feels like making a snack of them."

"Good."

"Or they might arrange for pickup at a public place like a restaurant or a hotel lobby. It varies depending on the circumstances."

"You've done this before."

"Oh, yes. If you must deal with them, never allow yourself to face them alone. It's much too dangerous."

Julie slipped her arm through his, and she gave him a smile. "Well, let's hope we never have to. I took self-defense lessons when I was in college, but I don't think they'd work against a werewolf."

Paul kissed her lightly on the cheek. "A good revolver with silver bullets would, though."

# Chapter Twenty-one

Catherine's love affair with Ian was basically under the radar because of the Institut's policies, but one evening he surprised her with tickets to a performance of *Tosca* at the Met and she couldn't bear to refuse. As Ian himself pointed out, they might encounter the werewolf on the prowl, so therefore it was entirely a business matter.

Elegant in a fine gray wool crepe dress with diamond and pearl earrings and necklace, Catherine attracted many admiring glances as she and Ian made their way up the grand staircase. Before the performance they paused at the railing of the dress circle foyer and stood looking out over the crowd of patrons ascending the stairs.

"Do you like *Tosca*?" he asked. "It's always been a favorite of mine. I can still remember Caruso singing the part of Cavaradossi at the old Met around 1912. I was also fortunate to hear Callas in the lead back in the fifties."

They were chatting in French, and around them others conversed in German, Italian, Russian, and English, the opera being popular with an international audience.

Many Russians were there this evening, she noticed, the women seemingly all thin, young, blond, and dressed in the height of fashion.

"Yes. Tosca loves whom she loves and will do anything to protect him. I can relate to that," Catherine replied.

"So can I," Ian said with a nod. "I think that's why we're meant for each other. Indeed, I've always loved this opera."

"In a way Tosca reminds me of you. Very fiery. Very determined." He reached for her hand and held it tenderly. "It's amazing to think what this little hand can do," he said. "Just like Tosca."

"Darling, you are such a romantic," she said with a smile. "Only you would pay me such a compliment."

Later that evening, Catherine stood on the balcony of Ian's town house, arm in arm with her lover, the echo of Puccini's beautiful music fresh in their minds. On a more prosaic level, she was still waiting for word from Geneva that they'd received the DNA results. So far, nothing.

"Technically we can't eliminate him without proof," Catherine said with a shrug. "But those boys in the science lab are geniuses. I expect to be hearing from them anytime now."

Ian nodded. He'd already spent two centuries eliminating werewolf relatives, but this time he'd agreed to help Catherine and the Institut Scientifique. Not smart.

He had worked with them before on other cases, but this time he knew he should have resisted his lover's request. Once you worked with the Institut, you played by their rules. Ian hated these constraints. *Men make bad de-*

*cisions when the little head does the thinking,* he reflected. *Even vampires.*

He was quite willing to let Catherine eliminate the
werewolf; in fact, he looked upon this as his gift to her.
He just didn't like the Institut and its red tape.

"You seem very quiet tonight, *mon cher,*" Catherine
murmured as she wrapped her arms around him and
kissed him gently on the cheek.

"I'm just savoring the moment," he said simply. "You,
me, the city spread out below us."

Catherine knew Ian well enough to know when he
wasn't being truthful. "You're thinking you could have
already bagged the Montfort if I hadn't persuaded you to
join us on this one."

He smiled and pulled her into a warm embrace. "No
comment." Then he kissed her neck, just skimming his
fangs over the skin as he felt her shiver at the touch.

Catherine's arms held him fast as she kissed him hard
on the mouth, pressing against him as if she wanted to
merge with him right there, high above New York for anyone to see. Her pulse raced as Ian took hold of her as if
he never wanted to let her go.

"I could drink you like wine," he whispered as he
slipped his hand into the front of her dress and down into
her bra, seeking her tender breast.

"You have a wicked way with words," Catherine said
as she reacted and arched her back. "Are we mortals nothing more than liquid refreshment, then?"

"No, *ma chère,* not all of them. Not you," he murmured
as he kissed her, gently at first and then with growing passion, bringing her so close to him he could hear the beat-

ing of her heart, the source of all that intoxicating blood. "I want you so much, Catherine. You drive me mad."

She wrapped her arms around his neck and kissed him again, pressing closer and closer against him until they found themselves up against the railing.

Catherine pulled her mouth away from his and murmured, "Let's continue this someplace less dangerous." She didn't want passion to send her flying over the railing, several stories above the sidewalk. Vampires could float; humans would shatter on the pavement.

"My bedroom," he whispered as he scooped her into his arms and carried her there.

"Ian," she said tentatively as they sat down on the bed with its antique headboard and elaborate silk hangings, "you were quite taken with Julie Buchanan the other night. Is there something you would like to tell me?"

Ian stared at her in disbelief. Julie Buchanan? "She is a charming young woman," he said as he stood up and unbuttoned his shirt. He watched the feline expression in Catherine's eyes as she observed him. Women! Really, he still found them unfathomable at times. He wanted to make love to her, not talk about anyone else. Five minutes ago, they had been ready for sex on the balcony. How could the woman switch gears so fast?

"Yes, she certainly is. She seemed to like you very much, too."

"I should hope so. I always endeavor to make my guests feel at home."

Catherine's smile tightened. She stretched out on the fine comforter and watched as first the shirt and then the trousers disappeared.

"You seemed more than usually attentive to her," she persisted as he took off his socks.

Ian placed his clothing on a chair and turned to face Catherine in only his briefs. She sent him a smile that made him so hard it contracted his stomach muscles. After that, his briefs joined the rest of the clothing and Ian sank down onto the bed beside Catherine, wrapping her in his arms.

"Are you going to remain clothed?" he inquired as her hands caressed him all over, taking his breath away as she stroked him, explored him, teased him with her touch.

"Perhaps you could undress me," she whispered. "I'm so tired I don't seem to have the strength."

"Gladly."

"Julie doesn't know what you really are," Catherine whispered as he carefully removed her dress and tossed it onto a chair.

"I don't generally advertise," he admitted. "What a lovely bra. La Perla?"

"Yes."

He sent that to join the dress. "And I don't think you'll be needing these charming panties, either."

Ian pulled Catherine under the covers with him. When they were nestled into the soft cocoon, Ian kissed her possessively and pulled her close to him. "I have the only woman I want right here with me," he said in tones as silky as the bedding. "You, Catherine, are the only one."

"But you did enjoy Professor Buchanan's company," she said as she responded to him.

*"Ma chère,"* he said in exasperation, "it's because of the fine job she did on Paul's book. And the historical

connection. Her family shared in my tragic loss. I respect these things."

"Ah. No attraction to *her* then?"

"Nothing like this," he murmured as he kissed Catherine's breast and took her hard little nipple into his mouth, making her womb contract with the sensation.

With a gasp, Catherine forgot her quibble about Julie and abandoned herself to the pleasures of vampire love. By the time Ian had drawn blood and sent her senses spiraling out of control in the heat of lust, Julie Buchanan seemed like a very minor point indeed.

Much later, as they lay entwined in each other's arms, breathing normally again, Catherine nestled against her lover and asked softly if he was still awake. Ian grinned.

"Awake and ready for whatever you wish," he replied, kissing her breast and trailing more hot kisses down to her thigh.

"Information this time. Not sex."

"Really? How disappointing."

"I'm serious."

"All right. What kind of information?" He braced himself. Was she going to continue grilling him about Miss Buchanan? If only she knew how pointless her concern really was.

"We've been friends and lovers for some time now. But you never told me how you came to become what you are today."

Ian leaned back and sighed. It appeared that tonight his mistress was the one who was out for blood. "That goes back to the worst time of my life, Catherine. It's painful to recall."

"I'm sorry. I shouldn't have asked."

"No," he said. "It's a perfectly logical question."

Catherine snuggled closer to him and nestled her head on his chest as he caressed her hair. Ian smiled, touching her, enjoying her warmth and the scent of her perfume. This woman could get anything she wanted from him, he thought ruefully. He adored her.

"After my wife was killed, I was charged with the crime. My guilty cousin testified against me, forced others to say I had been seen as a large wolf and manufactured all sorts of crazy things that stirred up a wave of hatred against me."

"Nobody defended you?"

"My lawyer," Ian said grimly. "Unfortunately, he wasn't the best choice, since he was a rabid Republican, and with the revolution breaking out all across France, he didn't try too hard to defend an 'aristocratic werewolf.' It was a travesty."

"They put you in jail?"

"Of course. There was a wave of attacks on the aristocracy. People were rounded up and thrown into prison on the flimsiest pretext. By the way, one of your relatives, the Marquis de Villevert, had the good sense to escape to Spain by way of Bordeaux. The Reds were furious."

"Oh, yes. He settled there for a while until Bonaparte made life impossible about ten years later. Poor man. He had no luck."

"Life was a horror," Ian agreed. "But I still had a few friends who didn't believe the lies about me. One of them, a very intrepid lady, avoided prison by seducing a vain jackass who practically ran the local revolution. She managed to get him to transfer me to another prison, and on the way, I escaped. The guards swore I fell to my death into a raging river, and that was that. Good-bye aristo-cratic werewolf."

Catherine was now sitting up in bed, arms hugging her knees, watching Ian intently. He knew what she was thinking. If she had been alive in those days, she would have faced death or prison, too.

"On the run, I felt exhilarated. At that point, I thought my life would probably be short, but before I died, I wanted to see justice done for Marie-Jeanne. I returned to the château, made contact with a loyal servant, who pro-vided me with weapons and food, hid in the woods, and waited until Raoul shape-shifted. The night he did, I shot him with a silver bullet and left the body hanging from a tree by the side of the road. But by that time, he was pos-ing as a 'man of the people,' trying to avoid running afoul of the local Reds. He'd had a child by a peasant girl and passed on the damned gene."

Ian looked at his lover. Her beautiful face was grim.

"While I was on the run again, I sought shelter in an empty house. I assumed it had been abandoned by an aristocrat fleeing the Revolution. I didn't even realize anybody still lived there." He smiled wryly at the mem-ory. "Indeed, it was the home of a very ancient vampire. I told her what had happened to me and how I had killed my werewolf cousin. I didn't care any longer. My wife was dead. I didn't expect to survive, with the whole county in the throes of revolution and insane with blood-lust."

Catherine watched him intently, waiting for the rest.

"She listened patiently to my account of misfortune, then told me history moved in cycles, sometimes chaotic, sometimes calm. She made me understand that even though I was in the depths of despair, thinking that this terrible family curse would ruin lives for centuries without my being able to do anything to halt it, I was mistaken. If I were still around, I could avenge Marie-Jeanne's death by wiping out these werewolves each time they surfaced, no matter how long it took. And each one would be an offering to my lost love."

Ian looked up at Catherine from his pillow and gently reached for her hand. He seemed worn out, as if the telling of the tale had exhausted him.

"I listened to my hatred, my fury, my rage at losing my beautiful young wife, and I embraced this vampire vengeance. I swore I would make it my mission for eternity. If circumstances had been different . . ." His voice trailed off, and he tasted the bitterness of his choice, made in anger and desolation.

The silence in the room hung upon them like mist, both of them feeling it, neither one willing to speak. Finally, Ian gathered Catherine in his arms and kissed her tenderly on the forehead, pulling her close to him as she wrapped herself around him and let her tears fall on his chest.

There was nothing more to say.

# Chapter Twenty-two

Catherine had received an encoded message from Herr Doktor von Hoffman that demanded immediate attention. When she finally decoded it, she let out a little scream of delight. Their boy was not only a genuine werewolf, but an especially powerful specimen just coming into his own. He was the Montfort, the last one, a prime candidate for extinction. Then she stopped smiling and stared at the paper. Had Hoffman gone mad? He wanted her and Paul to try to capture the Montfort and bring him back to Geneva.

What did he think they were, big game hunters of the paranormal variety? When you got near a werewolf as powerful as this one, you didn't think about capturing it, you tried to kill it as soon as possible. If you hesitated, you'd be its latest victim.

"I would like to perform a series of experiments on this one," von Hoffman explained in the message. "For that we need him alive. The Institut will make arrangements for transport via a small airfield in New Jersey. I have dispatched additional operatives to assist you. This will be the most important thing ever to happen in our studies, so I know I can rely on you and Paul to be zealous in your work."

Paul responded to the news with stunned outrage.

"This time the old man's gone nuts. How the hell are we going to get a werewolf to fly back to Switzerland with us when he knows what's going to happen to him? It's a long flight. If we load him up with tranquilizers, we may kill him. Or if we misjudge the dosage, he may kill us. If he's in wolf form, he's dangerous, and if he's in human form and capable of transforming, he's doubly dangerous."

"Von Hoffman is out of his mind," Catherine said firmly. "I don't think he really understands what he's asking."

"I don't know about you, but I'm not ready to risk my freedom trying to capture and kidnap an American citizen who might eat me."

"No, it's crazy. We would need tremendous support to accomplish this mission."

"So we'll remind Herr Doktor von Hoffman of that fact," Paul said, "and the sooner the better." Then he glanced at Catherine. "What are you thinking? You look as if you might be considering a really bad idea."

She shrugged. "I don't think von Hoffman's idea will work. But if he could really get us some high-powered help, who knows? Maybe we could actually pull it off."

"No," he said firmly. "We could not. It would take too many helpers, too many levels, too much risk. I'm not going to jail for some werewolf."

She nodded. "Yes," she agreed. "You're right. Von Hoffman is old and doctrinaire. He's had his heart set on a capture since that other one escaped years ago. He's probably got his assistants standing by on twenty-four-hour alert."

"He'll have to settle for a corpse," Paul said. "We can use his assistance to ship Pierre's dead butt to Geneva, but that's the best we can do. I don't see a live capture as realistic."

"Umm. Probably true."

"Absolutely true," Paul corrected her.

Damn it, he thought. He hoped Catherine wasn't going to cave in to von Hoffman on this. They'd been through some dicey adventures, but kidnapping a live werewolf and shipping it out of the country was idiotic, not adventurous.

Pierre felt like a rock star after his kills and his growing success as a maturing werewolf. He now found it easier to take control and summon the beast or delay it. He had experienced the thrill of striking terror in his victims and seeing their pathetic attempts to escape him. So why the hell should he have to listen to Marianne yammer on about some cipher named Jim while they were together? Shit, he deserved more respect.

"I'm not jealous of this man," Pierre said testily as he and Marianne sat down to dinner in a favorite restaurant. "I understand he's your colleague. He has his work, and you have yours. It's just boring to hear about your workmates every time I see you. I don't talk about Keri," he said with an edge to his tone.

"Keri is a silly little girl who is remarkably uninteresting. My colleagues arrange for works of art to change hands."

"Keri graduated at the top her class at FIT. She's an artist with a good eye for color."

"That's nice," said Marianne through a stifled yawn.

"Jim is merely a broker. I am an artist," Pierre reminded her.

"So true, darling," Marianne agreed. "He is essentially a very good salesman."

Pierre felt mollified. "It's a nice evening," he said abruptly. "Why don't you come back to my place? Spend the night?"

Marianne smiled with regret. "No, I can't. I can stay here for only a little while. I have a big day tomorrow."

"Oh?" He paused. "What's going on?"

Marianne squeezed his hand. "Something exciting," she said with a smile. "Jim has arranged for me to meet one of his Hollywood clients who just happens to want to sell off some of his little knickknacks, including his Oscar."

"Who is it?" Pierre inquired. "Anybody I know?"

"I can't tell you right now. But he's very big. He's a living icon of the cinema."

"And out of cash?"

"No. He's gotten religion or something, and wants to spend his twilight years saving the planet to expiate years of spendthrift consumerism."

"Okay," he said. "Got the picture. But I still can't see why you think you have to get home early. It's not like you're gonna turn into a pumpkin if you don't make the curfew. Come on, Marianne."

Marianne looked into Pierre's eyes, saw his normal everyday lust and briefly spotted something else, some kind of erotic desire that lured her with a smoldering flicker of depravity that promised strange and novel sensations, so bizarre that she wondered where it came from.

Marianne's expression reverted to mild annoyance after this distraction. "You know," she said, "after we're married, I hope you don't carry on like this if I have to work late or go someplace with a colleague. I couldn't stand that."

"Sorry," he snapped. Then he softened his tone and said, "I don't mean to sound old-fashioned and possessive, but I love you so much I don't like to hear about you and other men. It's not that I don't trust you, darling. I just don't trust *them.* Men are dogs."

"They say some men are wolves," she teased.

Pierre's temper flared. "Can we stop this wolf crap? It's getting old."

"You're becoming obsessed," she said unkindly. "You can't even take a joke anymore."

"Oh, I can take a joke if it has some humor to it. This stuff is just plain stupid."

Dinner continued, and the strain of their argument lingered through the end of the meal.

When Pierre paid the bill and walked Marianne out to the sidewalk to hail a cab, he was filled with conflicting emotions. He loved her, but he sensed she was drawing away from him, and he burned with anger about her new fascination with this Jim.

When Marianne kissed him good-bye, he knew a wedge had been slipped between them. There was no heat, no passion in the embrace. It was time to deal with the intruder.

Pierre was sure that Jim was trying to seduce Marianne. Marianne might not see it, but a man knows when another man is sniffing around, especially when that man is a wolf with a sense of entitlement.

Marianne was his chosen mate. No furniture-loving, asshole was going to come between them. Not now, not ever. You try to put the moves on the alpha male's alpha female, and you better just roll over and play dead, because dead was what you were going to be.

On his way home, Pierre found himself fighting the impulse to let out the wolf.

*Not now,* he told himself. *When we do this, we do it right. Man, are we gonna do it right.*

The thought made him smile all the way back to his apartment.

Ian loved Catherine for her charm, her beauty, and her blood. He adored the taste of her, the feel of her, and the way she made love with abandon, always trying to outdo his expectations. She often surpassed them.

Despite all that, he couldn't get Julie out of his mind. One night, shortly after Catherine had received her message from von Hoffman, Ian read of an exhibit at James Miller College and decided to pay a visit. He called Julie, asked her if she was interested, and explained he wanted to see it.

"You like the art of Oceania?" she asked in surprise. "I had no idea."

"Yes. It's so different from what we are used to in Western art that it makes you rethink your ideas about form and meaning. Wonderful stuff."

"Well, I suppose it does, and perhaps I ought to take a look at it myself. We have several art exhibits going on right now. James Miller College has ties to museums around the world, as well as several very generous patrons."

"Impressive for a small institution," he said.

"Small isn't always bad," she replied with a smile.

Ian couldn't agree with her more. "Well, Professor, will you let me see the exhibit with you? Perhaps soon? What would be a good time for you?"

Julie was so rattled by the thought of playing hostess to this elegant man on her own turf that she was momentarily at a loss. "What about Thursday?" she asked, pulling a day out of the air.

"Thursday is wonderful," he declared. "I have business in the afternoon. May I meet you at your office in the evening? Say, seven o'clock?"

"That's fine. My last class ends at four, but I have papers to grade to keep me busy. I'll see you then." After they disconnected, Julie allowed herself to wonder what was going on.

She couldn't believe Ian wanted to come here. She also wondered if Catherine would be with him. Some part of her hoped so. She liked Catherine and didn't want her to think she had designs on Ian. Paul was enough for her.

When Ian arrived at the campus, he followed Julie's instructions and arrived without any trouble at the Administration Center, where she was waiting for him. He was pleased to see her, and Julie noticed that several of her students were eyeing him with approval.

"They've done a really professional job here," Ian said as he took in the rooms. "Nice placement of the objects."

"Yes. They always do good work. It's one of our best departments."

Julie handed him a program and began making the rounds of the exhibit, viewing a dazzling assortment of statues, beadwork, and everyday tools crafted by artists once considered primitive, now seen as sophisticated geniuses.

When they finished, Ian asked if she'd like to go for drinks or dinner. Having downed a sandwich earlier while she was working on her papers, Julie opted for drinks.

Sitting with Ian at a small table in a restaurant someplace in Little Italy half an hour later, Julie relaxed with a glass of Kir and smiled across the table at her companion, who was watching her with a charming smile.

"You're looking at me as if you think you know me from someplace," she said.

"In a way, I feel I do. You remind me of someone from a long time ago."

"I'm a modern woman," she said playfully.

"Yes, of course. But there is such a resemblance," he said quietly. "It's disarming."

"Was this person an old girlfriend?"

Ian nodded faintly. "She was very dear to me," he said. Then he seemed to shake himself out of a reverie as he asked abruptly, "You said once that your ancestor was killed by the Montfort werewolf, didn't you? That was the connection to your job as Paul's translator."

"Well, she wasn't a direct ancestor. She was a great-great-aunt. Her sister was my ancestor. Marie-Jeanne was the unfortunate lady who was killed, and her sister, Manon, and the rest of the family fled France during the Revolution and settled in England, where they established themselves and never went back. In the 1830s,

Manon's eldest son immigrated to the United States with his wife and started our branch of the family."

"So your ancestry is French and British."

"French and Scottish," she corrected him with a smile. "The Buchanans were Scots living in London."

"Ah."

"The Buchanans are proud of their Scots roots," she said. "In fact, it was while I was visiting Edinburgh years ago as a child that I decided I wanted to become a historian. I loved the romance of it, bringing to life the old stories and legends. . . ."

"I'll bet you saw *Braveheart* more than once," he teased.

"Twice in the movies and four times on TV," she admitted with a grin. "Loved it every time."

"History is a passion with me as well. It always has been."

"Did you study it in college?"

Ian hesitated. "Yes," he said. "I did take a few courses."

"Where?" she asked, interested.

"Oh, at a small college in Europe. My family lived there when I was younger."

"Then you've traveled a lot."

"Yes. A long time ago. I haven't been out of the United States in years now, though."

Julie reflected. She thought he had met Paul and Catherine over there. "Catherine said you knew quite a few of her relatives."

"Yes, from their visits to New York," he said smoothly.

Julie played with the wineglass as she looked into Ian's beautiful dark eyes. There was something there that drew her in, made her feel she was with a friend, even a protector.

"Paul and Catherine have an unusual vocation," he said. "It's demanding, it's dangerous. I try to give her my unflagging support. Paul needs that, too. He's a very brave man, but the work is lonely."

"I've gotten to know him over the past two years," Julie said. "And I've come to like him and respect him a lot."

Ian smiled. "I hope your friendship continues to grow. It would make Catherine and me very happy. For both of you."

Julie felt like a kid at a sit-down with her dad, talking about a serious boyfriend. Ian Morgan, the most elegant man in the room, was talking to her as if he were her father.

Maybe it was the sincerity of his tone, maybe it was the memory of her own late father, who would have liked Paul at first sight, but Julie felt some kind of bond with this man that had nothing to do with physical attraction. She felt at home with him, and she couldn't explain why.

# Chapter Twenty-three

As Pierre carefully crafted the pendant of Princess Sulame's coat of arms, he seemed to seethe with every movement. Sulame had bequeathed to him and all her marked descendants a breathtaking power. He was starting to feel more comfortable each time he used it.

Pierre had made a beautiful mold for the pendant, copying the design with painstaking attention. As he delineated the outline with tiny golden beads, he carefully placed small rubies and sapphires in channel-set rows on the shield. Above the shield was a phoenix in plumage, which represented the family's unending death and rebirth in foreign forms.

This pleased him. The more he thought of the unusual request, the more he felt it was a symbolic reminder of his roots, even a call to arms. Death to those who poached on the werewolf's territory, he thought grimly.

Sergeant Joe Brindisi of the NYPD had the assignment of finding the attacker or attackers of the young couple whose gruesome remains traumatized a stunned dog walker near the docks. It looked like murder, but it also seemed to him to be the work of something inhuman, a fact that worried the police as well as denizens of the dock area.

The man who had gone there with his pooch was in such a state he couldn't do anything but babble when he got on the phone to report the crime. It looked like a "nightmare in a butcher's shop," he had said. There were bodies with chunks of flesh thrown all over the place, and his dog got scared, too, and wouldn't go near the scene.

"So whaddya think, Joe?" asked Manny Rodriguez, a cop who had gone to the location with him. "Human or animal?"

"Animal," he replied. "And maybe a human directing the show."

"I dunno. Anything that could make such a mess of two people has got to be hard to control. I know I wouldn't stand around watching something that dangerous. It might decide to have another snack."

Joe agreed. "Wonder if whatever did this has a connection to those murders in Brooklyn. Two bodies chewed on by something with big teeth. Now we have two more."

"Aside from the reports about the coyote in Central Park, we haven't had any sightings of large animals. I read the newspapers. Scientists think the killers were big carnivores. Could another person be keeping a tiger in his apartment?"

"Like that guy in Harlem a few years ago?"

"Yeah."

"Hey, this is New York. Anything goes."

Sergeant Brindisi winced as he glanced at the sickening piles of flesh. How would a mortician even know where to begin with the reconstruction? He had never seen anything this bad in his whole career.

"We gotta find this thing," he stated quietly. "And we damn well better do it fast."

Paul DuJardin had accepted Catherine's affair with Ian, but when Julie told him Ian had called on her and visited the art exhibit, he was somewhat surprised.

"Do you think it was a bad idea?" she asked as she and Paul strolled along Fifth Avenue. "He was so nice."

"Ian is a world-class art collector," he said with a smile. "I guess he likes to see something new every now and then."

"He spoke very well of you," she said. "He admires you and Catherine."

"He's quite a guy. He can be a wonderful friend."

"He and Catherine make a beautiful couple."

Paul smiled as he nodded emphatically. "That they do."

Julie slipped her arm though Paul's and pressed him gently. "It's sort of strange," she admitted, "but when we were talking, he almost reminded me of my dad, even though he's not much older than I am."

At that, Paul grinned. "I don't think anybody's ever thought of Ian as paternal before. But it's a nice thing to say. And I have to admit, he does have a protective streak."

*If she only knew,* he thought. But even if Julie could accept the idea of werewolves on the prowl, the idea of a two-hundred-year-old vampire as an ancestor might make her run away. He didn't want that. Not now, not ever. Explaining Ian could wait a while.

A cool autumn breeze swept the sidewalk, surrounding them with the scent of roasting chestnuts. Lying abandoned on a park bench, a copy of the *Post* screamed the headline COUPLE CHEWED UP AT DOCKS.

Paul spotted it at the same time Julie did. He reached for it and held it up so they both could read it. The story appalled them.

A young couple, dating for only a few weeks, had gone to the docks to watch the city lights and enjoy each other's company when they were apparently overtaken by something carnivorous. Police reports stated they were badly mangled and identified only by the contents of the woman's handbag, which was untouched and contained her driver's license and other personal papers. Through that and dental records, they established the identity of the pair.

"This is horrible," Julie said in such a low tone it was nearly a whisper. "Do you think it's him?"

"Yes. Nothing else kills as ferociously as a werewolf."

"But he didn't look as though he could do that. I mean, he did look tough," she said, recalling Pierre de Montfort's glare that night at the bookstore, "but it's hard to picture a man turning into a beast."

"Geneva confirmed the DNA is lupine," Paul reminded her. "And this one is as dangerous as they get. The police are studying the crime scene and looking for any clues they can possibly find there." Paul paused and glanced at Julie. "I wonder how he arrived at the scene."

"If he did it as a wolf, he can't drive a car. He must have walked."

"But at what point did he change form?" Paul wondered. "And if he changed into a wolf near the docks, how did he get to the docks? Would he have taken a cab, with the chance that a cabbie would remember him? Would he drive himself to a place close by and walk into the area? We have to find this vehicle and take a good look at it," Paul said. "Soon."

"My dear," Ian said with a frown, "if you actually try to do what the old German asks, it will probably get you killed. You or Paul. Or both. It's not a wise choice."

"I'm not stupid. I will find a way to do this."

"You're an experienced hunter, that I'll give you, but you're letting pride get in the way of reason here, Catherine. They are pure evil, and they're impossible to control. It's kill or be killed when you deal with werewolves. There is no middle ground."

She sighed and turned her head briefly. She hated lectures. Men were too protective when it came to their women; it was a macho thing.

"It pains me to bring this up," Ian reminded her, "but you lost your own father to a werewolf years ago. And the Count du Vallon was a skilled tracker."

"Yes, he was," she replied coldly. "But he made a foolish mistake. I won't."

"Be careful of your pride. It will bring you down," Ian said sharply. "No one can foresee the circumstances of every hunt. Some small detail you've overlooked can be the source of your undoing."

She shook her head. "I won't go into this without a good plan, and good allies. If von Hoffman can get me the help I'll need to take him down and fly him out to Geneva, I can pull it off."

"And if not?"

Catherine said calmly, "Then I won't attempt it. I'm not suicidal."

Ian studied her expression. She appeared to be telling the truth. Good. At least she had some instinct for self-preservation.

"You may have competition from New York's finest," he said with satisfaction. "There's been another double murder, and the police are saying it appears to be the work of a large animal. Perhaps our werewolf is experiencing a craving for human flesh that won't let him rest."

"He's struggling with his hormones," Catherine said flatly. "All these years, New York hasn't had a single werewolf attack of record. Now Pierre arrives on the scene with a raging bloodlust. He's reaching his prime, can't control the urge, and runs around like a wild beast."

"Paul's book must have played a part," said Ian. "We provoked him more than we knew."

"There's more to it than that. It doesn't make sense to start devouring humans just when a book comes out calling attention to your family's lupine past. No, this is linked to his maturity cycle. He's grown up and he's having control issues. Something's gone wrong and the wolf is waging war against the human."

Catherine reflected on werewolves she'd killed before. All seemed disposed to attack when life dealt them a blow.

"Then we'd better try to grab him sooner than planned," Ian said. "He's too damned dangerous to be on the loose. If something is making him crazed, he's as unstable as mercury right now."

"I wonder how Pierre's love life is," Catherine mused.

Pierre de Montfort had done some fast research and found out where Jim lived—an apartment in Jersey City, a few blocks away from a bus stop. To get to that apartment, Jim walked past several old buildings that were slated to be torn down to make way for a new high-rise. Few people lived right around there, and if a man were to vanish into the alleyway between those condemned buildings, nobody would know until it was too late.

On a rainy autumn night, Pierre de Montfort drove his Jaguar to the Jersey side of the Hudson, found a parking spot two blocks from the condemned buildings on Jim's route home, and walked quickly to the place he had chosen for an ambush.

Settling into his position deep in the shadows, Pierre removed his clothing as he kept an eye on the street. When he had placed his clothes carefully on an overturned barrel halfway down the alley, he willed himself to change shape.

Straining from the pain of it, Pierre still maintained his vigil as his well-muscled human form underwent its transformation into a sleek, silver-furred wolf. Half an hour passed while Pierre waited anxiously for his prey, keeping an eye on the passersby, all of them more concerned about the rain than about the remote possibility of a werewolf lurking in the area. These were, for the most part, trendy yuppies who would have scoffed at the idea of a paranormal beast on their path. They walked quickly, heads down under umbrellas, fretting about the rain spoiling Ferragamo loafers, concerned only about reaching their destinations.

Pierre, now a majestic silver wolf, waited just out of sight, shivering a little in the damp cold. Finally he spotted his victim, alone and walking like a little munchkin under a Totes umbrella.

The wolf leaped from the shadows and knocked Jim to the ground, then dragged him by the neck into the darkened alley, where it hurled him against the nearest wall.

The munchkin was disoriented by the speed of the attack. He staggered, tried to find his assailant, then once his eyes adjusted to the dark, he screamed as he found himself facing a large, slavering wolf, its evil yellow eyes fixed on his throat.

Jim struggled to stand up as the terrifying wild beast snarled and advanced on him. "Oh my God!" he whispered in shock.

The wolf loped forward, then lunged at his prey, striking him in midchest and knocking him back to the ground. As its terrified victim tried desperately to grapple with it, straining to keep those wicked teeth at bay, the wolf clamped down on his throat, once, twice, severing arteries and sending blood spurting onto the damp brick walls.

The animal felt the prey go limp. It kept biting, almost in a frenzy, possessed by the desire for revenge. Satisfied he was no longer a threat, the large silver wolf ripped at his flesh, tearing through muscle and bone, ravaging the corpse until all that remained of the darling of Durand et Frères was a bleeding heap of flesh. *Sic transit gloria mundi.*

After taking a long time to control his jangled emotions, Pierre willed himself to assume his human form, then waited for the pain to come as his limbs twisted back into their normal shape, slowly but steadily. Exhausted by his exertions, Pierre dressed himself, took several deep breaths to clear his brain, made sure he still had his car keys in his pants pocket, and poked his head outside the alley to survey the street.

The rain continued to pound the sidewalk. Nobody scurried past the buildings now, as if they knew to avoid this place of death. Pierre had touched nothing on the way in. Now he avoided putting his hands on anything on the way out. With another long look outside at the street, he stepped out onto the sidewalk, walked briskly down the block, and headed for his parked car, two streets away.

For an instant as he unlocked his car, he froze in fear as he saw a police cruiser coming his way, but the cops passed right by, on patrol and searching for signs of trouble. Who had time to notice a lone, dripping civilian getting into his car? What could be more normal on a night like this?

He started the car and turned up the heat, chilled by the rain and his exertions. He was startled when the cruiser made a U-turn and came back toward him. The car pulled up alongside his Jaguar and the cop motioned for him to roll down the window. Sweating despite the chill, Pierre did as he was asked. He waited, heart pounding.

"Sir, just want you to know your right headlight is out. Better get it fixed. Nice set of wheels," he added with a grin.

"Oh. Thanks. Thanks for the tip," he said with a nod. "I'll take it in to be looked at."

"Okay. Drive safely."

"Right. Good night, Officer." He finally exhaled.

Driving back to New York, Pierre reveled in the thrill of a successful hunt. He had tracked his quarry, pulled him into his trap, and ambushed him, ending the ridiculous threat Jim posed to him and his mate. Let anyone try to take him down. . . .

# Chapter Twenty-four

The day after Jim died, Durand et Frères was awash with rumors. Jim Perkins, their golden boy, had gone missing, and the office was in an uproar. Guys like Jim didn't just cut out one day. They had appointments they kept, schedules they honored. People depended on them.

Everybody looked around nervously, lowered their voices, and whispered that something terrible must have happened for him not to call in. The guy never even took a sick day. Now he failed to show up for an important meeting and didn't call, and repeated phone calls to his place went unanswered. This was not normal.

Some worried souls suggested the man had gotten himself mugged and was lying unconscious in a hospital, waiting for a friend to find him. Others opined that some family emergency had called him home and he hadn't yet been able to get in touch with the office. It was all pure speculation, and the tension made the staff nervous.

Marianne confided her fears to Pierre at dinner, and he shrugged them off by saying they were all overreacting. Jim would probably show up with some excuse sooner or later. Anyway, he pointed out, she didn't need a mentor. She was a rising star all by herself, and it was time she realized it. That inflated her ego, but didn't quite squelch her fears. In fact, it made her angry because Pierre seemed so casually dismissive.

In spite of that, when he kissed her passionately and made love to her as if he were about to devour her, Marianne was so overwhelmed by the raw passion that she got carried away and matched his lusty performance.

The very next morning though, sober and a little sore, she called the police and filed a missing person's report.

At around the time Marianne was talking with the police, a drunk in Jersey City staggered into an alley to find a nice quiet spot for himself and his bottle of cheap wine. Within seconds, he could tell there was something odd about the place. There seemed to be chunks of slippery stuff on the ground beneath his feet and a strange odor in the air. Then he glanced down and saw what looked like a bloodied, shredded carcass. In a panic, he ran from the alley, and two cops found him blocks away, still shrieking and wailing about murder.

When they got him calm enough to lead them back to the corpse, they nearly threw up. It looked like the work of Jack the Ripper.

The following day, the *Post* announced the discovery of the body in a blaring headline: BEAST PUTS THE BITE ON JERSEY. It gave lurid details, interviews with the drunk, the cops, and even ordinary citizens on the street, who seemed to be thinking of buying guns in response to the attack. This time, however, the *Post* dropped the dog pack theory and began to speculate that a larger animal, or even a very disturbed human, had slaughtered the victim, who was as yet unidentified, pending notification of next of kin.

"First New York, now Jersey City," said one man. "What the hell is out there and why is it so hungry?"

Nobody could answer.

That evening Paul, Julie, and Catherine met with Ian for drinks at his place to discuss the newest development.

"This is creative," Paul said as he held up the *Post* so Ian could see the headline: BEAST PUTS THE BITE ON JERSEY.

"Nice touch." Ian smiled and reached for the paper. "Are they still insisting dogs are killing these people?"

"Some experts are saying the killings are the work of larger animals. Either way, the public is worried about wild dogs or large carnivores on the loose in the metro area. Nobody is mentioning the word 'wolf,' let alone 'werewolf.'"

"It would be too exotic," Ian said with a shrug. "Who would ever believe it, especially in Jersey City? No, this is another one of those staged killings. It's Pierre de Montfort. I'm certain of it."

"Or some other werewolf on the prowl."

"There's no other that we know of in the area, Paul. It has to be him."

"We have to get him before he kills anybody else. And if we have to scrap von Hoffman's plan in order to prevent more murders, we'll just have to take the heat."

Ian said, "I have a supply of silver bullets, and I have a weapons permit. I am ready."

"Pierre de Montfort knows he will be killed if caught. He has to be prepared for it, and that could be very dangerous. I also think the wolf is now trying to exert control over the man," Paul said significantly. "The balance of nature has shifted, and you know what that means. Major instability."

It frightened Julie that her friends thought these killings were the work of a werewolf, and the longer she knew Paul and Catherine, the more she worried about them.

As if he read her mind, Paul slipped his arm around her waist and gave her a hug. She smiled at him.

"Are you starting to regret working on my book?" he asked.

Julie laughed. "No, but I'm beginning to think I ought to stick to less flamboyant subjects from now on. Something that doesn't involve paranormal predators."

"We'll keep you safe," Ian promised. "I think it's fitting that you were the one Paul entrusted with the story, since it's part of your family's history. There's a poetic justice in that."

"Maybe," Julie admitted, "but I don't mind telling you, the idea of dealing with an honest-to-God werewolf terrifies me."

"You won't have to," Catherine assured her. "He's ours."

"Amen to that," said Ian.

There was something beside Julie's growing affection for Paul that delighted her. One day, a beautiful Russian Blue cat came up the stairs to her office at work and made himself right at home. He paid her a visit almost every day and somehow his presence comforted her amidst all the turmoil. She began to think of him as her own little guardian angel.

"I think our werewolf is in some kind of free fall," Catherine said to Ian the next evening in the bedroom of Ian's town house. "He's crazed. He's on a killing spree. This complicates everything for us."

"It may be time to tell von Hoffman his dream of capturing the wolf alive is going to have to give way to the reality that the Montfort is out of control and needs to be exterminated immediately," Ian replied.

"Do you have so little faith in my skill?"

Ian looked up at the ceiling. Starting an argument over this was not a good idea.

"I have faith in your skill as a hunter. You and Paul have done well. I simply think the old German is over-reaching himself with this plan. And unfortunately, it will affect you, whom I love dearly."

Catherine gave him a cool look. They laid curled up in his bed, looking out onto the balcony and the Manhattan skyline, which sparkled with a million lights in the downpour. A torrential rain pounded the French doors, creating a murky atmosphere inside.

"You say you love me, yet you seem quite interested in Paul's young translator," Catherine said bitterly as she propped herself up on an elbow and looked straight into his eyes. "Men who love one woman usually don't go courting another."

A heavy silence greeted that. Then to Catherine's extreme annoyance, she saw Ian grin sheepishly, as if he found the charge amusing but true.

"Ah, so you admit you fancy her. You went to her college to see her. Some things don't change, do they?" she said in exasperation as she sat up. "You always did have a wandering eye."

"Catherine," he said quietly, still smiling, "I admit I like Julie Buchanan. I even admit I have feelings for her that go beyond what you think I should have, but I swear to you, it's nothing that threatens my love for you."

"Of course," she said dismissively. "You're a male. You're entitled to a harem. It's nature's way of spreading the good DNA."

At that, Ian burst out laughing. "Have you been reading von Hoffman's work again? That sounds just like him."

"Don't make fun of me," she warned.

"Darling, I'm not. What I have for this young woman is the love of a great-grandfather for his charming great-granddaughter."

Catherine was so stunned, she stared in consternation. Had she had failed to hear him properly? Great-granddaughter?

"What do you mean? Julie is a Buchanan, not a Montfort. How could she be your great-granddaughter?"

"Ah," said Ian with a smile. "It seems I do have a few secrets after all, eh?"

"How? Julie is descended from Manon de LaVillette and her Scottish husband, Angus Buchanan. Manon was your wife's sister. How could Julie have Montfort blood?"

Ian replied, "When my cousin Raoul murdered Marie-Jeanne in his werewolf incarnation, I fled for my life. But Marie-Jeanne and I had a child, a baby boy. I had to do something to protect my son from Raoul, who would have killed him."

Catherine stared. "I didn't realize your child survived the Revolution. He disappeared from the records after birth. What did you do?" she demanded in fascination.

"I took a great risk and contacted Manon, who was about to escape the country with her parents. She screamed when she first saw me, and I struggled to make her understand that I didn't kill Marie-Jeanne. Finally she accepted the truth. I begged her to take my son, her nephew, with her, and raise him as her own, to protect her own flesh and blood from that monster who killed his mother."

"She took your son to England?"

"Yes. And when she married, she insisted that her husband adopt the child, which he did. So my son, Charles Henri de Montfort, became Charles Henry Buchanan, the ancestor of our little Julie."

"And you kept track of your descendants?"

"Of course. I have helped them throughout the years. And each time the eldest Buchanan daughter married, I sent her the traditional wedding present of an aristocratic bride, the *treizaine,* the thirteen gold coins."

Catherine stared at him. "When I first became friendly with Julie, Paul told me the eldest daughters in her family received those coins just before their weddings. And that her aunts had been rescued by men who appeared out of the blue. She had mentioned this to him."

"You see."

"She still doesn't know who you are?"

"Ah, Catherine," he said with a sigh, "how could I tell her?"

"Will you tell her now?"

Ian shook his head as he sat up and said, "I don't think so. How could she believe I am what I say I am? I was born in the middle of the eighteenth century, and I'm still alive today. Well, half alive," he said bitterly. "I live in the world of the undead. She'd think I'm a lunatic if I tell her this."

Catherine raised her elegant eyebrows. Yes, good point. The outlandishness of it would certainly prevent Ian from revealing his past, unless of course he ever felt Julie could handle it. Great-granddaughter. My God! No wonder he was so taken with her.

*Well, at least he won't be making love with charming Professor Buchanan,* Catherine thought with relief. She could scarcely begrudge him his paternal affection now.

"Ian, darling," Catherine said with a soft kiss as she wrapped her arms around his neck, "such a shame we weren't born in the same era."

"Yes," he murmured, as he playfully kissed her neck and brushed her delicately with his fangs. "But at least we're together in this one."

Catherine felt torn when she contemplated the act that would link her to Ian forever. She loved him with a fervor that surpassed anything she'd ever felt for a human male. Nothing in this world offered her the intensity of gratification except the capture and killing of a werewolf, and now, when she lay beside her lover in his bed, her head pillowed on his chest, Catherine found her joy in her work overshadowed by this other pleasure. Compared with what she had with Ian, dispatching a werewolf began to lose its appeal.

Almost against her will, Catherine realized she was tired of the hunt, a feeling she fought to keep at bay since it was her life's work, her source of satisfaction, her contribution to the betterment of mankind. One hour in Ian's bed could make her forget it all.

Catherine hated feeling dependent on anyone, and she recalled with bittersweet clarity that vampires were masters of manipulation, even when they pretended to be your friend. Or lover.

She had to shake herself free of this domination, she decided. She still had work to do.

# Chapter Twenty-five

Since Jim Perkins had been a man without known relatives, the police had resorted to contacting the workmate who called in a missing person's report. When the *Post* released the story, minus the name of the victim, the staff at Durand et Frères was the first in the city to know the identity.

"My God, I can't believe it. He's dead. Jim Perkins, who didn't have an enemy in the world, is dead and the police think he was chewed up by wild animals in Jersey City. It's insane!"

Marianne thrust the *Post*'s lurid headline at Pierre as they sat in her office at Durand et Frères. She had never looked so distressed, he noted with annoyance. He knew she had never gotten that worked up over him. He felt slighted.

"Aren't you being a little overwrought?" Pierre demanded. "I mean he was probably an okay guy, but you'd think it was Princess Di the way you're so hysterical over him."

"Jim Perkins was one of the nicest, kindest, most

considerate men I've ever met," Marianne snapped back at him. "He helped his colleagues, he worked at an animal shelter in his spare time, and he campaigned against subjecting rabbits to cosmetic testing."

"Oh, rabbits," Pierre said with a sneer, before he could help himself. *Little furballs,* he thought. They were nothing. You had to eat half a dozen before you felt like you'd had lunch.

"Yes. Rabbits," Marianne repeated.

Pierre flashed a gleaming white smile at Marianne and took her hand. "Let's get over all this wailing and gnashing of teeth, honey. We're young and healthy, and it's getting boring to hear all this hype over a guy who sold antique furniture."

Furious, Marianne snatched away her hand and stared at Pierre with shock in her eyes. "How can you be so callous? I'm in mourning over the loss of a good friend and colleague, and you tell me to get over it? Don't you have any compassion in you?"

Pierre rolled his eyes. "Come on, Marianne. I'm here and I'm worth ten of him. And you know it. He's bought the ranch. End of story. Get on with your life."

Nearly speechless for a moment, Marianne glared at him and said angrily, "You know what your problem is? You're so damned arrogant you don't know how repulsive you sound. I don't even know if I want to keep seeing you anymore. You have absolutely no heart."

At that, Pierre stood up and ran his fingers through his hair, a nervous trait. He paced for a few steps and turned to face Marianne, who was tight-lipped with anger. Pierre couldn't believe what he had just heard. Marianne thinking of rejecting *him*? Impossible.

"Now, I'm sorry I hurt your feelings," Pierre said. "I never worked with Jim, so I can't share your grief over his loss. And maybe I sounded a little hard-edged just before—"

"You sounded like an arrogant jackass," Marianne interrupted.

"All right. I'm sorry about that," he apologized through clenched teeth. "But I also think you're a little overwrought and that you need some rest. Go home early today. Maybe have a good cry. Then take something to calm you down and get a good night's sleep. Okay?"

Marianne shrugged in a noncommittal way. "Maybe I do need some rest," she said finally.

"Good. I'll take you home."

When Pierre dropped her off in front of her apartment building, Marianne barely glanced in his direction as she shut the door. "Good-bye," she said and walked off into the lobby without so much as a wave of her hand.

Pierre didn't take it as a good sign.

Paul heard the coded number of his contact in the NYPD and said, "Yes? Any news?"

"Not much so far, but an expert from the Bronx Zoo says it's definitely a wolf."

"That's a given," Paul replied. "What about tire tracks? Any hard evidence from the crime scene with the two kids at the docks?"

"Two sets. The vics arrived in a Honda with Goodyears. That was easy. We found tracks made by Michelins. Expensive tires need an expensive car."

"Find that car. It could be a rental, but most likely it's his own."

"We're on it. If we go there and tell him we're going to bring him in for questioning, we have to make it look good so he won't panic. He'll figure he'll make a call to his lawyer and post bail if it gets that far. No problem. But since it's off the record and unofficial, our boy just disappears."

"All right. We're working on something, too. We'll go with whatever gets him first. You know how to reach us."

"Right."

"And remember to carry the antibacterial injections with you. If he bites, it could be lethal."

"Will do."

Julie was busy correcting papers in her office at the college when the phone rang. She picked it up, said, "Hello," and waited for a response. What she got raised the hairs on the back of her neck. It was a strange panting sound, followed by laughter, then either a moan or the sound of an animal howling. The sound of a wolf.

Alarmed by Julie's visible reaction, the Russian Blue cat on her desk rose and stared at the her.

Slamming down the phone, Julie got up, paced back and forth, and looked stricken. Her office mate, Chuck Dailey, had gone down the corridor, so Julie found herself alone and looking at the receiver as if it were poisonous. As she stared at the black telephone, it rang again. Julie gave a little start and tentatively put out her hand as if to reach for it, then pulled back. If it was who she thought it was, why give him the satisfaction of answering and letting him hear how upset she was? He'd just get his kicks from that.

On the other hand, if she didn't answer, perhaps he

would think she was too scared. How dare he do this to her?

Convinced Pierre de Montfort had her in his sights and was toying with her, she reached for the phone and dialed the code to trace the last incoming call, then scribbled down the number she heard. Her next call was to Paul.

When she told him what just happened, he said, "Stay there. I'll be right over. Lock your door, and don't let any strangers into your office. You have a glass panel so you can see who's coming down the hall. Be aware. If anything looks suspicious, call one of those security guards who are all over the place."

"Like they can protect me against a *loup-garou*?"

"They have guns," he said. "You don't. It makes a difference."

When Julie hung up the phone, she opened her desk drawers and rummaged around for the set of brass knuckles a guard had taken off a kid and given to her as a souvenir. If that was the only weapon she had available, she might as well get it ready. The cat, she noticed, had placed himself beside the door, as if standing guard duty. Even he seemed on edge now.

She prayed Paul could reach her before the werewolf did.

Paul put down the receiver, grabbed a coat, checked to make sure he had his wallet with him, and raced out of his hotel room to hail a cab. The thought that Pierre de Montfort might target Julie next set off every warning bell possible. He had read the descriptions of the recent murders; moreover, he had seen the crime scenes of others firsthand, and it made his heart race to contemplate Julie suffering a similar fate.

The trip to the college took forever, but when he reached his destination, raced up the stairs to the administration building, and found Julie holed up in her office and clutching brass knuckles, he relaxed. She was safe. The sight of the cat surprised him but made him feel better. Catherine had told him of Ian's arrangement with the Russian.

Julie flung her arms around Paul's neck and hugged him. "I'm sorry I brought you all the way over here," she said apologetically. "Normally these things don't get to me, but there's nothing normal about any of this. That phone call was so creepy, it gave me the shivers. How does he even know about me?"

"I don't know why he should," Paul admitted. "He did see you the evening of the book signing, but he didn't realize who you were. For all he knew, you were a fan who had come to meet me, like anyone else. You were never introduced as my translator. Pierre has no connection to the college, does he?"

"No. He's not on the staff. But he might be the friend of somebody who is, and maybe that person told him your translator worked here. I'm just so creeped out by that howling. . . . My God, it was horrible, especially after what's been happening."

Paul felt Julie trembling as he held her. He didn't blame her. Nobody could fail to be rattled by the thought that they were on the werewolf's menu.

"Come, sit down," Paul said as he gently directed her to a chair. "Take a drink of water and tell me exactly what he said."

Julie unfastened the cap on a bottle of mineral water and took a mouthful. She swallowed and took another. Somehow it calmed her. Julie looked at Paul and said, "I picked up the phone and heard the sound of somebody panting. It took a second for me to realize what was going on. Then I heard laughter and the sound of howling, like he was trying to let me know who it was, and sending me a threat."

"Did it actually sound like a wolf?" he asked "Or just an imitation?"

"Well, it sounded like somebody doing a pretty *good* imitation."

"Did he speak to you?"

"No. Not really. I just heard panting at first, then laughter, then the wolf sounds."

Paul frowned. "Sounds more like a prank phone call. Maybe with all the talk of this mysterious creature killing people, he thought the wolf sounds would get a reaction from you. Actually," Paul said, "the creep might not even know you. It could very well be a random call, just to see if a woman answers."

"I have his number," Julie said. "We have a system that will give you the last number that called you."

"Well," Paul said with a nod, "let's ring him up."

"Yes," Julie said nervously. "Why not?"

As she watched, Paul reached for the telephone on her desk and dialed the number, a local one with a Manhattan area code. Julie leaned close to him and was shocked to hear the voice at the other end, one she heard every day. She couldn't believe it. The little bastard! He had used his cell phone to play games with her.

Taking the receiver out of Paul's hand, Julie practically

screamed, "Chuck Dailey, what the hell kind of half-wit joke was that supposed to be? You're not funny at all! I'm going to kill you!"

"You know him?" Paul asked in amazement.

"Know him? I work with him," she sputtered as she ran down the hall to corner her office mate and give him hell.

It was a joke, a stupid, dim-witted joke. Paul sank down into the nearest chair and exchanged glances with the cat, who seemed to be taking it all in.

He loved her. The thought of Julie in danger from the werewolf set his pulse racing and his adrenaline into overdrive. At that moment, he knew there was no sense in trying to be rational, to take things slowly, to wait for a time when things were calmer. Things were never going to be calm for very long, and he might be dead at any given moment.

When Julie returned, Paul didn't even let her finish her account of what she did to Chuck. He simply took her in his arms, kissed her as if he never wanted to let her go, and said, "Let me serve you the most romantic dinner in New York tonight. Come home with me. Or pick any restaurant you want. Right now I don't want to let you go."

"All right," said Julie, when she recovered. She entwined him in her arms again and said softly, "Room service at your hotel. And a Do Not Disturb sign on the door." She kissed him eagerly, making Paul want to take her right then and there. To his delight, she was as ready as he was.

That night, all Julie's doubts about Paul's intentions were put to rest. He loved her, he wanted her, and he made love so passionately that she knew she was the only woman in his heart. There might have been others in the past, but right now, she was his one and only.

Nestled in his arms, making plans for life beyond the Montfort werewolf, Julie realized how precarious their existence really was. There would always be another werewolf to hunt, more danger, and more adventure for him. It would never end.

"Do you think I might join the agency?" she asked as she lay in bed, propped up on an elbow as she caressed his hair with her free hand.

"Good God!" he exclaimed. "Never. Don't even contemplate such a thing."

"Just a thought," she said with a smile.

He responded by pulling her closer to him and covering her with kisses. "It's too ugly for you," he whispered. "I love you too much to want you hunting them. You have no idea how evil they are."

"Then when you are out in the field with a big werewolf in your sights, just remember who loves you and who thinks about you all the time. And come home to me," she said softly as she buried herself in his arms.

"I will," he promised.

Julie prayed it was a promise he could keep.

# Chapter Twenty-six

"Herr Doktor von Hoffman has given me the details of the extraction," Catherine informed Paul at a breakfast meeting the next day. "Everything will be in place in a few days, and then we can finally act. I'm tired of waiting for Montfort's next attack."

"Von Hoffman is crazy to think we can pull this off," he replied. "The more I think of it, the worse it sounds. Pierre de Montfort will never come quietly. He'll resist to the death. It's a suicide mission."

"Paul," she said reproachfully, "I've never heard you sound so negative before. This is not like you."

"Perhaps I'm becoming more rational," he said bitterly.

"Or perhaps you're becoming too involved with Professor Buchanan, and it's making you cautious."

He smiled sheepishly. "She means so much to me. I knew it all along, but last night, I suddenly realized . . ."

"Paul," Catherine said with a smile and a raised eyebrow, "how interesting."

"It's not what you're thinking."

"Oh? And exactly what happened last night that made you discover your feelings for her?"

Paul shook his head and laughed. "It was actually quite comical. She received a phone call at work that was from some idiot playing games, making breathing sounds and howling like a wolf. It rattled her, she called me, and I rushed over there ready to be her hero. When I saw her in her office, safe and waiting for me, I can't explain it, but everything changed in that moment."

"And how did you discover the hoax?"

"Julie got his number from caller ID, and I called back. She recognized his voice when he spoke to me, and she gave him such a tongue-lashing, I'm afraid he'll never play a joke on anyone again. It was quite amusing. However, it could have turned out quite differently had it been Pierre."

Catherine nodded. "Yes, of course."

She glanced at him with just a trace of nostalgia. How many times had he come running when she called for help, ready to face unspeakable evil to assist her? Paul was a man you could trust with your life. That was what had always endeared him to her. And now he found another woman who brought out the knightly instinct in him. Catherine was pleased.

Did Paul know who Julie really was? Had Ian somehow had a hand in this? she wondered. Vampires were such clever intriguers. Well, she wasn't going to be the one who told them. Let the Count de Montfort explain in his own good time.

"We have to stop Pierre before he strikes again," Catherine said.

"When are Maryse and her husband going back to pick up the jewel Pierre is creating for them?"

"At the end of the week. They'll ask him to bring it to their hotel, where they'll meet him in the bar. Our people will be waiting there. Someone will slip a drug into his drink, then carry him out when he becomes unconscious. A van will be waiting to pick us up, and we'll rendezvous with a helicopter, which will carry you, me, and Pierre to the private airstrip in New Jersey, where we board the plane for Geneva. Von Hoffman has arranged for our transport and will see to our security."

"I'd feel better if we had our usual team backing us up."

"He assured me that his US operatives are as reliable as our European team. You know his standards, Paul. We're in good hands."

Paul gave Catherine a smile. "Well, we've trusted him before. We'll have to trust him now. This specimen is pure evil. I can't wait to see the end of him. And I think von Hoffman is taking too much of a chance trying to capture him for study. Just kill him and run the tests on the corpse. You'll probably get just as much information."

Catherine shook her head. "No. All we'll get from a corpse is data. If we can get Pierre to talk, we can learn so much more: how they manage the change, how they discover their ability in the first place, how the lessons are passed through the generations or not. It would be a scientific breakthrough. Von Hoffman will consider it the crowning achievement of his career."

"And ours?"

"It will be our greatest accomplishment," said Catherine. "If we can do this, we'll revise the science of our profession and uncover secrets that have been hidden for centuries. I'm proud to take part in this."

Paul nodded. He knew he might be making history with this capture. Von Hoffman would be ecstatic. The Institut would achieve unsurpassed glory. He and Catherine would become legends in their field.

But Paul now had other things on his mind that troubled his concentration, a dangerous lack of focus right now. It made him vulnerable.

Ian Morgan also doubted the wisdom of the new strategy. It placed Catherine and Paul at risk in a way that maximized the potential for trouble. He could see nothing but disaster ahead, and he didn't hide his uneasiness.

"Paul and I are experienced hunters," Catherine said as she and Ian sat in the living room of his town house, overlooking the lights of Manhattan. "This is different, but I believe it's possible."

"Nobody has ever taken one of these beasts alive. It's him or you. And for many hunters, it's their last pursuit."

"I have survived many encounters with these creatures. I'm still here. I will be here after Pierre de Montfort is lying on a lab table in Geneva, being probed by Karl von Hoffman and his assistants."

"And how can you be certain Pierre won't escape from von Hoffman?"

"The old man won't take unnecessary risks with his trophy werewolf. He'll have enough manpower to contain him."

"Nonsense." Ian made a dismissive gesture and looked out at Manhattan's nighttime panorama. "A mature and calculating werewolf could easily overcome most restraints. And the Montforts are an especially dangerous lot. There is only one thing to do with them: Kill them before they can kill you. Otherwise you're lost." He looked Catherine in the eye and said, "I swear these beasts gather strength from generation to generation. Pierre is the end product of centuries of mutations and the repository of aeons of degeneracy, something that began when the world was young and will not end until he dies."

Catherine reached out and caressed her lover's face. "Ian," she said softly, "I know you love me and worry about me. It gives me strength and enables me to keep going, but it also makes me careful. I will not risk losing you because of a werewolf."

"My dearest Catherine," Ian said tenderly as he took her in his arms and gently kissed her neck. "This werewolf may not give you the chance to choose your fate. That is what worries me."

She murmured endearments as he gently brushed her neck with his fangs. She shivered as he caressed her breast, then moved his hand down along her thigh.

"If the werewolf ever gains the upper hand," she whispered, "then do what you can to help me. Use your powers, be my guardian angel, my knight in shining armor."

"My darling," he said with a growl in his voice, "do you ever think for a moment that I wouldn't?"

Then Ian decided to move the discussion to a more comfortable place, picked Catherine up, and carried her into his bedroom.

# Chapter Twenty-seven

Julie found herself getting pulled into the world of were-wolf trackers almost by default. Odd as it seemed, it was the life Paul and Catherine lived, and she loved Paul so much by now that she didn't care if he spent his working life pursuing things that were better left unnamed. She just wanted him to come back to her safe and sound.

One evening shortly before the planned takedown, Julie invited him over for dinner, a risky adventure because her cooking skills were a little underdeveloped. She got a recipe for chicken with rosemary, bought some pricey veggies at a gourmet deli, picked up really good bread and a dessert that cost more than the dinner. The wine came from one of New York's best wine merchants.

She needn't have bothered. Paul arrived with gorgeous peach-colored roses and he took her breath away. His kiss made her stomach dance and she instantly forgot about her nervousness and wanting to impress him. How could one man make her feel jittery and safe at the same time?

After their meal, they sat together holding hands and talking on Julie's sofa.

"You have a lovely home. It feels very warm and welcoming," he said. "You have surrounded yourself with the things that make you happy. I miss that. I've been living out of suitcases for too long. Unfortunately I hardly ever get back to the house in Vence that belonged to my grandmother. It sits way up on the Grande Corniche and offers a lovely view. That is the only place I can really call home. And I really miss it."

"Who takes care of it?" Julie asked.

"A very charming old lady who used to be my nanny. She needed a sunny place to live since the cold bothers her, and she runs the house for me in my absence. It's part of my family's past, so I would never sell it. But I wish I could live there more often."

"Do you think you will someday?"

"I hope so. It's where I wrote the books, you know. In the same kitchen where I used to sit with my *grand-mère* when I was a child and listen to her tell me stories of the old days."

"Grandmas always have the best stories," Julie said with a smile as she and Paul looked into each other's eyes and saw the promise of a future.

"My *grand-mère*'s stories were a little different from other people's," he said. "In our family there have been many hunters of the *loup-garou*."

They drank wine while Paul shared his family's secrets and stories. He was a natural storyteller with a seductive accent, an arousing combination.

Rain had begun splashing against the windows, and as Paul finished his story, Julie surprised herself by inviting him to stay until the storm passed.

"I'm afraid I might not leave if I stayed here," he said

honestly as he moved closer to her on the sofa and kissed her.

"That doesn't sound like a bad idea," she murmured.

Paul smiled and drew her toward him, and Julie felt as if she might melt with desire. When they kissed, she felt a shiver of anticipation as his tongue flicked over her lips and his strong arms pulled her closer and closer. They were in the bedroom before either one of them knew what happened and lying naked under the comforter in a passionate embrace.

"Don't take chances with the Montfort," Julie murmured after they made love. "I want you alive and well."

He playfully kissed her hand as she cuddled next to him. "So you can have your wicked way with me?"

"Of course."

"Then I'll be extremely careful," he said with a smile. "It's the Montfort who should watch out for me."

Catherine had spoken with Maryse and her husband, André, to set up a meeting with Pierre in the bar of a boutique hotel in SoHo, a place the Institut could control with the help of its owner, a man who owed von Hoffman for services rendered, and who remained a loyal supporter. Filling the bar with their operatives, they could overpower Pierre with a strong tranquilizer and bundle him into a waiting vehicle without a problem, the first step on his trip to Geneva.

When Maryse called Pierre at the Beau Bijou to set up the meeting, his assistant answered.

"Hello," said Maryse, "this is Madame Chevalier. My husband and I ordered a jeweled pendant from Monsieur de Montfort and we would like to arrange to pick it up. May I speak with him?"

"Oh, sorry, Mrs. Chevalier, but Pierre isn't here right now. He's been out of the office since this morning. But I'll have him give you a call as soon as he returns. May I have your number?"

Maryse indicated distress at the news and said, "Please don't forget. This is an important commission."

"Oh, absolutely," Keri said. "I watched him work on it. It's fit for a queen. You'll be so proud to wear it."

"Wonderful. I'm looking forward to seeing the finished product. Here's a number where he can reach me. . . ." And she gave a cell phone number with a Manhattan area code.

Catherine was not pleased when Maryse called to tell her of the hitch. They had to make a definite date with Pierre so they could tell their American colleagues and plan the capture. "Do you think he suspects anything?" she asked.

"No. How could he? For all he knows, we're just a couple of rich Europeans with money to burn."

"Perhaps, but he might be thinking it's too suspicious to have people come into his shop with that design. He could be obsessing over it."

"Catherine, *ma chère*, it was your idea," Maryse reminded her. "I'm not concerned. Men go out all the time and come back again. He'll return and give us a call. He wants the balance on that thirty thousand dollars."

"All right. Just make sure you call me once you hear from him."

"As soon as I hear from him, I'll relay the news."

"Good."

As Catherine clicked the END button on her cell phone, she felt a sense of unease, and then tried to shake it off. Maryse was right. Pierre's absence from his shop meant only that he had gone someplace and would return. He had no reason to skip town, no reason to deprive himself of the money he'd earn for creating the Sulame pendant. He had a thriving business, a reputation as an artist, and even a girlfriend who presumably loved him to no end.

Of course he also had plenty of provocation right now, which had resulted in a growing body count. Pierre was disturbed and increasingly agitated, due to their efforts. Catherine shuddered with disgust as she considered the possibility that perhaps that was the reason Pierre de Montfort wasn't in his boutique. Maybe he was out there, stalking, ready to pounce and tear some helpless citizen to pieces. No. It was daylight. His kind almost always struck at night, when the darkness provided a cunning shelter for their black deeds.

Thoughtfully, she pulled out her cell phone and punched in the number of an ally. "Did you find the car he used?" she asked without preamble. The man on the other end knew who it was and what she wanted.

"Yes. He keeps it in a narrow space behind his boutique. And in the parking garage at his condo."

"Is it the one he used at the scene of the last excursion?"

"Yes."

"Good. Put a GPS device on the thing in case he gets antsy. He's out there someplace right now, and we need to pin him down for the appointment. I don't want any more damage. If he starts cruising, make it too risky for him. Get in his way. Just don't get too close."

"Will do."

Catherine had a bad feeling about this. They really needed to keep him under surveillance until they grabbed him. Otherwise, God only knew what could happen.

"Marianne, are you there? Pick up. It's Pierre."

Pierre waited impatiently for her to answer. She was being difficult, he decided. Where the hell was she?

Oh, he remembered. Jim's funeral. She and all the rest of the movers and shakers at Durand et Frères would be there, shedding crocodile tears at his demise and plotting to get his job. Okay, he could wait until later, after things had calmed down and Marianne got home.

Pierre strolled along Madison Avenue and took a detour on his way back to the shop. He needed a drink. He was agitated, his wolf aching to be released.

He had done enough lately, had garnered too much publicity with his kills, and now the whole city was on alert. Pierre just wanted Marianne back in his life, ready to become engaged to him, marry him, have a family with him. He couldn't bear any separation from her, especially now, when he needed her affection so badly.

As much as he hated to admit it, he had made serious mistakes. He had been too honest; he ought to have been a hypocrite, pretended to admire old Jim, lament his death, offer some halfhearted praise for his dubious talents. That's how humans operated, he reminded himself. That's what they expected, not honesty, not the truth, not a realistic appraisal of a mediocre character, but a sentimental, shallow hypocrisy that allowed them to avoid reality.

He preferred his lupine nature. It was better, Pierre thought sadly as he ordered a whiskey in a chichi bar, more honest, more natural. And despite his self-imposed ban on hunting at the moment, he couldn't help noticing three or four people right in the same room who had potential as prey.

Damn, he thought as he nursed his drink and tried to concentrate on Marianne. It was hell to deal with temptation. They all seemed to be wearing targets on their chests. He could practically feel his teeth sinking into soft tissue and sinews, bone and muscle. Oh, if he could only let loose, he thought as sweat beaded on his forehead and upper lip from the torture of temporary abstinence. He wanted it so bad.

Some days, Pierre wished he had never been born with the mark.

# Chapter Twenty-eight

Karl von Hoffman rarely left his alpine retreat to go into the field, but sometimes, in response to a historic moment, he felt obliged to undertake the rigors of travel and go to the scene of a capture. True, this zest for the hunt hadn't seized him in about thirty years, but now, the more he thought about the Montfort, the more Karl realized he had to go.

The Montfort was the Holy Grail of werewolves, a powerful and ancient species. Ah, the Montfort was a classic, full of the kinds of secrets the Institut wanted to discover. He had to be there when Catherine and her helpers took him down.

The fact that he hadn't told Catherine or Paul didn't disturb him. It didn't matter to him if they objected. He could easily overrule his subordinates, and they would just have to accept his participation if they wanted to continue to work with the Institut.

Heinz, his assistant, heard of the decision and said nothing, but von Hoffman recognized the look.

"So, Heinz, do you have some advice to give me?" he asked, the irony in his voice not lost on the younger man.

"No, sir. I was just thinking of the logistics."

"Ah. Well, that's good. Prepare for departure as soon as I get word from the countess that the rendezvous is definite."

Von Hoffman always referred to Catherine by her title, despite her own use of Mademoiselle Marais. In Germany after the war he had rubbed shoulders with many bearers of titles, and to Karl it elevated them in his estimation and made his own "von Hoffman" seem like a membership in the club.

In his case, the "von Hoffman" was bogus, but it gave him a cachet that eluded him when he had simply been Karl Hoffman, the son of a butcher from Dresden. The tragic firestorm that incinerated the beautiful old city during the war also destroyed any inconvenient birth records that might disprove his cherished "von" as well, so Karl had been von Hoffman since the late 1940s with no one to say he wasn't, and now in his eighty-fifth year, he felt as if he'd been born with it. But Catherine was a legitimate Countess du Vallon, and it impressed him tremendously.

"I'll tell the pilot to be ready for a departure this week," Heinz said.

"Excellent."

Von Hoffman glanced at his assistant. "Heinz, you will accompany me this time. You've earned the privilege."

"Herr Doktor . . ."

"Don't be modest," he said dismissively. "You've done well here. You ought to have some field experience, too."

"I'm honored that you place such trust in me. I will do whatever you need." Heinz almost clicked his heels.

"Good. Now, see to it that you pack a suitcase with appropriate clothing for autumn in New York. Dark colors. Classic cut. Nothing to draw attention to you. We will try to blend in, eh?"

Heinz nodded, and von Hoffman could tell his assistant was delighted by the prospect of visiting the city that never sleeps. Heinz had his good qualities, but von Hoffman knew he had the soul of a tourist. Taking down a werewolf would occupy all his time, and Heinz had better realize it. To reinforce the seriousness of their task, von Hoffman said, "This is strictly a business trip. No time for personal activities."

"Of course, sir."

"We may get to rewrite the history of the species with this, Heinz. It will be the crowning achievement of my career."

*"Ja,"* said Heinz with alacrity as he gave his boss a sober look.

Von Hoffman hoped he would keep that in mind.


Paul was in touch with his contact in the NYPD and heard what the investigating cops had found out about the Jersey City killing. The victim was a rising star at a Manhattan auction house. His disappearance caused a coworker enough concern for her to phone in a missing person's report, and due to the poor condition of the corpse, ID came from his dentist. The *Post* had carried the same information, he thought.

"Was the coworker the vic's girlfriend?" Paul asked

curiously. "Most people don't like to get involved these days."

"She told the sergeant who took the report she just worked with him. She said she had a boyfriend."

"So she's a good citizen. The poor bastard was lucky someone was concerned about him."

"Didn't save him, though, did it?"

"Any tire tracks?" Paul asked.

"Nah. Not on macadam. And it was raining." The man paused. Then he said, "The Jersey City cops said they pulled a guy over a couple blocks from the scene that night, before they knew what was in the alley. He was driving a fancy Jag."

"Did they happen to notice the tires?" That was a long shot, but Paul felt he ought to ask.

"Yeah, as a matter of fact, they did. Michelins."

"Marianne, I'm so glad I caught you. How was the funeral?" Pierre asked when Marianne finally answered the phone. He'd been leaving messages for hours.

"How do you think it was?" she snapped. "It was very sad. We all cried. Jim was a man everybody loved and respected. And for him to die like that . . ." She paused to compose herself and blink back tears. "Well, it was cruel."

There was an ominous silence following the last statement. Pierre rolled his eyes. Shit. She was probably going to accuse him of insensitivity now.

"Marianne," he said into the phone, "if I hurt you, I'm sorry. If I did anything to offend you, I sincerely beg your forgiveness." Silence on the other end.

Desperately, he seized on the one thing that might interest Marianne, not because she was a greedy bitch who only wanted things she could turn into cash, but because she had such fine taste and could appreciate his art.

"Marianne," he said softly, "if you let me come over there tomorrow and take you out to dinner, I will bring you the most beautiful piece of jewelry I've ever created. I've been working on it for some Euro customers, and it's worth thirty thousand, but if you'll let me offer it to you as a reconciliation gift, it's yours."

"What's it made of?" she asked. Though irritation was still clear in her voice, her desire for the beautiful jewelry had won her over.

*Ah, thank God,* Pierre thought, bowing his head as if in prayer. "Eighteen karat gold, rubies, sapphires, and diamonds," he replied in relief. "It's a pendant with three fine strands of gold rope holding it up. It's the finest piece of work I've ever created. It's all yours if you'll let me take you to dinner tomorrow night."

With his heart beating wildly, Pierre held his breath. Marianne didn't answer at once. He listened carefully, wondering if something had happened to the phone. Had they been disconnected?

"All right," she said finally, petulance in her voice. "I'll see you and you can present me with this jewel at dinner. Where would you like to go?"

"I'll think about it and surprise you," Pierre said happily, looking forward to having Marianne in his arms again. "It will be memorable."

"All right, then," she said wearily. "See you tomorrow. You can pick me up at seven."

"Seven, it is," Pierre replied with a smile she could hear in his voice. "Good night."

"Bye."

# Chapter Twenty-nine

Ian knew that Catherine had made preparations for the takedown, and he wanted to help her even the score by sending her a specialist with field experience, just in case she needed an extra hand. This person already had an assignment, which he had fulfilled in exemplary fashion, and Ian felt he could now help in the conclusion. Of course, he had to clear it with Catherine, and she would probably say she didn't need his help. So stubborn, so adorable, he thought. He didn't want her and Paul to face down the Montfort alone when he knew of someone more than qualified to lend a hand.

Ian himself had played his part in locating the Montfort, along with von Hoffman and the Institut, but he wouldn't be available if the capture took place in daylight. However, Pavel, the Russian, had no such constrictions. Whether Catherine and Paul would want to add a new man to their team at the last moment was another consideration.

"Darling," she said to him when he broached the subject that night, "I really don't want to have to deal with strangers. Paul and I work well together."

"This one is very good," Ian said. "Russian Special Ops."

"In moments like this, you can rely on only yourself and your partner. That's Paul. I learned long ago that too many hunters spoil the hunt. And men get aggressive and competitive. With all the jockeying for position, sometimes the quarry escapes in the confusion. We have enough wild cards in play without your Russian."

"Catherine, this should be your finest hour."

"And I don't want to spoil it with a testosterone posse," she said.

Ian chuckled. "I'ved always admired your strength, Catherine, but I'd be wounded to think you've grown so confident that men and their testosterone are of no use to you any longer."

"No, darling. I'm just an old-fashioned girl who knows how to hunt with the best of them. My great-great-grandmother, Anne-Clarisse du Vallon, once shot ten wolves in the course of a hunting party on a country estate outside of Moscow. She was the woman of the hour, and the tsar himself honored her by dancing the opening polonaise with her at the next ball of the winter season."

"Nicholas the Second?"

"No, *chéri*. His father, Alexander the Third. It was back in the 1880s. And the grand dukes wined and dined her and her husband for the rest of the social season. Those men knew how to appreciate a skilled hunter."

"And how did your ancestor happen to be in Russia, by the way?"

"Oh," said Catherine with a wave of her hand, "she

was having an affair with Grand Duke Alexei. Her husband was pursuing the French ambassador's wife, so it all worked out."

"Ah," said Ian. "You know, the man I have in mind to help you has much experience in things lupine. Russians all hate wolves."

"Sorry," she replied. "I prefer to work with my own team, and that means just Paul."

"You're a very stubborn woman."

"I'll take that as a compliment," she said as she leaned toward him and gently took his face in her hands. "You can give me more compliments if you'd like. In fact, you can spend the whole night doing just that," Catherine murmured as she kissed him gently on the lips, then wrapped her arms around him as he drew her toward him and kissed her with passion.

"Darling," he whispered as he covered her neck with kisses, "I don't want to lose you. The thought terrifies me." He meant it.

"Don't worry. No werewolf will ever take me down."

Ian kissed her throat, then started to unbutton her blouse as Catherine shifted position and ended up lying beneath him on the sofa.

"I want to keep you with me forever," he murmured as he brushed her throat with his fangs while she caressed his hair and whispered endearments.

"No," said Catherine as she shook her head. "I love you, but I was born human and I plan to die human."

"Catherine," he murmured, cajoling her, caressing her with tenderness. "We could be together for eternity."

"Don't tempt me, my love. Never did I say I'd cross over to the dark side."

"It could go on forever, my darling. You, me, for all eternity. Endless love."

"Endless night," she replied softly. "No sunlight. Never a caress of the sun on my face, fear of too much light. Ian, I love you, but I can't do that. I offer you my love, even my blood, but I can't forsake this world for yours."

At that, Ian pulled away from her and lay back on the sofa, drawing Catherine to his chest in a tender gesture that spoke of his sadness and his genuine affection.

"So," he said with a sigh after a long silence, "I'm merely your walk on the wild side, a dalliance of the shadows."

He glanced at Catherine out of the corner of his eye as he said it. To his amusement, she was grinning from ear to ear.

"Oh, *mon dieu*," she murmured. "They told me vampires loved to be melodramatic. How right they were. Yes," she continued, "I suppose you're my dalliance of the shadows. That's perfect for you, Ian."

"Well then," he said cheerfully, "if that's the case, why waste any more time trying to define our love? Let's just dally."

"Ian! Were you really going to try to take me over to the dark side?" Catherine demanded, as he picked her up and carried her into his bedroom. She loved him to do this. It always reminded her of Rhett Butler sweeping Scarlett off her feet and up the stairs in that stunning red velvet gown.

"Of course, my darling. I will always try," he replied. "And someday, maybe not now, but possibly in the future, you will say yes."

"Vampires never give up," she whispered in his ear, kissing it, "do they?"

"No. They're a lot like you," he answered with a wicked wink and a smile. "I think that's why we're so fond of each other."

No matter what Catherine had told Ian, he did not want her and Paul to have to confront the werewolf by themselves, since the Montfort was the worst of the breed—clever, devious, and ruthless. And he didn't care how many local operatives were in the party. He shared Catherine's opinion that small was better when it came to the actual takedown.

My God, the woman was stubborn. Of course she knew her business; he had to concede she was a pro, but he loved her, and consequenty, he worried.

He summoned Vladimir and asked him to have Pavel come pay him a visit. He was going to instruct him to continue monitoring Julie on video while keeping an eye on a much more difficult character. That was a top priority now.

# Chapter Thirty

Paul and Catherine felt that Maryse and André ought to make another attempt to contact Pierre. So to remind him of the money that hung in the balance, Maryse dialed his number again. After three rings, his assistant, Keri, picked up and said, "Beau Bijou, how may I help you?"

"Hello, this is Maryse Chevalier. May I speak with Pierre?"

"Oh, I'm sorry, Mrs. Chevalier. He's still not in. He went out to see a diamond dealer this morning. I don't know when he'll be back."

"Well, we're pressed for time," said Maryse. "My husband and I have to fly back to Germany tomorrow, and we want to make an appointment to come get the necklace he's creating for me." She paused and added, "Has he finished it?"

She rolled her eyes and shook her head in annoyance as André, Paul, and Catherine glanced at her, trying to read her reaction. They could tell things weren't going well.

"Damn," Paul muttered. "The Big Bad Wolf must be avoiding them," he whispered to Catherine.

"Mademoiselle," Maryse said as politely as she could manage, "we did have an agreement with Monsieur de Montfort. He told us the necklace would be ready by the time we had to leave. I'm so disappointed he can't keep his word." Hoping to encourage cooperation, she added, "If I can't have the necklace by this afternoon, I'm afraid I'll be forced to cancel the order. What time shall I come by to pick up my deposit?" That usually worked.

Maryse waited for the threat to sink in. To her surprise, Keri merely sighed and replied, "Well, Pierre hasn't actually finished it, and since he's been busy with his annual conferences with the diamond dealers, I'm afraid I'll just have to accept the cancellation."

Maryse wanted to blurt out, "Are you crazy? What kind of businesswoman cancels an order for thirty thousand dollars?" Instead she said in a perfectly normal tone, "Isn't there some way he could find to finish by this afternoon? I really would hate to forego this jewel. And it's a substantial sum of money for him. Do you have authorization to accept cancellation?" As she said this, she flashed her audience a look that suggested she was dealing with a loon on the phone.

"Oh, yes, ma'am. I'm his assistant and I have full authority to speak for him," Keri replied, leaving Maryse wondering what to say next.

"All right," said the Frenchwoman, "what about this? Could he possibly finish it by tomorrow? That's the last possible time I could come get it."

"No, tomorrow wouldn't be any better," she said. "He'll never be able to wrap it up by then."

"Is there any way I can speak to Pierre?" Maryse asked, hoping maybe the woman could give her a cell phone number where he could be reached.

"Sorry, ma'am. When he goes to do business with the diamond dealers, he refuses to be disturbed. Says it makes him lose his concentration."

Maryse had never dealt with anyone like this. No jeweler she knew would so airily write off a sale like this. Not unless he had an ulterior motive. Maybe Pierre liked the necklace so much, he felt he could do better than the price he'd given them. Greedy werewolf trait, she thought.

"Well, I'm sorry, too," Maryse said with more truth in her words than Keri realized. "Perhaps another time."

"Sure. Well, good-bye. Some people just came into the store and I have to wait on them. Come see us next time you're in New York." And then came a *click*.

"Stupid little cow!" Maryse exclaimed as she snapped shut her cell phone. "Can you imagine that? Losing an important sale like that without consulting your boss? I'd fire her in a minute."

Paul shook his head. "She's lying. Pierre must have decided not to part with the necklace for some reason. We've planted a GPS device on his car recently and it places it right behind the Beau Bijou. Maybe he's re-thinking the deal."

"Yes," said Maryse. "He's probably going to sell it to somebody else for a higher price."

"Or he smells a rat," Catherine added.

"Why should he?" asked André. "We appeared to be wealthy tourists who liked his work and were able to give him top dollar for it. He's in business to make money, not lose it."

"Yes, and we just happened to drop in with a sketch that probably set off alarms in his head. He looked stunned when he saw it. He's probably changed his mind about it and wants nothing more to do with us."

"Werewolves are greedy," Paul said. "If he already accepted the commission, that meant he wasn't scared off by the sketch. No. I think this means he's found somebody else to unload it on."

"Very enterprising of him," Catherine remarked with a wry smile. "Well, the Montforts always did have a knack for business. That's how they acquired all those vineyards in the old days. Apparently, our boy has inherited this trait, along with the less desirable one."

"Damn. What are we going to do now? The Americans will think we're hopeless."

"We'll just have to find another way to get him. We can kidnap him from his place of work after closing time. We can follow him home and do it there. We still have options."

Paul glumly shook his head. "This would have been so easy," he said. "If we can't absolutely control the area for the takedown, things will be a lot more difficult. Too many variables."

"Including helpful citizens who want to call the police to prevent Pierre from being abducted," Maryse added. "We have to rethink this very carefully."

"The Chevalier woman again?" Pierre asked Keri after she hung up the phone.

"Yes. She really wants that necklace. I felt bad for her," she admitted.

"Well, I'm sorry, but I love it so much I can't give it to her."

Keri asked, "Are you going to show it at the next design competition?"

"Oh, no," he replied. "I'm giving it to Marianne."

When he realized Keri's mouth was hanging open at that statement, Pierre frowned and said, "She's the love of my life. Why shouldn't I give her the finest jewel I've ever created?"

"You were going to charge thirty thousand dollars for it," Keri replied. "That's some nice gift."

"I'm not starving. If I can't make a loving gesture to the woman I love, what good is all this?" he demanded, making a sweeping gesture to encompass his shop with its gorgeous jewelry and exorbitant price tags. "Besides, that's nothing compared with the engagement ring I'm planning."

"Okay," said Keri. "It's none of my business. But you could get some bad publicity if these people start spreading the word that you can't be trusted to deliver the goods. I'm just saying . . ."

"Well, I'm sorry. But Marianne comes first."

The young woman stared at him. "I hope she appreciates the gesture," she said.

Paul didn't like the sudden setback the werewolf had handed them. Grabbing him at a prearranged meeting was smart. Cobbling together a new plan on the spur of the moment was risky. Granted, one had to possess a certain amount of flexibility, but solid planning guaranteed at least a chance of success. This was just too haphazard. Of course, they did have a fallback option: Their moles at the NYPD could always go pick him up for questioning and turn him over to them.

"Is it getting down to the wire with you-know-who?" Julie asked, sitting across from Paul at a small Italian restaurant.

Paul smiled. "Yes. Only there's a last-minute problem, and we haven't yet reached the proper solution. We're back to square one. I don't like it."

"Be careful," she said as she reached across the table to take his hand. "I don't want to lose you."

"Thank you. I want to survive this, too," he joked. Then he looked at her and said quietly, "You know, you have been such a light in the darkness for me. Every moment we've spent has given me such happiness. I can't wait for this assignment to be over so we can be together.

"I live in France, you live in New York," he said, shaking his head. "It won't be the easiest thing in the world, but somehow we can figure out a way to be together. You never know what the future holds. Perhaps you could take a job in France."

She smiled dubiously. "I hear it's a lot harder for a foreigner to find work over there."

"Does James Miller College have a branch in France?" he asked seriously. "Some American colleges do."

"No. But perhaps I could look into taking a leave and finding another translation to do."

Paul looked down for a moment and then looked at Julie. "Do you think you could take a leave and go on the book tour with me?" he asked.

"Do you mean it?" She felt flattered and a little shocked. She hadn't expected that. But she loved it.

"I'm old-fashioned about some things," he added. "I would never ask a woman to do this unless I intended to have a serious relationship."

Julie smiled in bewilderment. "How serious?" she asked.

Paul looked her in the eye and replied, "Very serious."

The waiter seized that moment to come over and refill their glasses. Julie nodded, and Paul couldn't figure out it she intended that for the waiter or for him.

When the man disappeared, Paul said, "We've known each other for two years now, and I know I love you, and there is no one I would rather spend the rest of my life with. I've been in love before. I've known other women, but I've never felt so certain about anything."

Julie glanced at him, remembering how he had responded to her call for help, remembering the fun they had working on the book. She could picture herself spending the rest of her life with him. But more important, she couldn't picture the rest of her life without him.

"I've searched in many places, but now I've found what I've been looking for. But I don't want to get ahead of myself. Before we get caught up in our future, we have to finish this business with the Montfort," Paul said.

"I love you so much. I'm so scared for you. Please, Paul, be careful. We have some unfinished business of our own, you know."

# Chapter Thirty-one

Julie felt as if she were living a scene out of a war movie. When Paul took her back to her apartment that night, they began to kiss at the door, continued into the living room, and ended up in the bedroom, unable to let go of each other.

"I wish you could stay all night," she whispered as they made love with an urgency that surprised both of them. "I hate the thought of you being in danger out there."

"This is what I do," he said. "But you give me a reason to make sure I return."

Later, lying in each other's arms and playfully kissing, Paul and Julie were tired but happy as they made plans for the post-werewolf period. Then Paul caught sight of the time; with regret, he got up and put on his clothes.

"I have to report to a strategy meeting with Catherine and the other partners in Team Werewolf."

"That's what they're calling it?" Julie said with a giggle.

Paul smiled, bent down, and gave her a tender kiss on

the forehead. "Yes. I think it was one of the locals who came up with that. We're all due at a meeting at midnight, probably for the dramatic effect," he said with some irony. "Personally I think a morning conference would do just as well."

"When will I see you again?" she asked as he paused before leaving. Julie pressed herself tightly against him, hating the moment she had to let go and send him off to this strange war he waged against evil.

"Just as soon as we take him down," Paul replied.

"Be careful," Julie whispered tenderly.

"We'll capture him, get him onboard the plane, and fly to Geneva. I ought to be back within the week."

Julie held him close to her and rested her head against his chest. "I want to give you something to keep with you until you come back to me. A good-luck charm."

"Thank you," he said, deeply touched. Going up against the Montfort, Paul thought he might just need it.

When he left Julie's apartment for the meeting, he carried with him a French 1878 twenty-franc gold coin, bearing the figure of an angel, a talisman said to bring good luck to the bearer. He would find out.


What awaited Paul and Catherine at their meeting left them stunned. Herr Doktor von Hoffman himself greeted them at the door, flanked by Heinz, his shadow and chief flunky. These two had flown in from Geneva, something that had never happened before. The old man supervised from afar; that was his style these days. He hadn't gone out into the field in at least three decades.

"Hello, Countess," von Hoffman greeted Catherine,

kissing her hand. Then he shook hands with Paul as he waved them in. Heinz flashed a cheerful smile.

Von Hoffman clearly intended to take over the hunt. Damn. He hadn't pulled this in years. She felt betrayed. And angry.

"So the werewolf has brushed you off," Heinz said by way of making conversation. "Perhaps he feels threatened. Perhaps he senses imminent danger."

"Perhaps he just thought he could get a better price for the bauble somewhere else," Paul replied. "He's a businessman. The customers were foreigners who wouldn't be around to bad-mouth him because of his change of heart, so he felt he could get away with failing to keep his promise."

"Just because he wouldn't speak to Maryse on the phone doesn't mean he isn't around. He was probably avoiding her on purpose."

"From what I heard, it sounded as if the assistant had orders to get rid of them. He lost interest for some reason. He didn't want to be bothered with them any longer," Catherine added. "I really doubt he's very far away or in hiding. We've placed a tracking device on his car and it's parked behind his shop."

Karl von Hoffman listened from a comfortable sofa and inquired if his guests would like something to drink. He seemed less tense than he had seemed just minutes before, when he thought they had lost their best chance at capturing the Montfort.

Paul and Catherine both opted for a glass of wine, which Heinz produced from the minibar in the hotel suite's living room. With glasses in hand, the group seemed slightly more relaxed.

"I think if one of us were to go to his shop and look at his work and ask for him, he would probably come out and talk to his customer," Paul said. "In that way we could verify his presence and get a good close look at him. Unfortunately, Catherine and I can't do it because he met us at my book signing."

Von Hoffman nodded, then glanced at Heinz. "What do you think?"

"It is a good idea. Makes sense to me," Heinz agreed. "Who will do the scouting?"

Catherine and Paul exchanged glances.

"I will go," von Hoffman said. "Heinz, you will accompany me."

Heinz appeared pleased by the idea of a visit to the werewolf's den.

"So, Heinz, do you think we could play the part of tourists bent on acquiring presents for our women back home?"

"Oh, *ja*," he said. "I'm always looking for something to bring my wife."

"What a prince," said Catherine. She had never liked Heinz, always felt him to be a complete brownnoser, sticking to von Hoffman like Velcro, sucking up to him at every opportunity.

Von Hoffman eyed his assistant with a sly expression. "Then we shall pay a visit to this boutique tomorrow," he said.

The next morning as von Hoffman and Heinz were on their way to the Beau Bijou, Paul received a call from his mole in the NYPD telling him Officers Brindisi and Rodriguez, who were investigating, had been in contact with a woman named Marianne McGill of Durand et Frères. She was the person who had phoned in the missing person's report and she appeared to be a close friend of the vic.

The cops thought she might be able to provide them with details of his background, hobbies, enemies, and they had made an appointment to see her. They discovered he was an animal rights activist and had protested against some powerful drug companies. Brindisi wondered if his death was some kind of warped payback.

"All right," Paul said. "Keep me posted. And keep an eye on the officers. Don't let them get too close to Pierre unless they have backup. Monitor the investigation. You don't want our boy to dine on New York's finest."

Around ten a.m., two tall, slim men of athletic build dropped by the Beau Bijou and began to browse through what Pierre referred to as the "wife/girlfriend pleaser" section of bracelets and necklaces. He observed them on his monitor in the back room and noticed that they appeared to favor the semiprecious stones set in silver. He saw Keri do her best to steer them toward the higher-end selections in gold, but they resisted and lingered among the topaz, coral, and quartz.

In his workroom, Pierre listened in as he applied the final touches to the Montfort pendant he intended for Marianne. As a final embellishment, he had added a diamond eye to the phoenix in the center; now he slowly and carefully threaded the triple chain of eighteen-karat gold through the loop. Magnificent.

Whatever had possessed him to create this for some foreigner? This belonged to the Montfort's mate, a beautiful and striking emblem that linked her to the family, its history and her future in it. When she saw it, Marianne would understand how much he loved her, how her destiny and his demanded unity, how passionately his heart beat for her. There were glints of pride in his eyes as he kissed his creation tenderly and then arranged it lovingly in a dark red velvet case lined with white satin. He would proudly offer her a masterpiece of art and love.

About ten minutes after the two young men entered the boutique, two more customers arrived, an elderly white-haired man who looked like a banker and a younger blond man who appeared to be his son. Keri hastened to greet them, ever the gracious saleswoman.

"Hello," she said with a smile, addressing the older of the two.

In the back, Pierre glanced up at the screen and noticed that the white-haired man looked like the one in charge. He had to be at least seventy, but he appeared quite fit, as if he exercised every day of his life. The younger one did, too, although he lacked the commanding presence of the older man.

In fact, all four customers looked like walking advertisements for clean living and fresh-air exercise. Cool. If they were accompanied by a couple of sexy fashionistas, it would make a great ad for the Beau Bijou.

"Good afternoon," the gentleman said with a charming smile. "I was just passing by when I spotted your wonderful display in the window. Would it be too much trouble to ask you to show me that magnificent amber necklace? My daughter loves amber pieces and it might be just the thing for her birthday. And my son Jurgen needs something for his wife."

"Of course, sir. I'd be delighted," Keri replied as she reached into the window and removed the necklace, a truly regal creation featuring an Art Nouveau silver setting with various-sized chunks of dark green amber interwoven in the floral links.

The man studied it appreciatively.

"So, Jurgen, what do you think?" he asked the younger man.

He blinked and said, "Very fine. Very fine, indeed. I think Helga would love it."

The older one nodded, as if considering the effect of the gift on his daughter. Then he said, "It is quite beautiful, but you know your sister has so many pieces. Do you think she would like to receive one more?"

"Oh, *ja*," he replied with a decisive nod as he looked at the necklace. "Helga collects these. She can't get enough of it."

The old man asked Keri to model the jewelry for him and eyed it appreciatively as she fastened the clasp around her neck and showed it off. "Beautiful, absolutely first-class," he declared. "That is a work of art."

"Does the jeweler make all these pieces himself?" the younger man asked as he, too, admired the necklace. "My wife adores amber."

"Every one. Pierre is a genius. He's always creating, always looking for something new. Sometimes he'll take a style like Art Nouveau and put his own stamp on it. He's so versatile. I just love working for the man."

The young man saw something that interested him and wandered off to another display case. Keri unfastened the clasp of the necklace and glanced at her customer.

"Let me think about it while I see what else you have," he said pleasantly. "I do like the piece."

In his back room, Pierre suddenly realized he had four customers wasting time looking and not buying. He hated that. Robbers had done a smash and grab last month at a store two blocks away and the police had sent out flyers with their photos, taken from the store's video camera. Could the Beau Bijou be next in line for plundering? Not if he had anything to do with it, Pierre decided. Little Keri was no match for a quartet of robbers; he had to go out there and make his presence known. Of course, the licensed handgun he kept in the drawer would help, too.

As he stepped out into the showroom, Keri whirled around and smiled at him. Pierre knew she hadn't expected him to put in an appearance, and she was always begging him to come out and interface with the customers to generate some purchases. Customers loved to meet him, she told him, and when they did, they often bought things. Today, though, Pierre was on the alert for trouble.

"Ah," said the old man, looking as if he'd just found the Holy Grail, "is this Mr. de Montfort, the creator of so much beauty?"

"In the flesh," Pierre replied, taking in the four men, apparently not together. He stood behind the counter, within reach of the drawer and its Glock.

"I'm so glad to meet you," the old man said, flattering Pierre with a look that suggested he was a huge fan.

The younger man ceased studying the merchandise and looked instead at Pierre, moving next to the old man as he did.

"This gentleman liked your Art Nouveau green amber," said Keri.

"Yes. It's stunning. My daughter loves amber, and I think I might purchase it for her. She has nothing like this, as far as I know. Where did you find the stones?"

"They come from the Baltic," he said. "That's a great source of amber. The Dominican Republic also has quantities of the stones. I use both."

The old man smiled affably at Pierre and then he said politely, "Would you do me a favor, sir?"

"If I can," he replied, somewhat puzzled.

"Would you sign your business card for me when your assistant wraps up the necklace? I'm sure my Helga would love to have your autograph along with the necklace."

"My pleasure," he said with a smile as the old man indicated to Keri that he would be taking the jewelry with him.

Jurgen hastily selected two medium priced bracelets, one in silver with brown quartz, and the other in silver with citrine.

After they left the store, the other two men selected lesser baubles and departed as well, leaving Pierre relieved he hadn't been the intended victim of a robbery after all.

Keri seemed delighted. "You always have that effect on customers. You come out and talk to them and they buy. I keep telling you, it's good for business when you show your face and chitchat. People love to meet the artist. It makes the shopping experience more intense for them."

"The shopping experience?" he repeated. "Where did that come from?"

"Oh, everything is an experience these days," she said. "You buy a cup of coffee, it's a taste experience. You buy something you can wrap up and take home, it's a shopping experience."

"It sounds so prepackaged," he commented dismissively.

His petite, dark-haired assistant gave him a big smile. "Pierre," she said, "you're so cute, but you have to stop being such a backroom guy and come out and schmooze the clients from time to time. You can't be a lone wolf and hope to become a major player."

For a moment he wondered suspiciously why she had chosen that particular expression. Could she have any idea of how close to the truth she was? He studied her carefully and decided against it.

"It's finally ready," he said, switching the conversation to a theme that interested him.

Keri glanced up.

"Marianne's necklace," he announced, surprised that he had to remind her. It was all he thought about.

"Oh. So tonight's the night?"

"Yes. I'm taking her out to dinner, and then I'm presenting her with my masterpiece. What do you think?"

Keri reached out to take the open velvet box containing Pierre's work, and he noticed with pleasure how her eyes widened when she beheld it.

"It's the most beautiful necklace I've ever seen," she said. "Marianne won't be able to resist it."

# Chapter Thirty-two

Catherine hated to rely on other people, even von Hoffman, and especially on Heinz. Speaking of the plans, she said to Ian, "After this, I'm going to think seriously about starting my own company. Just me and Paul. Nobody to overrule us."

"It will be a big step," Ian commented, not displeased. He'd long thought von Hoffman was getting too old. He was pedantic and stuck in the past, although the excellent equipment available at the Institut Scientifique was world-class. He did have a true scientist's interest in keeping current with the research, although Ian had heard unsettling stories about some hush-hush experiments on cloning that made his skin crawl. He knew Catherine hadn't participated in any of these and would not, but the knowledge of the experiments made him glad she had begun to think about ending her association with the Institut.

"When will you grab him?" Ian asked.

"Just as soon as von Hoffman think it's right."

"Any danger of him running away in the meantime?"

"Why should he? Von Hoffman, Heinz, and two backup types paid a visit to the Beau Bijou and met him. He didn't react to them in any way and there was no hint that he was planning to close up shop for a time. They said he was in the back working on jewelry, probably his normal routine."

Ian smiled. "And I imagine von Hoffman's heart was beating so hard at the sight, he could barely contain his emotions. He must have wanted to terminate him on the spot."

"He did," she said mildly. "He told me it took all his self-control not to kill him right there. He only mastered the impulse because the Montfort was in human form."

Ian gave her a skeptical glance. "The old man thought he could take the werewolf all by himself? He's at least eighty now, and not as spry as he once was. He'd better be careful not to get carried away."

Catherine smiled. "He's in good shape. He could pass for ten years younger than his age, but he's still an old man. That's why he's keeping Heinz around to fetch and carry."

"Do you think this Heinz could take over?"

"No," Catherine said firmly. "He's strictly von Hoffman's gofer. If they ever made Heinz the boss, half the staff would quit. He's a pretentious little brute."

"What about you?" Ian asked. "I always thought you'd be running the Institut one day."

She hesitated. "I once had ambitions in that direction," Catherine admitted, "but, as I said, I'm now thinking of branching out and starting something on my own. And of course, I love the field work. I wouldn't be content with an administrative job, not at my age. It would be too confining."

"Perhaps twenty years down the road," Ian said with a smile. "You're still a young woman, my dear."

"Not that young," she replied.

"Darling girl, from my perspective, you're practically a child. A rather dangerous youngster, but still very young. Of course, if you'd let me help, you could continue at the same age forever."

At that, Catherine had to laugh.

"I know," he said with a theatrical sigh, "you merely wish to keep me around as your New York fling."

Catherine burst out laughing. "You can be so maddening at times. Next you're going to say I want you only as my boy toy."

"Oh, that, too," Ian replied with a wicked twinkle in his gorgeous dark eyes. "Thank you for reminding me." He moved closer to Catherine and nuzzled her neck, leaving a trail of kisses down her throat, her shoulders, and as he undid the buttons on her blouse, down her breast as well.

"Ian," she murmured as she found herself entwined in his arms, while he kissed her, moving his mouth to hers and exploring it greedily while he caressed her breast, sending familiar signals down to her sensual center, making her willing to fall into bed right now, no questions asked.

"I want you," he whispered. "I want all of you, every delicious part of you lying in my arms, loving me, not thinking about anything but us. Not work, not friends, not careers, just us, you and me alone."

Catherine felt too weak from need to do anything but

nod as she somehow got from the salon to the bedroom, guided by Ian's strong arms and their mutual desire.

If this was going to be one of her last nights on earth, Ian Morgan made it worthwhile. When she rose from his bed shortly after dawn, once Ian had already left to go to his daytime lair, Catherine knew that whatever fate had in store for her in her hunt for the werewolf, she had already experienced more sensual bliss than a human had a right to.

This would sustain her to the end.

After von Hoffman and Heinz paid the werewolf a visit, von Hoffman decided a surprise raid on the shop at closing time would work, since it was the one place Pierre could be counted on to be each day. The assistant could easily be overpowered and rendered unconscious inside the showroom, while a team headed by Catherine and Paul would burst in the back door and take Pierre down at the same time. He'd be bundled into the trunk of his own car, which was parked in back, and driven unconscious to the prearranged hangar near the Hudson River, where he'd be loaded onto a helicopter and flown to the New Jersey landing strip for transport back to Geneva. Tranquilizers would be administered as needed.

Paul knew something was up when the spotters who had taken up position near the Beau Bijou reported Pierre had gone AWOL.

"What do you mean?"

"Never showed up this morning."

"Maybe he's coming in late. The guy goes there every day. It's his territory and he likes to control it."

"Yeah, but it's already eleven o'clock and he's not there."

"Shit."

Catherine raised an eyebrow and glanced his way. "Trouble?"

"Pierre's not in yet."

"You're joking."

Paul raised his free hand in a gesture of frustration as he spoke into his cell phone. "Keep up the surveillance and keep us posted. The party's still on."

When he ended the call, he turned to Catherine and said, "Let's check the GPS monitor."

After they did, they found that Pierre's car was moving through Long Island.

"What the hell is he doing there?" Paul marveled.

"Who knows? Maybe he's making a delivery. If he has a special creation for a millionaire, he could be providing personalized service."

"Today?"

"They have remarkable intuition. Maybe he feels threatened."

"He can't know what we have planned."

"He doesn't have to. He may just have a feeling that he ought to be out of there for the day. You know how they are."

Paul shook his head. "We'll have to let the old man in on the news. See what he wants to do."

On a pier near the Hudson, von Hoffman, Heinz, and the chopper crew waited for a progress report from the field.

"Well, today's the day," Heinz said. "I wonder if he'll put up much of a fight."

Von Hoffman heard the remark and turned to give his subordinate a gloomy look. "Of course he will put up a fight. He is the last surviving Montfort werewolf, a legend among the species. He will fight to the death, attempting to tear us limb from limb if he can."

"*Ja,*" Heinz added with a nod and a glance at his colleagues. "This one will be a real terror. He'll attempt to inflict as much damage as possible."

Still, as von Hoffman stood at the water's edge, looking across the river to New Jersey, he wondered if they had really taken everything into consideration. With werewolves, there was always the chance of the unexpected. With a Montfort, it was almost a given.

When he got the call on his cell phone, von Hoffman tried to maintain a stoic expression, but the others could tell there was a glitch. They watched anxiously in the background, a few of them smoking cigarettes as they waited for the news.

Finally, von Hoffman ended his call, slipped the cell phone into his pocket, and turned to his men. "The subject is away from the pickup spot and shows no sign of returning to it. We will continue to monitor him."

An audible murmur of disappointment greeted that statement.

Von Hoffman's expression darkened. "He will come back to his shop, and when he does, we will get him. In the meantime, we watch and wait."

He hoped the damned werewolf hadn't been keeping track of *them.*

# Chapter Thirty-three

Paul, Catherine, and their backup team of the Institut's local operatives sent messages back and forth as they tracked Pierre's progress via their GPS monitors. A helicopter followed overhead, and the pilot radioed in reports on the subject's progress.

Pierre's car had stopped at a residence for half an hour, and then proceeded to a restaurant on the water, where it remained parked for an hour. He was now returning to Manhattan.

"Is he going to the shop?" Catherine asked when the pilot notified them the wolf had reached the city.

"Doesn't appear to be. Nope. He's heading for his condo."

"What do you think?" Catherine inquired. "Should we try to take him down at his place?"

Paul shook his head. "We haven't planned for it. Too many variables in a large building. Hard to secure. If somebody sees us capturing Pierre and calls the cops, it would compromise the Institut and we can't do that."

"Then what do we do?"

"Watch and wait. Then try again tomorrow."

Catherine didn't like the idea of giving up on Pierre so easily. She dispatched a scout to linger in the area of his condo, and after about two hours, she received a report that the wolf was again on the move. It was now about four thirty in the afternoon and she wondered if Pierre was going to stop in at the Beau Bijou to check on things.

"Paul and I are on our way," she said. "We'll cruise the area near the shop. Keep him in your sights."

The Institut's local operatives continued to pursue Pierre as he left the East Side and turned left at Fifth Avenue, driving past the Metropolitan Museum in lanes of traffic filled with cars and buses. Other drivers showered them with curses and several interesting hand gestures as they swerved to change lanes, trying to get close enough so as not to lose him, yet keep far enough back to be anonymous.

"Where the hell is he going?" Paul demanded back in his car as he and Catherine kept track of Pierre's progress on the GPS monitor. "He didn't go to the shop today, went tooling around Long Island, and now he's roaming Manhattan. These things kill only at night, so I don't believe he's done that."

"They could change."

"Yes, but our guys on Long Island checked out the restaurant after he left. Nobody was screaming about being attacked. No corpses in the men's or ladies' rooms."

Catherine shrugged. "Who knows? It could be related to his business."

Blocks away from them, Pierre's green Jaguar took a right turn on West Sixty-fifth Street and headed into Central Park. When he exited the park he drove onto West Sixty-sixth Street, turned onto West End Avenue, and then finally onto Eleventh Avenue, surrounded by cars that bore New Jersey plates. It was the route to the Lincoln Tunnel.

"Shit," exclaimed one of the trackers. "Is he going to New Jersey for a repeat performance? That was the scene of his last kill."

Pierre detached himself from the traffic and pulled neatly into the driveway of the largest Jaguar dealership in New York, disappearing from sight into the depths of the huge, multistory building, a tower of glass and steel.

When the trackers notified Paul and Catherine, they got a quick response. "Try to cover all exits. He has to come out someplace."

"Only two of us here. Will you join us?"

"We're on our way," Paul replied.

While the Institut's operatives tried to find parking nearby, they were forced to circle the block until they could locate a tight space not far from the entrance to the dealership. From there, they could keep an eye on the driveway Pierre had used, but they couldn't watch the opposite side of the building. They were torn between waiting for Paul and Catherine to show up and cover the other side or simply splitting up, with one of them going on foot.

"We'd better not lose him. I'll get out and go around."

By the time Paul and Catherine arrived, Pierre had dropped off his Jaguar to have its headlight replaced, picked up his prearranged burgundy rental Jag, and driven out of the dealership while the Institut tracker was still walking.

Pierre had been out of the car dealership about twenty minutes before Team Werewolf came to that conclusion and realized they'd blown it. Some desperate tracking produced no results, even though they fanned out in several directions, two of them going back to the area of the Beau Bijou and two others to the area of his apartment. The werewolf had given them the slip, and worse, if he rolled out of the dealership in a rental car, they now had no idea what his ride looked like.

Marianne waited in the marble lobby of her high-rise, chitchatting with the concierge about the next extravaganza Durand et Frères looked forward to in the spring: her very own show featuring the worldly goods of a very fashionable, very decadent American novelist whose private life made the news just as often as her books. It would be *big*, Marianne assured the man. And it would be hers. She couldn't wait.

"Well, good luck, miss," he said with a smile. "You know, I heard that last show of yours about Christine Bellerive was quite a sensation. I went down there to see the preauction display. You know, I was a fan of hers. Man, she was something."

"She certainly was," Marianne said, slightly distracted. She could see a man in a dark burgundy Jaguar outside, waving frantically. She looked again. "Pierre!" she exclaimed. "Oh, look at that. He's got a new car."

"Nice set of wheels," the concierge said appreciatively. "Here, let me get the door for you."

Marianne thanked him, scampered outside, let the

concierge open the door of the Jag, and jumped in. "You bought a new car? You could have told me. I was looking for the green one," she said as they pulled away from the curb.

"Sorry. I had to take it in for repairs. This is mine until tomorrow."

"It's nice." Then she wanted to know, "What happened to the other one?"

"Nothing much. I just had to get the headlight changed."

"I like the color. What is it, burgundy?"

"Yes, it probably is," he said with a smile, "but in dealer speak it's called aubergine."

Marianne ran her hand over the smooth leather and nodded. "Feels great. So tell me, where are we going?"

"Ah," he said, "that's a surprise. But I promise it will be a dinner to die for."

She laughed, ran her fingers through her long blond hair, and settled in for the ride. "I can't wait," she said flirtatiously as she darted Pierre a melting glance.

She couldn't wait to see that necklace.


Paul and Catherine received a call from Ian's Russian contact while they were conferring with von Hoffman and Heinz, reporting what they already knew about Pierre. His car and its signal were in the Jaguar dealership. He advised them to take all precautions while Pierre was unaccounted for. Then he added, "Tell Paul I continue to have Professor Buchanan on video surveillance, too. She's fine."

Then Catherine heard a click.

With a slight motion of her head, she gestured to Paul

to come closer. "Somebody working for Ian just called to tell me what we already know. Pierre's car is in the dealership and we don't know what he's driving now."

She gave Paul an odd look and said, "The man also said he's keeping watch on Julie."

He glanced at her in surprise. "I ought to give Julie a call and tell her to go someplace else tonight if she can. Just in case."

"She'll be all right," Catherine said. "If Ian has somebody keeping track of her, she won't be harmed."

"We don't know who he is."

"Paul," she said quietly, "I think it's the Russian he uses from time to time. If he's good enough to work for Ian, then I think he must be top-notch. Unlike our present company."

Heinz happened to catch that, and he gave Catherine a vicious little smile.

She didn't care.

The Jaguar powered its way from the Upper East Side, as lights sparkled in all the high-rises and crowds filled the sidewalks, eager to make their way home. It took a few turns in the west forties, and then merged with hundreds of other cars fighting for a place in the lanes heading into the Lincoln Tunnel and across the river into New Jersey.

"I've never liked the tunnel," Marianne reflected as she glanced out at the acres of tiles and railings rolling by. "I was in a traffic jam here once when I was a kid, and my sister screamed the whole time. I always think of that when I have to go through here. And the fumes."

"Traffic's good tonight. Everybody's moving at a nice, even clip. No problems."

"Thank God," Marianne murmured as she leaned back against the soft leather and glanced at Pierre. "Now are you going to tell me where we're going?"

"Not until we get there," he teased. "I told you it was a surprise."

Marianne looked out the window and saw the state line of demarcation picked out in tiles beyond the yellow reflections in the windows. "It says we've just crossed the border, pardner. We're in Jersey now. Will that unlock your lips?"

"Not yet. Be patient. We'll be arriving in about half an hour."

"What sort of place is it?" Marianne persisted as they left the tunnel long behind and cruised along I-95 South, heading toward Newark. When she saw the sign, she exclaimed, "Newark? Are you serious."

"Are you speaking of atmosphere or cuisine?" he inquired.

Marianne gave him an incredulous look. "Both," she said anxiously.

"All right, since you're so impatient," Pierre teased, "I'll give you a little hint."

"Yes?" she replied.

"Very elegant, very Continental, and very elevated," he said mysteriously. "Happy?"

He could tell she felt a lot happier when she saw the signs changing to I-280 and then veering away toward the Essex County suburbs of first Cedar Grove and then West Orange. Marianne had relatives in Essex Fells. She could relate to this area.

When Pierre's borrowed Jaguar made a left turn onto Crest Drive and headed into a suddenly wooded location, Marianne brightened up. They were entering the Eagle Rock Reservation, home to one of the state's finest and most elegant restaurants. When Pierre grandly drove his Jag up to the entrance and Marianne saw the parking attendant come forward to open the door for her, she turned and gave Pierre a beatific smile.

"Oh, you darling," she gushed. "This is heaven."

# Chapter Thirty-four

The sight of Marianne's delighted smile gave Pierre a big boost of confidence. She approved his choice. She loved it. He was already ahead in the game.

He felt like a *GQ* model as he and his lovely lady paused briefly at the headwaiter's station, received a smile of welcome, and followed a gracious host to their table, a good one with a magnificent view of the distant New York skyline. He noticed admiring glances from other men as Marianne made her way to the table, a blond goddess in a black-and-white wrap dress from an up-and-coming SoHo designer. Very chic.

"Enjoy your meal," said the host as he escorted them to their seats and then sent the busboy to fill water glasses before their waiter could come to take their order.

"Well, this is really spectacular," said Marianne as her eyes surveyed the horizon, alight with stars and the distant lights of the city. "It's made my day."

"My pleasure," he said sincerely. If it brought joy to Marianne, nothing was too much. He was already thinking of bringing her back here to present her with the engagement ring he hadn't yet designed.

He reached across the table and took her hand. He gave it a little squeeze of pure emotion and saw her lower her eyes and glance down. She was moved. He enjoyed the way her long lashes covered her eyes when she did that. She was so lovely, so adorable. And all his.

The waiter interrupted to announce the evening's specialties, hand them their menus, and disappear again to allow them time to choose after he took their beverage order.

By the time he returned with their drinks, they had decided on entrées and were ready to order their meals. When the waiter took their dinner order and left them again, Pierre raised his glass to Marianne and said, "Love you always."

She smiled back by way of reply and didn't meet his eyes, an omission that Pierre attributed to an overload of emotion.

In Karl von Hoffman's hotel suite, the top echelon of Team Werewolf sat around the salon hurling accusations at one another, or at the very least trying to assign blame for the debacle. They had lost their quarry and the team was frustrated and tense.

"Montfort is someone who will change plans on impulse," Catherine said. "He already proved that when he refused to hand the necklace over to Maryse and her husband even though he had created it for them on commission. He's not someone you can rely on to go from point A to point B without a few detours. We've had men watching him for several days. They should have been aware of this."

"My men can't read minds," Heinz reminded them.

"No," Paul said, "but they might have been able to plant a listening device in his boutique or tap his phone."

"If you think that's the way to go, why didn't you do it?"

"Oh, is it Paul's and my job to run every aspect of the operation? It's not enough that we'll risk our own lives to bring him down, but we're also responsible for the preparations behind the scenes?" Catherine snapped in outrage.

She gave Heinz a look that would have daunted a lesser soul. He merely shrugged, pulled out a pack of cigarettes, and selected a smoke.

"We need to get back on track. Have someone call up the dealership to try to find out the status of the car. Someone who can pass as his assistant. We need to know why he went there and how soon he will get his car back. Maybe he simply needed an oil change."

"Is this something important or just a housekeeping detail for him?" Catherine wondered aloud. "Does it have any bearing on his other life?"

"In what way?" Heinz asked.

"I don't know. Perhaps he's trying to have evidence of some kind cleaned off."

"He could just run it through a car wash," Heinz said dismissively as he smoked his cigarette.

"You're right. Perhaps he needs something repaired so he can continue to use it to roam the city in his search for prey."

Catherine glanced at Paul. He looked as if he just had an unpleasant thought.

"Do you think that since this Montfort is so flexible, he might be planning on using an alternate vehicle for his hunting expeditions, in case anyone has noticed his own car?"

Catherine hadn't thought of that. "You mean like renting one from time to time for variety?"

"Yes."

"It's possible. But would he really want to have it in the records of an auto rental company that he used one of their cars?"

"No," said Paul. "Too risky. Leaves too much evidence behind."

Catherine felt uneasy. If the Montfort had sensed any attempt at surveillance, what might he be up to this evening? This dropping out of sight could be aimed at them, all of them, just letting them know he was smarter than they were and a lot better at tracking them than they were at hunting him.

Paul looked at his partner and Catherine could almost read his mind. He worried about Julie. He was in love, and even though Julie had a better chance of being hit by lightning than attacked by the werewolf, Catherine wanted to put his mind at rest. She needed him focused.

"Paul," she said, "I'm going to call Ian and ask him to let Julie stay at his place this evening. Would you feel better if she were locked up there? Nobody can get into that house."

When he hesitated, Catherine said, "Paul, step outside with me for a minute. I have to tell you something."

Mystified, he followed her while Heinz and von Hoffman eyed them suspiciously.

Once in the next room, Catherine said, "Paul, I don't

know how you're going to take this, but I think I ought to tell you something Ian just revealed to me. Julie is his great-great-granddaughter. Manon de LaVillette took Ian's son to England with her, and her husband adopted him. That makes Julie a direct descendant of Jean de Montfort, and that's why he's so fond of her. No harm will come to her in that house."

Paul was so stunned, he simply stared. He was in love with somebody whose living ancestor was a vampire Montfort and whose family tree contained several branches of werewolves. Talk about ironic.

"Paul? Are you all right?"

"I'm fine," he said. "And I don't care who her family is; I love her." Then he looked at Catherine and asked in amazement, "Does Julie know any of this?"

"No. Ian is afraid to tell her. I think he's scared she might reject him."

"Well, they'll have to work it out later. Right now, I just want her someplace safe. So if Ian wishes to shelter her for the time being, fine. I'm all for it."

"Good. Then I'll make the call. You call Julie and tell her Vladimir will drive to her apartment and escort her to Ian's home."

She pulled her cell phone out of her pocket and punched in Ian's private number. When he answered, she asked, "Would you let Julie stay at your home tonight to assure her safety? The Montfort's gone missing and we don't want to leave anything to chance."

He told her to tell Julie he'd send his servant to pick her up.

When Paul telephoned Julie and explained the new de-velopment, she sounded relieved that they wanted her someplace safe. She appreciated the seriousness of the situation and agreed to pack and leave as soon as Vladimir arrived.

Catherine gave Paul a smile. "It's the best place for her tonight. You have no idea how possessive the Montfort men can be when it comes to their women."

# Chapter Thirty-five

Dinner had gone well and Pierre sensed a new bond with Marianne that could only be increased with the presentation of his masterpiece. As the waiter arrived with the dessert menu and Marianne opted for coffee instead of the dazzling array of high-calorie carbs he offered, Pierre decided the time had come for the offering of the gift that would make her his forever, the ancient family crest set in rubies, sapphires, and diamonds.

As Marianne watched with interest, he reached into his jacket pocket and extracted his signature burgundy velvet box. Her eyes glittered in the candlelight as he extended his hand and the treasure across the table.

"Oh, Pierre, thank you," she said as she reached for the case and pried it open. Her blue eyes widened with genuine pleasure as she reached in and removed the jewel to hold it up in front of her and admire it in the soft light.

"Do you like it?" Pierre asked anxiously, feeling almost giddy to see it in her hands and savoring the expression of bliss on her face as she stared at it, surveying it from side to side, lifting it, feeling its weight and taking in the splendor of the stones.

"You're right," she said simply. "It is the most beautiful thing you've ever done. I'm honored. Really. It's breathtaking."

"You deserve it," he said. "It belongs around your neck. You are the only woman who can do it justice."

Marianne responded by unfastening the clasp of the gold necklace she wore, putting it in her handbag, and replacing it with her new present. She took out a small mirror and studied the effect, preening for Pierre.

"What do you think?" she asked coquettishly.

"Magnificent," he said truthfully. The triple strands of gold seemed to caress her neck as they supported the fabulous Montfort family crest picked out in precious stones, a symphony of taste and brilliance. The phoenix seemed to symbolize not only the eternal rising of the Montfort's destiny but also the rebirth of Pierre's hopes for his future.

"Darling," she said simply, "you are a genius."

Julie felt a little odd about accepting Ian's offer of shelter for the night, but fear of the missing Montfort rattled her, recalling the fear she felt the day Chuck played that stupid practical joke. With the werewolf on the loose and Paul and Catherine unable to locate him, Julie felt surprisingly vulnerable. If Paul considered Ian capable of safeguarding her, she would take his advice. The man had an impressive security system at his town house. Nothing would get past the front door unless he allowed it in. Cameras tracked every visitor from the moment they arrived. And Vladimir seemed to exude a reassuring strength himself.

Okay, she thought, Ian's beautiful home was like a luxurious fortress and she was about to go there in a kind of private protection program. As Vladimir chauffeured her there in a Mercedes, drove into the underground garage, parked the car, and then escorted her into the house through the locked passageway that led from the garage to the first floor, Julie wondered if the owner of this little palace lived in expectation of assassination.

She wondered again what Ian's profession could be. The luxury of his home and the refined display of art on his walls could come only from vast wealth. Then she remembered that Catherine was a French aristocrat, so it was natural that she moved in very rarefied circles.

And despite their short acquaintance, Julie felt a sense of security with this man, as if he were someone she could truly trust. Paul was her love, but Ian was an ally, and he would take care of her while Paul and Catherine tracked the elusive werewolf. She knew one thing: She had absolutely no desire to share the fate of her tragic ancestor.

Pierre was eager to leave the restaurant and spend some time alone with Marianne. When they got into the car after the meal, Pierre surprised her by driving deeper into the wooded area rather than finding the main road and heading back to the city. To his amusement, Marianne seemed startled, even a little nervous.

"Do you know where you're going?" she asked as she glanced out the windows into a bewildering darkness. "I don't think this is the way out."

"I'm going to show you a favorite spot where we can get a view of the New York skyline. It's unforgettable," he said. "You'll love it."

"All right, but then let's go right back to Manhattan. I have an early-morning meeting."

He was disappointed that she wasn't feeling quite as romantic as he was, particularly after the presentation of his gift. Pierre leaned over and kissed her neck, hoping to arouse some heat in her.

When the Jaguar finally came to a stop at a spectacular overlook, nestled among some trees, even Marianne had to admit it was heavenly. She let him draw her closer to him on the soft leather seat, wrap his arms around her, and kiss her passionately as he caressed her breast, slipping his hand into the low neckline of her dress to explore the soft curves.

After a while, Pierre felt something pushing against his chest as he kissed Marianne ardently, savoring the taste of her, the scent of her, focusing on nothing but his raw desire.

"Pierre! Pierre. Stop. I have to go to work tomorrow." She was practically beating against his chest, jolting him out of his happiness. "Come on. You're behaving like a college kid. Let's be grown-ups. We've had a lovely evening. You've made me very happy. Now, let's go home."

Pierre stopped kissing her and with an effort pulled back from her. He couldn't believe this. No matter what he did, it was always wrong. He suddenly began to feel cheated.

"I love you," he said simply as he reached out and stroked her cheek. "I thought you loved me, too."

Marianne sank back against the leather seat and she looked out to the distant skyline. Pierre thought he heard a sigh.

"Don't you?" he asked with a building sense of uncertainty. "I want to marry you. Don't you realize that?"

"Oh, for God's sake," she said at last. "I'm sorry, Pierre. I thought I was in love with you. I tried to be. I loved all the beautiful things you created for me. You're a genius. You're a wonderful man. You deserve somebody who adores you."

"I want *you*," he said.

Marianne turned and faced him in the darkness. "I can't do this anymore," she said. "I can't pretend."

"What do you mean?"

"Pierre, I don't want to keep seeing you any longer. It's not working out for me."

"How can you say that?" he demanded.

"Because it's the truth." She paused and said, "You know what it's like going out with you lately? It's like having a big, jealous old dog tagging around behind you. I want more than that."

"Dog?" She referred to him as a dog? Like he was some kind of goofy old mutt? Pierre experienced a rush of adrenaline shoot through his body. To his horror, he felt the familiar sense of bones starting to change, of fur growing on flesh.

"Stop!" he shouted, more to protest the transformation than anything else. Marianne took it another way.

"No," she replied. "I am not going to stop. I've been holding this in for a long time. It was when poor Jim was killed that you showed me just how callous you could be. Do you think I want to go through life married to a man who has no heart?"

"I have a heart," he shouted as he lost the ability to control his shape-shifting and felt his bones begin their transformation. It was the stress. His hormones whirled in a deadly tornado of emotion as he stared at Marianne in the darkness, his anger threatening to tear him apart. "You broke my heart when you started to spend so much time with that jerk!"

"What? We had drinks together. Twice. We were colleagues," she shouted back. "Jim was a real gentleman, but it was you with your jealousy and your petty condescension that ruined this relationship!"

"I gave you the best I had," he moaned, from the pain of his limbs contorting as much as from the anguish he felt at her words.

"Yes, you did," she said furiously. "You gave it to me when I didn't even want it. Even when I was trying to get away from you. But, Pierre, I promise you, you're going to get it all back, starting with this." And she angrily unfastened her necklace, the masterpiece he had worked on so carefully, and she threw it at him.

With a scream that sounded like a roar, Pierre opened the car door and jumped out, tearing off his clothing as he did. Marianne watched him through the window of the closed door, unnerved. She struggled to locate the car keys, expecting to find them in the ignition. To her shock, they were missing. Where had he put them?

She searched frantically on the floor in the dark; then, as she heard horrific sounds coming from Pierre, she threw open the passenger door to turn on the interior lights, desperate to locate the keys. Marianne intended to slide over to the driver's side and take off with the Jaguar if she could, leaving him to find his way home and calm down before they met again. He was out of his mind right now. For the first time in her life, she felt blind panic.

"Damn it! Where are they?" she sobbed with terror as she kept crawling all over the seats, patting down the floor mats, thrusting her hands into the space under the seats. Nothing. Not a trace of the keys.

Without warning, something seized her leg as she scrambled around on the seat, head nearly on the floor, legs hanging out the door. She screamed in fright and glanced over her shoulder. She could see nothing at first. All she could do was experience the worst pain in her life as something sharp and pointed sank into the flesh of her calf, let it go, and fastened onto it again, harder this time, repeating the pain again and again.

As Marianne shrieked in agony, she caught a glimpse of what had grabbed her leg. Her adrenaline took over as she saw herself looking over her shoulder into the fierce yellow eyes of a wolf. In an instant, she managed to pull her leg away as she made a superhuman effort and kicked it frantically with her good leg, sobbing with terror.

The beast fell back momentarily, and as it started to recover and lunge at her, Marianne sobbed with pain and twisted herself around to grab the door and slam it shut just in time to feel the impact of the wolf colliding with it.

Irrational with pain and fear, Marianne scrambled across to the driver's-side door and opened it to scream for Pierre to come and help her. The wolf took another leap at the car and came crashing back to earth, its eyes glittering in the dark outside the passenger window as it focused on her, frantic inside the Jaguar.

Then, as the great beast disappeared briefly from sight, Marianne realized to her horror that the driver's-side door was open. She grabbed at the door handle and tried to slam the door shut on her attacker, but she was a second too slow. Out of the dark came the flash of amber eyes, a terrifying growl, and the feel of its teeth sinking into her soft flesh as the wolf leaped into the car, intent on its prey.

Nearly suffocating beneath the warm, shaggy body of the wolf, Marianne fought for her life, punching, twisting, hitting the door handle to force open the door and try to escape. As the animal's jaws clamped tight around her shoulder, she gave a primal cry of pain and grabbed it by its leg, sinking her own teeth into the wolf's sinewy limb.

For a moment, the beast seemed stunned. Marianne took advantage of its surprise by smashing it across the muzzle and dragging herself out from under its weight and through the car door.

Desperate with pain and fear, Marianne's legs gave way as she struggled to escape from the bloodthirsty monster. With the sound of its chilling growls rumbling in her ears, Marianne crawled along the ground as fast as she could. Then she collapsed, utterly spent, her body in agony, her mind in chaos. The last thing she saw as she lay bleeding under the stars was the gigantic dark shadow of the wolf as it paused to circle her, then leaned back on its haunches and leaped.

The kill took only minutes.

# Chapter Thirty-six

Standing over the bloody, torn corpse of its victim, the great gray wolf panted from the force of its fury. It looked down upon the body and poked it with his paw, searching for a sign of life. It found none.

Slowly, deliberately, the wolf sat back on its haunches and let loose a howl of emotion that sent night birds scattering from their perch on a nearby tree. Its wails startled a raccoon that roamed the woods.

Time passed while the wolf sat there next to its kill, guarding the body after the first wave of murderous frenzy subsided. Moonlight filtered through the trees. Night creatures called to one another. The wolf suddenly felt the pain of its injuries from the collision with the car door and from the woman's bite, and it lay down next to the corpse, pillowing its head on her chest.

Pierre didn't know how much time had gone by, but when he opened his eyes and realized he was back in human form, he was lying next to a bloodied corpse. The kill had been fast and furious; now Pierre would have the rest of his life to reflect upon the insanity of his act and the collapse of his hopes for happiness. He had killed the woman he loved, the one he wanted for his mate, the one whose love would have given meaning to his life. Now he had nothing. He looked into a black and bottomless void.

"Oh my God! Marianne!"

He had killed her.

"Marianne!" He stood up and stared at his work, hardly able to recognize her in the darkness. But he could feel that she was covered in blood when he touched her. Repulsed by the sensation, Pierre began to shake uncontrollably as he stood there, naked and chilled by the cool autumn air.

His mind seemed to reboot as he stared at what was left of the woman he loved. She was dead and he had destroyed her. She had insulted him and he had reacted by reverting to werewolf form and annihilating her.

"Marianne! I'm sorry!" Pierre sobbed, half doubled over in grief. "You were everything to me. Why did you say those things?" he demanded of the dead woman. "I loved you more than anything. I would have given you everything I had. . . ."

He experienced a surge of terror as he looked at Marianne's dead body, at his own body, at the car. He had to get out of there. He didn't dare let anyone find him like this, naked and so close to the corpse.

Stumbling in the dark, Pierre made his way back to the car and he found his clothing scattered on the ground next to it. Some of it was torn, some was intact. He hurriedly dressed as best he could, frantically searched for the keys, found them in his pants pocket, and jumped into the Jaguar.

Still shaking from nerves, Pierre started the engine, checked the time, calculated that most people would have left the area by now, and drove carefully out of the reservation with headlights off until he reached the city streets and headed back to New York.

The first thing Pierre did when he reached Manhattan was to go to an all-night car wash and try to remove any trace of the kill. There was blood on the front seat, a hideous reminder of his crime.

"Ah, do you understand English?" he asked the attendant. When he got an affirmative response, Pierre said, "I cut my hand and it stained the seat. I need you to clean it."

Without commenting, the man applied a solvent that seemed to make it disappear, but Pierre felt uneasy until he drove away in his shiny car after paying cash for the work. He thought the man gave him an odd look.

He drove for hours in the middle of the night, trying to understand what he had done and what he must now do to survive it. Should he call his lawyer? Should he call the police and give them some story about being stopped and assaulted by carjackers? Well, he still had the car, so that didn't seem too smart. What could he say about Marianne? She had been kidnapped? They'd had a lovers' quarrel and she'd run off to go back to the restaurant to call for a ride home? Then on the way she'd been attacked by some savage beast, probably the one who killed those people near the docks and over in Jersey City.

He had to think of something. People had seen him with Marianne. Keri knew he was going to take her to dinner. Hell, Marianne's friends at Durand et Frères probably knew she was going out to dinner with him, too. The whole restaurant had seen them together, all lovey-dovey and romantic.

Pierre's brain tried to cobble together some story he could peddle to the police. He, the last person to see Marianne, was the prime suspect. He knew this. The police knew this. Everybody who ever watched a detective movie knew this. The trick was to turn it to his advantage.

Every one of those people who had seen him with Marianne could testify to the fact that Pierre was head over heels in love with her. Keri would say so, Marianne's assistant, Flora, would swear to it; even all those strangers at the restaurant would affirm it. Therefore, since he was so much in love, how could he possibly have done his darling any harm?

Could a man, even an angry man, an enraged man, have inflicted injuries on Marianne like the ones she suffered? No. They were not consistent with human activity. Even a first-year med student would know that. A respected medical examiner would do the autopsy, make a list of all the injuries, and say conclusively that the deceased had suffered death at the hands of a wild animal.

Yes. A wild animal. Perhaps a wolf. Certainly not a well-known jeweler who adored her and lived to make her happy.

With a sigh, Pierre felt he might just manage to salvage his reputation and keep the authorities at bay despite this evening's tragedy. If things heated up, he was going to say farewell to this town and remove himself to a place without so many painful memories. He had plenty of cash; he also had offshore accounts in the

Caymans and on the Isle of Man. A little vacation at this point would be a very good thing. Some good investments and advance planning enabled him to pick and choose his destination.

# Chapter Thirty-seven

Team Werewolf had not slept well and were inclined to place blame on one another. Paul and Catherine left the temporary headquarters after seven in the morning, returned to their own hotel, showered, put on fresh clothes, and went to stake out Pierre's business. They were fed up with von Hoffman and Heinz. They needed a break and some fresh air.

Shortly after eight thirty, from their observation post inside a dark-windowed SUV, they saw a young woman—the assistant, Keri—approach the shop from the subway station and let herself in.

"Business as usual," Paul commented. "Nothing out of the ordinary."

"She probably doesn't know anything about her boss's alter ego," Catherine replied. "If she did, do you think she'd work for him?"

Paul laughed. "I know I wouldn't," he said.

An hour later, a late-model burgundy Jaguar made a turn out of the traffic lane and eased its way into a narrow driveway next to the boutique.

"Look! It's him. He's got a new car," Catherine exclaimed. "Well, at least we know where he is now."

"Call headquarters. The old man will be happy to find out the werewolf has turned up."

"My pleasure," she said, taking out her cell phone and punching in the numbers.

After Catherine spoke to her boss, who was relieved to learn that Pierre was still in town, Paul asked his partner what von Hoffman said.

"Keep up the surveillance and plan for the takedown at the earliest opportunity."

"Works for me," he said.


When Pierre let himself in through the back door and walked into his workroom he felt like a living corpse. He knew he looked haggard. The mirror showed a man with dark circles under his eyes and a lifeless expression, a cross between a drug addict and a zombie.

He disappeared into the bathroom, shaved, washed at the sink, took off the clothes he had worn the night before and threw them into a plastic garbage bag. Then he changed into fresh clothing he kept stashed in the shop for emergencies.

"Keri," he called when he emerged, "I'm in the back. I'm going to be busy today. Tell the clients I can't come out and chitchat, if anybody asks for me."

Keri strolled in to say good morning and paused as she came face to face with her boss. He could tell she was shocked. Her eyes widened and she looked at him as if she were seeing him for the first time. Instinct told him she felt uneasy.

"Pierre, are you all right? You look terrible."

"I'm okay. It was a late night. Could you go to the coffee shop down the street and get me a double latte? I could use it."

"Sure."

Something in her face told him he made her nervous right now. Well, why not? She was just a puny human he could slay with a couple of bites to the neck. She should be fearful. She should show him the respect a major predator deserved. He savored that fear, was almost aroused by it. That flicker of trepidation fed his ego.

Ah, what the hell. He liked Keri. He could allow a little mercy in her case. She was loyal—unlike that bitch he'd just killed.

In their SUV parked down the block from the Beau Bijou, Paul and Catherine drank coffee from paper cups and waited for some sign of activity. They had seen Pierre and the assistant. All seemed normal. In the meantime, Paul took the opportunity to call Julie on her cell phone and check on her.

"Everything's fine," she replied. "Ian was a very gracious host. We talked about art and he showed me some of his collection." She lowered her voice in awe. "You wouldn't believe some of the paintings he has. The kinds of things most people see only in museums."

"He's been collecting for years. And I think he inherited some of them, too."

"I felt honored to see them. It was so extraordinary. And he makes you feel like part of the family," she said.

Paul coughed a little. "Yes," he agreed. "He does. He makes me feel that way, too. So where are you now?" he asked.

"Back at my office at the college. Vladimir drove me there. And security guards are nearby."

"Good. Glad to know you're safe. I'll call you again as soon as I can."

After the first customers of the day had entered the Beau Bijou, Paul and Catherine kept a discreet watch on the place, but failed to spot anything out of the ordinary. Presumably the jeweler and his assistant were simply doing whatever they did each day. Then out of boredom, Catherine got out of the car and took a stroll down the street past the shop and spotted the burgundy jaguar, with the girl in it, leaving by the alleyway that cut through to the street behind the boutique.

She pulled out her cell phone and punched in Paul's number. "I just saw the assistant driving the Jaguar out the back exit."

"Where's Pierre?" he replied.

Catherine glanced into the shop. At first she didn't see him, and then she looked again and saw him talking to a customer. When she strolled out of view, she reached for her phone again and said, "He's in there with a client."

"I'm going to call the Institut guys to keep an eye on that car. They're on the next block. They can follow it."

When Catherine got back into the surveillance car with Paul, she shook her head. "Do you think he's playing some kind of game with us? Could he know we're trailing him?"

"No. He's probably just sending the girl back with a rental car. In an hour or so we're going to pick up the signal from the green Jaguar heading this way. I guarantee it."

"I hope so," said Catherine. "It would make things easier."

Pierre had reluctantly taken over the front showroom of the Beau Bijou while Keri ran his errand. After the disaster of last night, he didn't want to be there if they discovered any stains on the upholstery of his loaner car. He couldn't deal with it.

He actually didn't know if they would be able to tell there was a problem, but he put his faith in the less-than-thorough inspection he hoped it would receive upon arrival. With luck, nobody would find traces of his crime until after it had been loaned out to at least five other people. Then let them try to figure out where those stains came from.

The thought of that made him feel back in control once more, not like the poor jerk whose true, pure love had been kicked aside, spat on, defiled by the manipulative witch he had chosen to lavish his affection on.

Had any man ever been so cruelly deceived by the woman he loved? Had any Montfort? Pierre didn't think so. He had paid her the ultimate compliment, chosen her to be his mate, his beloved, and she had insulted him by calling him a dog. A dog! The kind of mutt whose devotion the master takes for granted because it's always there, always ready to do his bidding. Shit.

That woman didn't deserve to be the mate of the last Montfort werewolf. Thank God he had seen her true nature before he had married her and made her the mother of his offspring. An unworthy mother would only breed inferior children, not the kind who could, in later years, make their father proud of them.

No. He had to choose wisely the next time, pick a mate who could fulfill his destiny, love him, and revere him. He should have realized how weak she was. What had he been thinking?

Pierre took the spectacular gift he had given her out of his pants pocket and studied it. He had been stupid enough to offer it to her. Well, now it was his again, and he would retain it. Or perhaps he would sell it. The memory of Marianne flinging it at him disgusted him; he no longer treasured the pendant. He had cleaned her blood and fingerprints off it, but it seemed bad luck to keep it.

*Get rid of it,* he told himself. *You can always do another one.* This one is cursed.

That couple who commissioned it had been so disappointed when he had Keri inform them he couldn't deliver it. Pierre wondered if they were still around, even though they said they had to leave New York by now. What if something had come up to delay their return? What if they still wanted it?

The idea of ridding himself of this bad-luck jewel and gaining thirty thousand dollars appealed to Pierre. Out of sight, out of mind. Marianne's loss, his gain.

Morose and silent, he stared at the necklace and he knew deep in his heart that no matter what lie he told himself, he had loved her. Marianne was his one and only.

Every time he felt the pain her teeth had left in his arm when she struggled for her life, he felt a bittersweet guilt. He had killed his mate, but until his attack he had no idea how perfect she had been. A woman fierce enough to fight a werewolf! Where would he ever find her equal?

# Chapter Thirty-eight

Catherine answered her cell phone and found Maryse on the other end. The woman could hardly contain her delight.

"Guess who just called to ask if I am still interested in the Montfort pendant."

"Pierre?"

"That's the one."

"I can't believe it. You told him you were leaving the country. How does he know you're still in New York?"

"He said he just took a chance. I told him I had the number routed to my home phone and I was speaking to him from Germany."

"And he accepted that?"

"Of course. I don't think he cared if I said I was on Mars. He really wants to sell that pendant."

Catherine drew in her breath. Unbelievable.

"What do you think we should do?" Maryse asked.

"Did you give him an answer?"

"No. I wanted to let you know first."

Catherine hesitated. "Of course we would like to use

a meeting as the basis for our plan." She didn't have to go into details. Maryse knew what they had intended to do once they got him to the rendezvous. "But if you're supposed to be in Germany, it's going to be difficult to set it up."

"Not if I designate someone to act on my behalf. I could say I have to contact a friend I can trust and then wire them the money. He can meet this friend at a specific location, and then bada bing."

Catherine looked at her cell phone. Did Maryse, who had studied English at Oxford, actually say "bada bing"?

"Where does that come from?" she inquired.

"What?"

"Bada bing."

Laughter broke through, and Maryse sheepishly confessed she was addicted to American TV.

"Well, come meet with us and we'll make plans for Pierre," she said. "This is wonderful. It puts the ball back in our court. Von Hoffman will be pleased."

"I'll be over this afternoon. You're in the same place?"

"Yes. At the place we use in SoHo. We'll be expecting you."

Confident that Pierre was secure, Paul and Catherine returned to their hotel. Paul couldn't believe their luck.

"I can't help but wonder why he suddenly reversed himself."

"Who knows?" Catherine said with a shrug. "The important thing is he's ready to hand it over."

"Yes. Now all we have to do is make the arrangements for the purchase of the gem."

"We'll need a proxy for Maryse."

"That's easy. We'll use somebody else from Team Werewolf," Paul said, with a slightly ironic inflection.

"One of the local operatives?"

"Yes. There are a couple of guys who could play the part," said Paul.

"He could be a businessman with a taste for travel. He met Maryse at Monte Carlo and became friends with her and her husband."

"All right," Paul conceded. "Walker is a smooth conversationalist. It's plausible."

Catherine glanced at him. He didn't seem convinced. "Don't hold back," she said. "Who would you recommend?"

"Let's send one of the Europeans. It would make more sense. Somebody who can be passed off as a moneyed gentleman from over there, the sort who attends the opera, the ballet . . ."

"We could use Heinz."

Paul was about to agree; then he remembered that Heinz and von Hoffman had gone to the Beau Bijou and met Pierre. Perhaps it would seem too much of a coincidence.

"On second thought, perhaps we ought to stick with our first choice. Just because he's American doesn't rule him out as a friend of Maryse. And, of course, Pierre might think old money once he hears the Boston accent. It wouldn't make sense for a woman like Maryse to have friends without money, would it?"

"No. She plays the part well," Catherine said with a smile. "Now let's see if Walker jumps at the chance to be the main player in a sting operation."

"I think he'll love it," said Paul. "He's such an alpha male."

"Yes," Catherine agreed. "And so is our quarry. He'll be well matched."

The next morning, while an energetic group of suburban housewives were doing a run through the Eagle Rock Reservation in West Orange, New Jersey, one of them spotted a group of birds clustered around what she thought was a kind of garbage spill. Dismayed by the sight of trash spread over the grass, she pointed it out to her friends.

"Look at that mess."

One of the others glanced at the spot and looked confused. "It looks like old clothes," she said uncertainly. "Why would anyone dump them here?"

"Kids being stupid?"

Now the women stopped their exercise and walked with halting steps toward the mess on the grass. They saw the dark birds take flight as they approached. Then they got a good look at what they had been feeding on.

"Oh God! Oh God! I think I'm going to be sick!" wailed Marci. "Let's get out of here."

"What is it?" asked one of the women at the back of the group."

"A body," replied another one. "Let's call the cops. Fast."

"Oh, jeez," whispered her friend right before she threw up.

Two hours later, Paul received a call from his mole in the NYPD informing him of the newest attack. The hairs on the back of his neck stood up. The latest victim had died during the time they lost track of Pierre.

"Shit!"

"Our guys heard from the West Orange PD and checked with Jersey City. Same kind of attack. Same bites, tears, rips. She was in pretty bad shape."

"Any idea about who she was?"

"Nothing definite yet. But one thing for sure. She wasn't poor. The jewelry was expensive. So was the label in her dress."

"Anything else?"

"Yeah. Brindisi and Rodriguez went to talk to the woman who was friendly with the last vic, the one from Jersey City. Guess what? She went on a date with Pierre last night and hasn't been seen since. She was his girlfriend, and the relationship was getting rocky, according to her assistant."

Paul felt his pulse race. The Montfort was responding to stress. The hormones were out of control and he was losing all restraint. If they didn't take him down now, the Metro area would be swimming in victims. With Pierre so crazed that he would attack and kill his girlfriend, nobody was safe. Paul was convinced the missing woman at the auction house and the newest victim were one and the same. How could they not be?

Von Hoffman responded to the news with barely concealed frustration. "We have to speed things up," he ordered. "The Montfort is going into the classic berserk phase of his life cycle, where he will attack and kill as he pleases for the pleasure of it. He had to have considered this woman his mate if he had invested so much time and effort in the relationship, and it is unprecedented for one of them to kill a mate. Our wolf is exhibiting a rare degree of hysteria, perhaps exacerbated by fear of capture."

"Then we have to get him to the meeting as quickly as we can."

"Yes. Just don't scare him away by pressuring him. We have to reel him in carefully."

When Paul ended the call, he wondered where he might draw the line. Apply enough pressure to get him to turn up with the necklace; be mellow enough to let Pierre think he could set the agenda.

What kind of werewolf would savage and kill its mate? Okay, nothing could be proved until tests were done, but the circumstances seemed to point to it. Pierre takes his girlfriend on a date and the woman doesn't show up for work the next day. And a fresh corpse turns up.

Never in Paul's experience had a werewolf killed its own mate. It just wasn't done. They could slay half a village and leave their mate safe and sound. Historically there was no record of it. Until Pierre.

Was the last Montfort werewolf such a perverse and horrifying mutant that it would do the unthinkable?

After a conference with Catherine, Paul decided to go along with her suggestion to keep their local operatives sticking close to Pierre while Maryse set up the appointment. If their men could keep him in view, they could interfere with any attempts at murder. If Pierre shape-shifted and went after a victim, shoot to kill.

The next morning, when Catherine had already had breakfast and seen the news about the "wild beast's" latest victim, she cursed Team Werewolf for having been so lax. The Montfort had given them the slip while he changed cars right under their noses, and some poor woman had paid the price. Disgusting. And now the werewolf's territory had expanded into the suburbs of New Jersey. She could almost see an article materializing for Paul's favorite American magazine, *Weird New Jersey*. Now the Garden State could boast of not one but two mysterious slayings in the space of mere weeks and drop hints of bizarre paranormal doings in the suburbs.

The Montfort wallowed in this kind of thrill seeking, she reflected. Striking where nobody suspects; then do it again and again, until the public wakes up to the fact that there's something evil out there in the shadows, waiting to rip them to pieces.

Catherine felt the urge to have a conference with Ian, but he was deep in his daylight slumber. The Russian wasn't, she thought. She dialed his number and heard his charming voice say, "Pavel."

"Hello, this is Catherine. Have you seen the local papers?"

"The latest attack? Yes."

"We have to put a stop to it now. If we wait too long, he'll kill dozens of innocents."

"Your boss wants him taken alive," he reminded her.

"Yes. But if that proves too difficult, we'll just have to make an on-the-spot decision when the time comes."

"I still have the reading for the car. It's back behind his shop now."

"Keep monitoring him. And keep me posted. Any movement, let me know."

"Of course, mademoiselle. And watch out for your American operatives. Some of them are so thrilled to be working with von Hoffman on their home ground that they might get overly confident," he warned. "This Montfort is truly evil and merits the greatest caution."

"Yes," she said. "And thank you for your concern."

# Chapter Thirty-nine

The local tabloids continued to let the citizens know they were in danger by splashing the newsstands with attention-grabbing headlines such as SOCIETY GAL SLAUGHTERED and PREDATOR LOOSE IN JERSEY. Breathless accounts described how a blue-blooded mover and shaker in the upscale world of Durand et Frères had died in a wooded area of West Orange, savaged by a wolf or wolves, chewed, mutilated, and left to die. Police had spread out a dragnet and discovered she had been seen at an elegant restaurant nearby in the company of a gentleman the night she died. As it happened, the restaurant was having a raffle on behalf of a trendy Save the Rainforest charity and the victim had purchased several tickets. The host remembered that because she was so striking and was able to give the police her name and address when they canvassed the area the day after the crime. Her parents identified the body by means of a still visible scar on her arm and a ring she wore. Dental records confirmed it.

"She was a real hottie," one of the waiters commented. "Gorgeous. The guy was one of those moneyed types, and nuts about her. You could see it by the way he looked at her."

After hooking the reader with a scary headline, the writer let it be known that experts were still analyzing the kill, but most considered it the work of a wolf. She hadn't actually been devoured, they explained, but killed with vicious bites to the neck and then chewed up pretty badly during the attack. Police veterans of many years' experience reportedly wept at the sight. A sergeant was moved to say he'd never seen such a vicious attack in his whole career.

"Reliable sources" identified her as Marianne McGill, a rising star at Durand et Frères. For added titillation, an interview with her assistant let the world know that Marianne had worked with Jim Perkins, another victim, and was close to him, going so far as to call in the missing person's report when Jim went missing. Death appeared to be stalking the venerable company. Was there some kind of curse on Durand et Frères?

"It was sort of ironic that they were both killed like that," stated Flora O'Connnor, the dead woman's assistant. "The atmosphere in the office is pretty grim these days. They were both such professionals. Such straight arrows."

"Did Ms. McGill have any known enemies?" the reporter inquired.

"Oh, no. People just loved her."

"Was she romantically involved with Mr. Perkins?" the reporter asked.

"Not at all. She had a boyfriend. She went out with him the night she disappeared. His name is Pierre de Montfort."

\* \* \*

"Julie? Are you there?" Paul spoke into his cell phone as he stood on the street corner near her apartment building. He hadn't planned on seeing her until after they took down the werewolf, but right now, he needed to be with her. He couldn't explain it; he just wanted to see her, speak with her, kiss her. In a way, he already knew she was *his* mate, and he had to make sure she was safe.

"Paul? Where are you? Did you get him?"

"Not yet. Can I come up and see you? I have a few hours, and I would love to spend them with you."

He heard the smile in her voice. "Well, come right on up," she said.

Julie had thought she wouldn't see Paul for several more days and she was thrilled at the unexpected visit. She flung herself into his arms as soon as she opened the door.

"I've been so frantic about you, especially after I read this morning's news. I keep thinking of that creature and how it kills. It makes me crazy to picture you and Catherine near it."

Paul kissed her tenderly, passionately, wanting to hold her so close to him they could blend into one. He nuzzled her, taking in the scent of her perfume.

"Are you on a break?" she asked.

"Sort of. I have to report back in a few hours. Other people are keeping him under surveillance right now."

"Would you like something to eat or drink?"

"No, I just want you," he said truthfully. "Come. Sit down with me. I have something very important I want to ask you, and I couldn't wait another minute."

Julie led him over to the sofa and sat, looking at him with a quizzical smile. She took his hand.

"Darling," he said, "I know we've been talking about what we're going to do after this case is over, but we haven't made things definite. I want to. I want you to know just how much I love you and want you with me. Always."

Julie looked into his eyes and kissed him. She loved Paul. She had thought he was the sexiest man in the world since they first met, she respected his work, and she loved every romantic encounter in the past few years. She didn't want anyone else in her bed or in her life.

"This sounds serious," Julie said.

"It is. I'm asking you to marry me." He leaned over and kissed her, gently at first, drawing her closer as his kisses deepened.

He reluctantly stopped the kiss before things could go any further. Paul reached into his jacket and pulled out the jeweler's box.

"Is this what I think it is?" she marveled.

With a swift gesture, Paul opened the box, withdrew the diamond solitaire, and placed it on her ring finger. "Will you marry me?" he asked. "I know I have a very strange job, and it will take me away at times, but Julie, you're the only woman I want to spend my life with. Whether it's long or short," he added poignantly. "And tonight I felt compelled to say this to you so you have no doubts about just how much I love you."

Julie threw her arms around him and buried her face in his chest. "Yes," she said. "I'll marry you. I love you. I fell in love with you the first time we met, and then it became so much more during the past two years. You're my soul mate. There's nobody else for me."

"We'll make the announcement right after I finish this mission," he said. "And we can start planning the wedding."

When Julie finally got to sleep later that night, she found herself back at the Château Montfort in her dreams, walking near the spot where her ancestor met her fate. The day was bright, the skies were clear; it seemed perfect.

"You ought to have the honeymoon here," a voice said. When Julie looked around, she didn't see anyone. Then she realized there was a man standing several feet away, his face turned toward the château.

"Do you work here?" she asked.

"No," he replied. "I used to live here. You would have lived here, too, if things had worked out differently. But it's useless to complain about what cannot be changed."

For the first time, Julie looked carefully at the man and was startled to see that he was dressed in all the finery of the late eighteenth century: blue silk coat and vest with fantastic floral embroidery, cream-colored breeches, and a fine white linen shirt with expensive lace at the neck and cuffs.

"I wish you well, *ma chère*," he said. "Paul is a fine man. He will make you happy."

Then he disappeared, and Julie drifted into a deep and peaceful sleep, thinking of Paul, the château, and their future together.

When Paul rejoined Team Werewolf after his visit with Julie, Catherine remarked that he looked as if a weight had fallen from his shoulders.

"I finally came to a decision," he said. "I asked Julie to marry me. We have been talking about our future, but I never came right out and asked her to be my wife. Tonight I couldn't wait any longer. I had to make it definite. We belong together and I want to do it right."

Catherine's eyes sparkled at the news. "And?" she asked.

"She said yes."

"*Félicitations!* I can't think of a couple more suited for each other. It's fantastic news."

"Now all we have to do is deal with the wolf," he said.


"Pierre! Are you there?" From his worktable in the back of the shop, Pierre heard Keri calling him. "Pierre?"

He couldn't respond, couldn't tear his eyes from the photo on the front page of the *Post*.

"Oh my God," she gasped, looking at the paper and seeing Marianne's ravaged face and the headline LADY EXEC SLAIN.

He raised his head briefly to look at her. Then the effort sapped his strength and he slumped over the desk, sobbing with grief.

"Oh, Pierre, I'm so sorry," Keri whispered as she stepped behind the desk and put her arms around him. "I'm devastated, too. How could it happen?" Keri wondered as she held Pierre close to her. "It just doesn't make sense."

He pulled away and made a manful effort to sit up and speak to her, despite his grief. Keri looked at him like a student, waiting for her teacher to explain a puzzle.

He knew he stunned her by saying, "Marianne broke up with me."

"What?"

"We went to a wonderful restaurant that night, some-place in New Jersey. The food was delicious and the view looked out over the New York skyline. I felt on top of the world," he continued, choking back tears. "I gave her the necklace. She loved it."

"And then?"

"Afterward we left and we drove to the top of the mountain to look at the skyline. The city is so beautiful from there," he said wistfully.

"Okay," Keri said. "You had dinner; you looked at the view. . . ."

He wiped the tears away with his sleeve as he turned his face away from her.

"And then?" she prodded, sounding uneasy.

Pierre felt a surge of power when he smelled her fear. The wolf in him raged to be free at the sight of Keri's vulnerable, pale face. He could see her pulse beating wildly at her throat, and he could barely concentrate on his story.

"And then Marianne told me she was tired of me, tired of my presents, tired of my devotion. She just wanted to break it off."

He turned to look back at her, schooling his expression to one of brokenhearted grief.

For a long time, Keri said nothing, waiting for Pierre to continue. Finally he did. "I begged her to reconsider. I told her how much she meant to me, how much I loved her. She wouldn't listen."

Now her heart was beating so fast, he feared he might not be strong enough to control the wolf. Dear God, her fear was exhilarating. It excited him.

"I had to listen to all these insults. She actually said I

reminded her of some stupid old dog," he whispered with feeling. "A dog."

"Dogs are very loyal," Keri responded passionately. "They love people and never desert them."

That made him smile.

Then he lowered his head and said, "I was so angry, so hurt, I didn't think. I just told her if that was the way she felt about me, about all the love I had for her, she could just walk home."

When Pierre said that, Keri's mouth dropped open in shock. "All the way from New Jersey?" she gasped.

"Well, I wasn't thinking clearly. I told her I'd drop her off near the restaurant and she could call someone to take her home. It was the last time I saw her," he said, breaking down once more. "The beast must have killed her and dragged her away after I left in a huff. It's all my fault. I let my anger overpower my common sense and look what happened to poor Marianne. Keri, she was the love of my life! I can't live with myself after this."

Pierre knew he'd played this as well as he could. The pain of losing Marianne was still raw, but killing her had changed him. The power and the passion had blurred in him, and he was hungry to taste it again. He needed to control his wolf and keep Keri alive, at least until she helped him solidify his story. Soon the police would be coming to question him, he knew, and convincing Keri of his innocence was essential to his plans.

An awkward silence followed Pierre's confession. Keri finally sat down and just stared at the newspaper on his desk. "I think you ought to tell this to the police," she said. "People know you went out with her that night. You'll have to let them know what happened."

"Yes," he said. "I will, later. Right now, I can't face it."

Keri nodded. Then she asked, "Do you want to open today? Maybe it's not such a good idea. I don't think you're up to it."

"I'm not," he agreed. "But you can handle the customers. I'm going to stay back here for a while. Then I'm going home."

She had to ask. "You're not going to do anything rash, are you?"

Pierre shook his head. "I just need time to mourn by myself. I can't deal with anything today. It's too raw."

"I'll take care of the shop. Just go home and try to pull yourself together. But you have to call the police to let them know what happened between you. It's only right."

"Yes, of course I'll let them know," Pierre promised. He sounded sincere.

Catherine received a call a few hours later from one of her NYPD contacts who reported that Officers Brindisi and Rodriguez had paid a visit to Pierre's shop and had spoken to the assistant about his car. The young woman told them he had needed to have a headlight replaced, so he'd rented another Jaguar. It went back to the dealership the next day and she brought back his own Jag with the new light.

"Did she show any nervousness about her boss?" Catherine asked. "She must have read all the headlines about the dead girlfriend by now."

"She told us he was pretty shaken up by the woman's death. She looked uneasy when they kept reminding her that he was the last person seen with her. The guys laid it on thick by reminding her that most vics are killed by people they know."

"She could be next on his list. Keep up surveillance on the shop. Get a camera in there, if possible. He's out of control and she's accessible. Bad combination."

"Okay. We're going to step up the pressure on Pierre with a visit by Brindisi and Rodriguez. He's been mentioned in the papers as her boyfriend and her dinner companion that night. He's got to be sweating it. You keep the monitors on him. He might decide to get out of town after our guys drop in. You could follow him and grab him."

"Just don't let him grab your cops. Even the NYPD is no match for a werewolf."

"Oh, by the way," said the mole, "we got into the crime lab in West Orange and took a sample from the vic. She had the Montfort DNA all over her. Geneva sent us their records and it was a match."

"Good work."

"Von Hoffman himself trained me back in the eighties. I never forgot what he used to say then: 'Be one hundred twenty percent certain—then nail him.'"

She smiled. "That's our boss."

# Chapter Forty

Paul and von Hoffman decided that if the Montfort would agree to deal with an intermediary, Walker could fill in as the rich American who knew Maryse and could act on their behalf. Team Werewolf could set up a meeting place, take it over with the help of local operatives, and trank the suspect when he set foot in the room. All very cut-and-dried.

"What if the tranquilizer dart doesn't work on him?" Catherine inquired. "We don't know enough about his chemistry. We've never had to worry about keeping one alive before."

Von Hoffman shook his head. "*Nein.* We know enough. He can be subdued by the dart. It won't be a problem. As soon as he is, we load him into a van and drive him to the airport at the New Jersey location."

"Will there be a cage onboard to contain him while he's in transit?" Paul asked.

"Yes. That is an additional security measure we've decided on. You know how these creatures can be," he said with a shrug, as if dealing with frisky, drugged werewolves were so common, a child could understand the risks.

"Well then," Catherine said, "I guess we'd better tell Maryse to make the call."

Paul glanced at his partner. "The woman in West Orange is probably his fourth attack in under a month. He seems to be in a killing frenzy. Police departments in at least three cities are looking for whoever or whatever murdered those people. We need to move quickly before he kills again or the police step in and endanger their own lives."

"All right, then. I'll tell Maryse to call him up," Catherine said. "This will be the last meeting Mr. Montfort ever attends."

Paul nodded and said, "We'll grab him before he knows what hit him."

Pierre knew the NYPD would pay him a call— boyfriend of the victim, last person seen with the victim. Hell, he practically had "Guilty as Sin" stamped all over his forehead. Any kid who watched *CSI* would check him out. Even little Keri was looking at him differently now. It excited him.

He was a Montfort. Let the cops grill him. Let Keri's knees shake when she looked at him. He could brazen his way out of it. Or just shape-shift and head out of town if it came to that. He had plenty of cash and several good destinations in mind.

But he couldn't rid himself of the memory of Marianne. The way she fought him, the way she struck back, biting him, hitting him, slamming him with the car door, for heaven's sake. She was a wild woman, so savage that he had to admit there was nobody else like her. And now, because he couldn't control his damned hormones that night, he had killed her. God, the two of them could have produced one hell of a superwolf!

Because she liked to get involved in causes, she had purchased half a dozen tickets for some charity that night at dinner, which led the cops straight back to her address, which led them to her office and her talkative coworkers.

Damn that Flora, he reflected. He ought to pay her a visit and chew on *her.* She couldn't wait to start blabbing to the tabloids and mention his name. But that was all right. He had lawyers. He had balls. And best of all, he had an escape route.

Yeah. He would fly to Florida, hop over to the Caymans, do some shifting of funds, and head for an exclusive expat compound near Rio. No extradition treaty, *no problema.* So what if Rio had a crime rate that would make the South Bronx look calm? He was a Montfort werewolf. He lived to kill. He could kill for years and get himself applauded for wiping out the criminal element as a lone crusader. There was no downside.

All these thoughts of killing left Pierre so aroused he had to struggle to prevent himself from letting the wolf out. He had to keep it in check for a while, at least until he could sell that bad-luck necklace, collect some more cash, and head out of town. He could never have enough cash.

He wondered if he might be able to sate his hunger before he left town. He knew where Keri was, alone and defenseless at the shop. She'd make a nice snack, always eating that vegan stuff. He wondered if her flesh would taste of carrots and celery. Too tame for him really. He craved something tangier. As a human, he really liked her. As a werewolf, he might not be able to hold back. Poor Keri; she was a walking appetizer.

When Sergeant Joe Brindisi and Officer Manny Rodriguez arrived at Pierre's apartment with a warrant to search the premises and conduct a search of the Beau Bijou as well, he wasn't all that intimidated. To make it look good, he tried to give the impression of a man overwhelmed by grief.

"Come in, Officers. I was going to call you later, when I felt I could handle it," he said pathetically.

"Sir?"

"I was probably the last person to see Marianne alive," he explained. "Yesterday I saw the pictures in the paper, and I'm still so shaken up, I can barely think straight."

"We heard you and Miss McGill were very close," Joe said diplomatically.

"Yes," Pierre said with a nod. "I loved her."

Pierre let his body language suggest dejection, despair, all the things one could expect from a man who had just lost the love of his life. He was grief personified.

"You say you were the last person to see her alive?"

"I had to be. Except for the one who killed her," he said pointedly. "And if I hadn't been so stupid and let my pride take over, she would still be alive today. I don't know how I'll ever live with this."

Brindisi asked permission to sit down and ask a few questions, and Pierre graciously pointed toward a sofa that probably cost more than the cop's monthly salary.

"Mr. de Montfort, can you tell us exactly what happened between you and Miss McGill on the night you went to dinner with her?"

"We drove over to a restaurant in West Orange, New Jersey, at a place called Eagle Rock Reservation. The restaurant is terrific. The food is great, and the view is fantastic. Perfect for romance," he recalled somberly. "During dinner, everything was fine. She seemed to be happy. She enjoyed the meal. We talked about so many things. . . ."

"So you had a romantic dinner with no sign of anything wrong."

"Yes," he said. "It was perfect. Afterward, I drove to a spot where you get a great view of the New York skyline, not too far from the restaurant, and we sat in the car and talked some more."

"And what went wrong?" Joe asked kindly.

Pierre flicked him a glance and then lowered his head. "We had a fight."

"Did this fight get physical?"

"No. It was verbal. I should have said 'argument.' Marianne wanted to go home. She had a lot to do the next day. I just wanted to linger and enjoy the scenery." He shook his head. "I guess she got annoyed with me and started to tell me everything I didn't want to hear. She was bored with our relationship. I was boring." Pierre shook his head as he told the story. He tried to choke back the emotion.

"You loved her and she told you it was over," Joe offered.

"Yes. I couldn't take it. I loved her more than life itself. And I bored her?" His voice rose in a plaintive wail. "She might as well have pierced my heart with a dagger," he said.

The cop nodded. Pierre wondered if he had gone over

the top with that last remark. Very romantic and loaded with despair, like something a teenage Goth might say.

"So," Brindisi continued, "after Miss McGill told you it was all over and whatever else she added, what did you do?"

Pierre attempted to look embarrassed.

"Mr. de Montfort, I'm not judgmental, but I have to know. For the record," he added.

"I told Marianne I was hurt, she was cruel, and if she had that low an opinion of me, then she could have an even lower one. I told her I was going to drive her back to the restaurant and she could call for a ride home. I never wanted to see her again." He looked ashamed. "I left her there with nobody around. The animal could have attacked then and dragged her off," he added.

"You told her to find her own way home from New Jersey?" Pierre saw both cops look at him as if he were scum.

"It was the anger. I must have been out of my mind when I realized she never wanted to see me again. It hit me out of the blue. I barely knew what I was doing."

The cops tried to keep their expressions neutral, but Pierre knew they thought he was terrible. Dumping "the love of his life" off at a restaurant and telling her to get home on her own? Hell, it was lame, but it beat telling the truth.

"Mr. de Montfort," Brindisi said after an awkward silence, "we have a warrant to search your vehicle. Can you show us where it is?"

Sighing as if weighed down by grief, Pierre rose from

his seat and nodded to them. "It's in the parking garage attached to the building. I'll take you to it."

"We're going to call the forensics crew and have them go over it," Sergeant Brindisi informed him. "It's all part of the procedure."

Pierre couldn't have been more accommodating. "I understand perfectly, gentlemen. I was the boyfriend, the last person to see Marianne. You'd be remiss if you didn't check my car. No hard feelings."

He should have been a little more reluctant, he thought immediately. Who wants the police all over his car? Then again, if that person committed the crime in another vehicle, why shouldn't he look innocent?

"It's a Jaguar," Pierre added. "I hope they'll be careful."

"Oh, they will be, sir. That's their job."

Then, almost as an afterthought, one of the cops looked at him and said, "Would you happen to have a pet? A large dog, maybe?"

Pierre stiffened at the dog reference. "No," he said brusquely. "No pets at all."

Paul reached for his cell phone later that day and heard the voice of his NYPD contact. He said Officers Brindisi and Rodriguez visited Pierre and took his car in to search it for evidence.

"They won't find much. He rented another Jaguar the night of the crime."

"Do you want them to know that?"

"Not if it interferes with our work," he answered. "Let's use the cops as beaters to scare our wolf out into the open. Get Pierre moving into our trap. He's going to make an appointment with one of our guys to sell him a necklace. We'll take him down there. Don't let the NYPD grab him first. Once we get him, he'll be off your streets and you'll never hear from him again. Problem solved at no cost to the taxpayers."

"Gotcha."

Catherine felt the whole hunt was getting away from them. First they had to deal with the addition of the Institut's American operatives, and then von Hoffman and Heinz decide to show up. What else could insinuate itself into the takedown? Catherine hated the entire procedure right now. It was taking too long and she was frustrated that she and Paul weren't in control of it.

"Catherine, you're taking this too hard," Ian consoled her. "No matter what happens, you will soon have the pleasure of eliminating this Montfort. Of that, I'm certain."

"But it's all wrong. It ought to be just me and Paul. We don't need this circus."

"But apparently, von Hoffman does."

"Silly old fool. He's too old. He ought to retire. He never did things like this before, and worse than that, I think he's listening to Heinz, that shameless sycophant."

Ian put his arms around her and drew her closer to him in bed. Catherine sighed with pleasure and nestled against him, enjoying the warm afterglow of two hours of fevered lovemaking.

"I would like to help you, you know," Ian said. "If only to watch you in action."

"I don't need any more helpers," Catherine said, smiling. "And you're crazy, wanting to see me in action. I can't decide if you're looking to get turned on watching me take the Montfort down or get in my way to protect me."

That made him smile. "I worry because I love you," he said simply. "Just like any other man."

"Oh, darling," she said with a chuckle, "you may worry, but you're unlike any other man I've ever met. Nobody can do what you do to me."

Ian smiled, kissed her neck, and felt her nestle closer to him. "I love what I do to you, *chérie*. I'm glad you love it, too."

Catherine moved over and crawled on top of him, kissing Ian fiercely, possessively, as they tangled in the sheets. "I adore you. I am desperate for this mission to be over so we can be together without the distraction of these idiots."

Ian wrapped her in his arms. They kissed passionately, and Catherine slid beneath him and murmured endearments as he turned his attention to her neck and the seductive pulse that beat beneath it. She gasped in shock when Ian brushed her lightly, teasingly, with his fangs and drew blood with a move that sent fire rushing through her body. Then he moved inside her, delivering a second shock that nearly made her faint. She lost all sense of time and place and cared only to repeat that wicked, iniquitous, sinful coupling that left her so drained she no longer knew where or even who she was.

Afterward, with Catherine lying limp and exhausted in his arms, Ian felt he had satisfied her so thoroughly he had exceeded expectations.

In fact, he would need a day's sleep to recover from it. She surprised him when she sat up in bed, wrapped her arms around her knees, and asked, "What kind of werewolf would kill its mate? This is the first time it's ever happened, and it just goes against everything we've ever learned about them. Have they ever done it in another century?"

Ian looked up at Catherine and wondered when women became able to switch so seamlessly from lovemaking to interrogation. "No Montfort ever killed its mate," Ian replied. "At least not from the late eighteenth century till now. I have no firsthand knowledge of earlier Montforts, but there is nothing in our history to suggest it ever happened. As a race, we are so attached to our families that it would be unthinkable for any of us—including the werewolves—to do so."

"What about your cousin Raoul?"

Ian flicked her a disdainful look at the mention of cousin's name. "That idiot took a peasant girl as his wife to fool the local Reds, and he never harmed her. Some people even said he loved her. They managed to produce a son before I killed my cousin in retribution for my wife's murder. My bad luck that I never got the son before he reproduced."

"And you never heard of any ancestor who killed his wife?"

"Not one. It would have been a blessing for us all if my ancestor, Count Albert, had killed Sulame before she passed on her cursed DNA, but tradition says he adored her."

"So Pierre is some kind of bad seed."

"All werewolves are evil spawn," Ian reminded her.

"Do you think it means the breed is having some kind of breakdown?"

"I think it means Pierre never received proper training as a cub and he's floundering, unable to control his impulses or his hormones. He's in free fall, and when he dies, the bad genes die with him. So, my love," Ian said quietly, "make certain he does."

# Chapter Forty-one

By the time Pierre showed up for work the next day, the Institut's local talent had bugged the place with a mini-cam that recorded sound and video.

Paul, Catherine, and the others could tune in on a laptop, but the job of monitoring the Beau Bijou fell to Heinz. He actually enjoyed it, since his usual duties consisted of fetching and carrying for von Hoffman, and with this, he felt he had been entrusted with an important mission. It also reminded him of a reality show with higher stakes than usual: *The Girl and the Werewolf.*

With Heinz watching Pierre's shop on a double screen focused on the showroom and the back room, other members of Team Werewolf fanned out in the immediate vicinity, available in case Pierre let out the wolf and turned on Keri.

Catherine received a call from Heinz and quickly switched on her viewer as she and Paul sat in a car. They observed Pierre in conversation with his assistant. Suddenly they heard her say, "Oh, I forgot to tell you, a policeman spoke to me about Marianne. He wanted to know about you, what you were like. He was interested in your car, too. He wanted to know if it was the only one you ever drive."

They saw Pierre pause, glance up from the necklace he was examining, and turn to face Keri. Catherine felt a sudden chill as she studied his face. That struck a nerve with him.

"And what did you say?" he asked casually. The expression in his eyes hinted at something more intense.

"I told him the truth, that you have a green Jaguar and the only time you ever drive anything else is when you have to take it in for repairs. Like the other day when you had your date with Marianne and they loaned you that gorgeous burgundy car and I brought it back the next day."

"Oh," he said. He looked at his assistant with grim intensity. That seemed to rattle her. "You told them I was driving a rental car when I went out with Marianne?"

"Did I do anything wrong?" she asked.

"No, no," he said grandly. "You just told the truth."

Catherine started to reach for her cell phone to call in a prearranged signal to send agents to the shop. Then she stopped. Surprisingly, Pierre didn't seem aggressive.

She heard him say, "Excuse me, Keri. I have to make a phone call. I'll use the one in the back. You stay here and go over the inventory. Okay?"

"Sure."

On the second screen, Catherine saw Pierre enter the back room, sit down at his desk, take out his BlackBerry, and scan down a list of telephone numbers. When he found what he was looking for, he punched it in and said,

"Hello, Mrs. Chevalier? It's Pierre de Montfort. How are you? How's the weather in Europe right now?"

In the car, Catherine grabbed Paul by the arm and said, "He's taken the bait. He wants to get out of town before the cops come back with evidence from the rental car. He's ours!"

"Allo." Maryse answered her cell phone and listened hopefully. The Montfort still hadn't called to set up a date for delivery, and she and the guys from Team Werewolf were beginning to wonder if he ever would.

"Hello, Mrs. Chevalier?" the voice said. "It's Pierre de Montfort. How are you? How's the weather in Europe right now?"

"Absolutely lovely," she said. "We're having what you Americans call the Indian Summer. The last glow of warmth before the frost sets in."

"Nice to hear it," the voice said. "I was wondering. . . . Did you find someone I could meet with to hand over the necklace?"

"Yes, as a matter of fact, I asked a dear friend of mine to serve as my emissary. Could you meet him at his hotel? He'll pay you the remainder of the thirty thousand in cash and I'll reimburse him."

"That's a lot of money. He must be a very good friend," Pierre marveled.

"Oh, he is. Robert went to school with me in Switzerland, and André and I have been friends with him and his wife for over thirty years. We've often stayed with him at his home in Boston's Back Bay."

"Well, all right, then. Where is he staying?"

"He'll meet you in the bar of the Hotel Montaine near

West Eighty-sixth Street. Do you know it? It's one of those small boutique hotels. Very nice."

"Yes," Pierre said. "I've passed it a few times. I'll find it."

Maryse looked at her audience consisting of Walker, von Hoffman, and Heinz. She motioned at the clock, indicating she wanted to know what time to suggest for the meeting.

Walker put up one finger. One o'clock.

"Could you meet him there in the bar at one o'clock in the afternoon tomorrow?"

"I can't see why not," he responded cheerfully.

"Perfect," she said with a smile in her voice. "Then I'll call him and tell him. Look for a tall, slim man in his thirties with dark hair who looks like a lawyer."

"Okay. And let him know what I look like, too. We don't want him handing the money over to the wrong man," he joked.

"Heaven forbid," she laughed. "That would never do."

"All right, then, Mrs. Chevalier. I'll send you my necklace along with my best wishes. Wear it in good health."

"Thank you," she said. "I'll tell all my friends where it came from."

When Maryse hit the button on her cell phone to end the conversation, she glanced around the room and said, "It's on. Tomorrow we reel in our werewolf."

Pierre felt elated. He terrorized an entire city. He ruled the night. What more could one ask for? And he wanted to go out a winner.

Of course, with the police investigating the killings,

there was a chance of linking the crimes to him, especially Marianne's murder. He had been careless there. With no advance plan to commit the crime, he hadn't been able to cover his tracks as he should have, but still there was no way to prove he had killed her or anyone else. Did Pierre de Montfort have the kind of teeth the killer had? Did he leave paw prints? No. So let them investigate. The only danger to him was the strain of being taken to a holding cell in a courthouse during the course of an arraignment. That could get hairy and lead to a little stress-induced shape-shifting. At that point, it was all over. He'd be target practice for a whole platoon of excited court officers. Not gonna happen.

He had long considered that a flashy string of killings in New York would bring together the very best of the NYPD to deal with him. Even though some of the deaths had taken place in New Jersey, they all bore the same telltale signs, and sooner or later the police would confer and possibly start tracking him. It appeared now that at least two officers already had their eyes on him. He was certain he could beat the rap, but it would be stressful. Why put himself through all the hassle?

It was time, Pierre decided, to take that trip.

Robert Walker had no trouble with the role of wealthy go-between. The man walked, talked, and looked like the personification of old money. Polished, urbane, and self-possessed, he could incapacitate a target as quickly as other men might light a cigarette. He also projected the nonchalance a man would need when dealing with other millionaires, though this came from Walker's own personality rather than from any personal fortune. In his line of work, a furtive, nervous persona was a death sentence; Walker exuded casual authority.

"What if he asks you about your friendship with Maryse and her husband?" Paul inquired.

"I lie and tell him we go back a long way, beginning with our school days in Switzerland. We went to the Lycée La Fontaine in Montreux, a boarding school that catered to foreign students. Maryse's family sent her there during the family troubles, and my father the diplomat sent me there to acquire some European polish and rub shoulders with the international set."

"Very good. Now," said Catherine, "here's an obvious, but dangerous question. Can you actually speak French?"

*"Bien sûr, madame. Je suis allé en Suisse pour faire mes études. Pourquoi pas?"*

"Robert," she exclaimed, "I had no idea. Where did you study?"

"Not at some school for rich boys in Switzerland. At the Monterey Language Institute. For an assignment in Southeast Asia, in my other life," he added with a wink.

"Very good. That would certainly provide credibility if Pierre de Montfort decided to throw a few phrases at you to test you."

"Oh, I doubt he'd do that. He wants the money," Walker said with a shrug. "But I can talk him blue in the face if I need to."

"My guess is, Pierre might agree to a drink to be polite, but his object is to get the money and run," Paul ventured.

"Exactly. So we're going to spike his drink," Walker said. "One of the crew will play bartender and the rest of them will serve as customers. A deserted bar would be a dead giveaway. We have to make it look real."

"Where will we be?" Catherine asked. "We're in on this, too."

"You, Herr Doktor von Hoffman, and Paul can be one flight up, monitoring things on a screen. As soon as Pierre's head hits the table, we grab him, put him in a straitjacket, cuff him, and bundle him into the van for the trip to meet the helicopter. We then fly to our base in New Jersey to load him onto the plane for his trip to Europe."

"Do you think the tranquilizer will hold him?"

Walker looked somber. "If it doesn't, we'll have a major problem, so we're going to make sure we give him enough juice to flatten three werewolves."

"Just be careful you don't kill him," von Hoffman said cautiously. "This is going to be a historic experiment, and we can't afford to take chances."

"I hear you, sir. We agree completely."

Paul worried about the dosage. In his experience, a werewolf was ferocious enough to withstand just about anything a tracker could come up with. That was why almost nobody had ever tried to capture one. With werewolves, you didn't plan too far in advance. You either killed them or they killed you. Temporary storage seemed a fool's fantasy to him. They would have to rely on drugs and a straitjacket until they caged the creature. Good luck to them.

"Be careful you don't rattle him or scare him off," Catherine said. "They have a built-in sense of entrapment. And you know what an angry werewolf can do."

"Mademoiselle, I plan on living to a ripe old age. You know I'll be careful. And so will my team."

*Yes, that's what anybody would say. And it might turn out to be your last statement,* Catherine thought.

She sincerely wished men weren't so cocky.

# Chapter Forty-two

The next day, in the midst of the preparations for the take-down, Paul's cell phone rang as he sat eating a sandwich during a break in the meeting, and to his delight, Julie's voice greeted him.

"Hi," she said. "Am I disturbing anything important?"

"Nothing." He laughed. "Absolutely nothing important. How are you?"

"Missing you. Is everything all right?"

"Yes. I can't talk, but I'm fine."

"I can't wait for you to come back," she said softly.

"Neither can I. And when we see each other again, we can start planning the wedding."

"I love you, Paul. You and Catherine be careful. Don't take any chances."

"We'll be fine," he said quietly. "I have too much to live for to be careless right now."

"Remember that," Julie said.

"It's uppermost in my mind, believe me."

"Then I'll say good-bye and let you get back to your

work. My prayers are with you, and so is my golden angel. Keep it close to your heart."

"You'll be in my arms very soon," he promised. "Just as soon as we eliminate this creature."

When Paul slipped his cell phone back into his pocket, he closed his eyes and remembered how beautiful Julie was and how much he wanted her. He hoped with all his heart he would be able to keep his promise.

Truthfully, he had never felt so many misgivings about a takedown as he did right now. He couldn't wait to be done with it.

Catherine heard the ringtone she used for her informants. When she fished her phone out of her bag, she got the news that the cops on the official investigation had visited the Jaguar dealership, gotten a lab unit to check out the car Pierre rented the night his girlfriend was killed, and hit pay dirt. Her blood was all over it once they used the black light. They were going to get a warrant and take him in on suspicion of murder.

"He may kill them if they try. Can you delay this until after he has his meeting with us? That way he'll be gone, out of their jurisdiction, and permanently removed from the scene."

"It could take a few hours to get the warrant. What time's Pierre's date with destiny?"

"One o'clock this afternoon."

"Shouldn't be a problem. Just get him out of New York fast."

She turned to Paul. "The NYPD wants to bring him in for questioning. They found the girlfriend's blood on his rental car. We'd better hope he gets to the meeting before they get to him. Jersey City and West Orange will also be anxious to question him."

"Shit!"

"Exactly."

"Call the guys observing his shop. Let them know about the new development. They may have to attempt a flying intervention if they spot the cops coming their way. Have them check their supplies. If they need a couple of more shots to trank him in an emergency, let us know."

"Right."

Paul reflected. "We'd better check with the helicopter crew at the pier. Tell them to be on full alert from this point on, just in case."

"I'm so glad Doktor von Hoffman insisted I accompany him this time. Field work is so much more exciting than administrative duties in Geneva."

Paul and Catherine both flicked Heinz a scornful glance as he sat watching Pierre's boutique on the mini-cam.

"Yes," Paul said. "The paperwork can't bite you."

In the Beau Bijou, Pierre felt quite pleased with himself. In a few hours he would be fifteen thousand dollars richer, useful for bribes on his trip, done with that cursed necklace, and on his way to *la vida loca* in Brazil. He had his passport, cash in a money belt, a pouch containing hundreds of thousands of dollars in gems, and a suitcase all ready to go. A phone call last evening to a colleague in Rio prepared his way by arranging for a well-connected lawyer to meet him upon arrival and whisk him through customs by dispensing enough cash to welcome him to the country without distasteful inquiries about visas. He was about as ready as a man could be.

And then little Keri got on his last nerve.

"You don't look well today," Pierre said, giving Keri a suspicious once-over. "You look as if you haven't slept in a week. Everything okay?"

"Sure. Just too much caffeine," she said with a shaky smile. "I have to cut down on my visits to Starbucks."

Pierre gave her an intense look. He could see that she was rattled. She looked nervous now.

"Keri," he began somberly, "we've worked together for five years, now, haven't we?"

"Yes. Five years in February."

They stood behind the counter, facing each other, surrounded by beautiful jewelry.

"I hope you've been happy with my work," she said uneasily. "You always said I had a good eye."

He could see her pupils dilating in slight fear, and he felt power surge through him. It excited him when they stared at him like terrified rabbits, all quivery and shaky, their voices registering sheer panic, their limbs trembling with horror. God, he loved it.

Pierre moved closer to Keri, making her back up a little. She started glancing around nervously, as if she hoped to see somebody come to her rescue, but she had nowhere to go. The glass counter lay behind her.

"Why are you so nervous today?" he asked gently. "Do you have something you want to tell me?"

"No." She looked up at him as if she were looking at a stranger. "Why would I keep anything from you?"

"What did you really tell those cops you talked to?" he asked as she wriggled away from him and stood with her back to the door of the boutique with nothing behind her to block her exit. Pierre noticed that and stepped closer, putting his arm around her shoulder.

"Pierre, What's going on? Didn't you shower today?" she demanded, trying to shrug off his arm.

"What?" he demanded in shock.

Keri seemed to forget her fear and she continued, apparently fascinated, "You're different. You even smell different. Like a dog," she blurted out before she could stop herself.

He reacted as though she'd slapped him. He felt the desire to bite her, tear out her throat, shut her up forever. He lusted at the thought of the kill.

"You have the nerve to tell me I smell like a fucking dog?" He was a wolf, a predator, a merciless destroyer. The dog reference drove him wild. The lack of respect sent his temper into the stratosphere. Dog! What was it with these damned humans?

"What's gotten into you, Pierre?" she wailed. "I told everybody you couldn't have killed Marianne, but you've been acting crazy ever since that day." Keri edged toward the door and he grabbed her again and pulled her back, sweating now, the hormones rising in him.

"The cops think you did it," she said, in a blind panic as he clutched her wrist and dragged her toward the back room.

"And of course you had to tell them everything you could think of to incriminate me, you little bitch."

"No! But I had to tell them the truth. Pierre, you didn't kill her. You couldn't have," she sobbed now. "I don't believe you did it. I told them that. I told them how much you loved her."

"Yeah. You think I'm so innocent you made sure they knew I took Marianne out the night she was killed. That's loyalty."

"It was the truth. But what does it matter if you didn't do it?"

"You believe me, then?"

"Yes," she said emphatically as she fought to break away from his steely grip. "Please let go of me," she begged. "You're hurting me."

He wanted to kill her now. The rage possessed him, superseding any rational thought. She could have lied for him like a loyal employee, but no, she'd blabbed whatever she knew and helped the cops. He had let it slide before, heroically maintaining his calm, but today the thought of that betrayal roused him to homicidal rage. Hormones called to him, demanding to let out the wolf, to attack this pathetic little creature who dared to help his enemies. He leaned over her and tried to sink his teeth into her neck.

Then Keri did something Pierre never expected; she let out a screech and kneed him in the groin, making him double over with rage and pain. As he crashed to the floor, winded and almost nauseated from the shock of the blow, Keri threw a few countertop displays at him, going wild, cursing him, shrieking that he was a madman.

"You may want to look at this," Heinz announced gleefully.

"What's going on? Have the cops arrived?" Paul demanded.

"Much more interesting. Look."

As Paul glanced at the computer screen, he saw the

young girl who worked for Pierre engaged in a screaming match with him while Pierre flailed around on the floor, groaning with pain and cursing savagely, threatening major mayhem.

"Oh my God," said Catherine. "What happened?"

"They got into it," Heinz said with delight. "He accused her of saying too much to the cops. She claimed she thinks he's innocent. But of course she was probably only trying to humor him because he scares her so much. Then they got physical, he tried to drag her across the room and she kicked him in the family jewels. What a superb creature she is. And she seemed so sweet and gentle when I met her," he exclaimed. "What a tiger."

"Alert the guys on the street. This is bad news. Get somebody in there before he kills her."

In the boutique Pierre sprang to his feet as he struggled to dominate the pain and then lunged after Keri, who was already running for the door. "You're not going anywhere, you bitch!" he screamed. He felt the fury of being bested by his formerly docile assistant. *Never trust humans,* he reminded himself. *They're all bad, ready to turn on you in a heartbeat.* He shouldn't have fought the wolf in him; he should have allowed him to emerge and deal with her.

Keri flung open the door just seconds before he could reach her and raced screaming down the street, begging passersby to call the police, claiming she had nearly been murdered in the jewelry store.

Pierre stared out the window, saw at least three people reach for cell phones, and said, "Shit!"

He hurried to the door, locked it, bolted it, and looked

once more out the window to see Keri carrying on and beginning to attract a crowd.

*They'll use this to take me in,* he thought angrily. How the hell could this have happened? He killed with impunity, scared the crap out of the greater Metropolitan area, and all they have is circumstantial evidence at best. Now he roughs up Keri and the NYPD will use it to toss his ass into Rikers. They do that, he goes werewolf, and he's cooked.

"Stupid worthless bitch!"

Pierre headed into the back room, pulled his cache of gems out of the safe, took one last look at his workshop, and left by the rear exit. The hell with humans. They'd still be wondering what happened to him when he was sunning himself on the beach tomorrow.

"We can pretty much count on him missing the rendezvous now," Paul said with disgust.

"He may feel he can outsmart the cops if he moves fast enough. They don't know where he's going. He could still show up here."

"I doubt it. He has to know the cops could arrest him for assault. He's not going to jail if he can help it. I bet he's headed out of town. We need to get observers at the airports."

Catherine looked at the still computer screen. "If he's greedy enough, he'll come to us for some traveling money. If not, we'll shadow him and take him as soon as we can. Call the guys on the street. Tell them he's moving now and using a different car, maybe another rental. Paul, you have the make and the tag number, right? Let them know."

While Paul was transmitting the message to the men on the street, Pavel called in to report he had placed a tracking device on the car earlier this morning when Pierre arrived with the new vehicle, one he'd rented yesterday.

"You're good," Catherine said with admiration.

"Old-school training," he replied. "Mark everything."

"Where is he now?" she asked. "Does it look as though he's heading our way?"

"Sorry. He's driving in the opposite direction. Looks like he's ditched the rendezvous."

"Okay. Keep us posted. I'll get back to you."

She lowered her head and cursed softly. They had planned the event, staged the scene, even counted how much time it might take before the Montfort's head hit the table, but it had all gone to hell in the time it took for the wolf to lose its temper with the assistant. And they said women's hormones made them unstable! *Merde!* This guy was as unhinged as a gerbil on crack.

"We're ready for liftoff," Walker said. "Why let minor details derail us today?"

"All right," said Paul. "Tell von Hoffman what happened. Get the SUV. We're going after him. Tell Pavel to keep trailing him on-screen and try to send the feed over to one of our laptops."

"I can help you there," Heinz said unexpectedly.

Catherine glanced at him in surprise. "Good," she replied. "You might prove invaluable."

Ian lay wrapped in his daytime sleep, slumbering among the remnants of two centuries of family history. Even in this dormant mode, his thoughts drifted to

Catherine and her chances of taking the Montfort were-wolf alive.

Stupid to attempt a kidnapping because of the old German and his insane dreams of glory, he thought restlessly. She should never have agreed to it. With their kind, you go in fast and furious and get the jump on them before they can retaliate. It was the only way.

Smiling faintly as he recalled Catherine's charms, Ian relived the day he exterminated his despised cousin Raoul, the werewolf of his generation, but alas, not before Raoul had passed on his warped genes to a son.

Although he had avenged his dear wife's murder, Ian had never managed to locate the child who was to continue the line of the Montfort werewolves. Raoul had hidden him away so well in the company of other werewolves that the boy survived to continue the family curse and pass it on to his descendants. Ian had killed many of these blighted souls; others had died naturally. All that was left of this withered branch of the family tree was Pierre, the tortured beast.

What had made him so reluctant to kill Pierre when he had the chance, long before he became such a threat to the world? Had he gone soft?

Ian remembered when he first learned of his existence, the night he tracked and killed Pierre's grandfather. The boy had been nearby, heard the shot, and came running to his grandfather's aid.

The youngster wailed as he threw himself on the old wolf's body, screaming with the pain of his loss. The silver bullets had done their work and the old man regained his human form as the boy watched, not knowing a killer spied on him from behind a stand of fir trees.

At that time, Pierre hadn't developed werewolf capabilities, hadn't been worth killing, and his grief at the old man's death had been so heartfelt and so devastating that it had touched Ian's heart.

Worse than that, it rekindled horrific memories of the evening Marie-Jeanne had died. Pierre's screams of pain and mourning echoed his own more than two hundred years earlier, reviving all the agony he himself had suffered. More alarming, it short-circuited his hatred at that moment and allowed him to see that even the loathsome and despised heir of a werewolf could love and feel the sting of loss. It was something he could never have imagined.

Ian resolved to be careful with the boy, to watch his progress and never strike unless he deserved it. When it became apparent that Pierre was indeed a true Montfort werewolf, he put aside his hesitation and offered the information to Catherine and Paul. By that time Catherine and he were lovers and he knew the kill would be a great coup for her.

Pierre was the spawn of centuries of evil; he deserved to die before he could pass on his warped heritage. Ian felt no hesitation about this. He was simply, after two hundred years of killing them, quite willing to let somebody else take this one down.

# Chapter Forty-three

Trying to decide how to play his new hand, Pierre swore at all the idiot drivers in his way and rejected his previous plan to go to Kennedy Airport and catch a flight to Florida. If the NYPD intended to arrest him on an assault charge so they could hold him and grill him more thoroughly about Marianne's murder, and possibly his previous killings, and then realized he'd flown the coop, they would naturally alert the airports and have every policeman and security guard at LaGuardia, Kennedy, and Newark combing the place for him. Too risky to chance the main airports.

While he considered the possibilities, Pierre fought his way through traffic, turned right onto East Ninety-sixth Street, and headed toward the FDR Drive. With one eye on the road and another in the rearview mirror, Pierre wondered if the cops had posted an alert for him after Keri reported what she would certainly call an assault.

He knew she'd call the cops on him now. Running up and down the street wailing and screaming for help? Oh yeah. She'd probably accuse him of everything she could think of. Too bad he hadn't been able to do any of it. So far, there was no sign of anybody tailing him. With luck, he could make it out of the city before they got wise.

Depending on how much time they chose to spend questioning his treacherous little assistant about her hissy fit, Pierre had a fair chance of giving them the slip. He hoped they hadn't thought to send out an all-points alert to the bridges and tunnels. If they did that, it could get sticky, but he doubted they could think that fast.

He even considered shape-shifting in an emergency, but that would handicap him, since wolves can't drive or handle money. And it would take forever to reach the border on foot. Besides, thanks to his well-documented exploits, anybody who saw a wolf would freak out and try to kill him. Not a good idea right now.

He took out his cell phone and proceeded to Escape Plan B: calling a friend and letting him know he'd be dropping by on business. Nobody would have the sense to go looking for him there.

"*Ach*, even after all these years, who can really penetrate the mind of a werewolf?" von Hoffman said in disgust. "The furry wretch is playing us for fools."

Paul and Catherine glanced at each other, at their boss and his assistant, and had to restrain themselves from rolling their eyes in repugnance at the catastrophe as it unrolled relentlessly before them.

Paul got up from the monitor to stretch his legs and as he did, Catherine's cell phone rang. She took it out, hit the button, and said, "Yes."

By the expression on her face, Paul could sense trouble. He saw her register exasperation, then anger. By the time she flipped the thing closed and turned to her partner, Paul knew they were in a kind of free fall.

"He's headed for New Jersey with the NYPD hunting him. They showed up at the shop ready to arrest him for assaulting his assistant, but he'd already exited through the back door twenty minutes before they arrived. He's in a rented Escalade, driving in the direction of the Henry Hudson Parkway right now. That will take him right to the George Washington Bridge."

"Who's your source?"

"Pavel, that Russian who works for Ian. He put a GPS on the Escalade and installed a minicam behind the shop. He's monitoring the cops and they're trying to catch up with Pierre, but the Montfort has a good head start."

"Damn!"

Von Hoffman looked at his subordinates and gestured impatiently. "Can you trust this Pavel?" he demanded.

"He's reliable," Catherine said. "And he's trying to send the tracking signal to our laptops so we can follow him."

"Then let's end this charade and get to the helicopter. We can track him from the air," snapped von Hoffman.

Walker stubbed out his cigarette, pulled out his cell phone, and made a short, energetic call to a pilot waiting for their news.

"The package has taken off on its own. We'll meet you at the prearranged spot and proceed by air."

"Roger," came the reply.

"Get the van," Paul ordered. "We're going to the pier."

Catherine didn't know where their chauffeur earned his driver's license, but he drove like a demon. She found herself leaning into Paul on the turns, while von Hoffman criticized every maneuver and muttered in German about reckless young fools trying to kill them all.

Walker seethed with fury at the Montfort's escape and ignored all the complaints. The bastard had cheated him of an opportunity to show the top brass what he could do, and it rankled.

"How many can we take onboard the chopper?" Paul asked. "Catherine and I want to be there, of course."

"You two, me, Herr Doktor von Hoffman, Heinz, and our driver. The others will meet us on the ground. We'll have to contact them when we find out his destination."

"You think he's trying for an airport?"

"No idea," Walker admitted. "If he is heading for the GW Bridge, he's going to New Jersey. That could mean Newark Airport. With the NYPD on his tail, he has to get out of the country or get caught."

"The cops have to know that, too," Catherine replied. "Do you think he's that stupid?"

"By this time, he's desperate. That doesn't help someone think straight. Right now, I'd be willing to bet he's so agitated he's worried that his hormones will start to kick in and turn him furry while he's still in the car. If that happens, it's all over for him. He'll crash the Escalade and we'll never get our shot at him."

"Or he could shape-shift and fool us all."

"Let's hope our werewolf has great self-control," von Hoffman said from the backseat. "I haven't come all this way to lose him."

"*Ja,*" Heinz said. "But who can count on one of them for anything? They're all just animals. Ah," he said cheerfully, "I just picked up the Russian's tracking signal. Pierre is going to the Henry Hudson Parkway."

"And you've devoted how many years to pursuing the species?" Catherine inquired acidly, unable to help herself. If this nitwit and the over-the-hill von Hoffman hadn't screwed up her plans, she and Paul could have taken Pierre already. That showed the folly of dealing with a bunch of bureaucrats. If they survived this idiocy, Catherine swore to herself she'd never work for anyone again.

"Countess," von Hoffman said in a warning tone, "I think you're becoming overwrought."

"No, she isn't," Paul replied. "She's just expressing what I'm feeling, too. This group effort is rubbish. From now on we work alone."

"You will do as I say," von Hoffman ordered.

"No, I don't think so," Catherine said angrily.

"Countess, this is not the time to become mutinous. First we will capture the Montfort, and then we will discuss your future."

"And mine," Paul added.

Heinz glanced at the French and exchanged a worried look with his boss.

"If you people don't mind," Walker threw in, "I'd like to concentrate on our mission. Save the intramural bickering for later."

"Not your problem," Catherine told the American as she looked out the window. "Get us to the helicopter and mind your own damned business."

At that, Walker threw her an amused glance, but said nothing. She promised herself that if this guy said one word about PMS or any other macho nonsense, she'd

reach around and belt him. The hell with good manners.
If it weren't for these guys and their antique boss, she'd
have already taken care of the Montfort and be back in
France, attending a couple of family parties she had
promised not to miss. Instead . . .

"I apologize, Miss Marais," Walker said unexpectedly.

That caught her off guard. Maybe he wasn't as dumb
as she feared.

"Accepted," she said laconically.

And she gave Paul a glance that suggested there was
hope yet.

In his Escalade, Pierre ran a red light near the approach to the Henry Hudson Parkway, clipped a college
kid with his side mirror, and sent him flying through the
air, straight into the path of an oncoming Chevy. The
young man landed on the hood, bounced as the startled
driver braked, then fell headlong underneath the wheels
while cars screeched to a halt and drivers got out cell
phones to report the accident and tried to get the number
of the car that hit him.

Cursing with fury, Pierre floored the gas pedal and
nearly collided with a Porsche as he took off onto the
Henry Hudson. He drove like a madman, weaving in and
out of lanes as cars whizzed by, drivers giving him the
finger as he cut them off, not caring about anything except reaching the bridge and the next state.

# Chapter Forty-four

Having arrived at the rendezvous with the helicopter pilot, Team Werewolf hurriedly boarded, the members bowing their heads under the stiff breeze of the blades. Walker greeted the pilot like an old friend, everybody found their seats, quickly buckled up, and then suddenly they were airborne, rising high over the Hudson and the skyscrapers of Manhattan.

"We have special clearance," Walker shouted at von Hoffman. "Highest priority."

"Good." The old German had difficulty hearing in the roar of the background noise, but he understood what the American said.

Catherine glanced down at the pattern of river, streets, and buildings below and she prayed they could find the werewolf and capture him. The Russian's monitoring placed him in a white Escalade heading toward the GWB, but how many Escalades might there be on that stretch of road at any given time?

"Look," Paul said as he gave her a nudge. "We have company. An NYPD chopper over there."

Catherine noticed it, radioed a message to someone on the ground, and within a few minutes, Team Werewolf observed the NYPD's helicopter make a sweeping turn and head back to Manhattan.

He gave Catherine a pleased grin. She nodded, glad that they had thrown off such a powerful rival.

Up in the sky, Team Werewolf flew over I-95, scanning the traffic for Pierre's white Escalade. Thanks to Pavel, the car was sending out signals that placed him on the highway and heading toward Route 80/Garden State Parkway.

"Hey, I think I know which one he is," Paul shouted.

"Yes. There's our boy. Now, where the hell is he taking us?"

"Can he get to Newark Airport this way?"

"Uh-huh," Walker replied as he observed the Escalade veering toward US-46/Newark. "Shit."

To everybody's surprise, Pierre drove on, avoiding the expected route to the airport. He eased into the I-95 south lane, drove like mad, and made a startling exit toward US-46, exit 68 and the Ridgefields.

Watching from above like a flock of guardian angels, Team Werewolf studied the lay of the land and experienced a moment of pure joy. Down on the ground, their prey raced madly toward his obvious escape route, like a pigeon to its nest.

"Teterboro Airport!" Paul shouted. "That's it!"

Traveling as fast as he could, Pierre barreled along US-46 without spotting any local cops or state troopers, luckily for him. He made a few turns, exited via a ramp, and made another turn onto Fred Wehran Drive. He drove onto the grounds of the airport as if he were crossing the finish line at the Indy 500.

Once there, Pierre headed for an office building and a pilot he knew, intent on persuading the man to fly him to Florida.

"Jack, where are you? I have to get to Florida. Now!"

"Pierre, is that you? What's up? You sounded kinda weird when you called me before."

Jack McGee looked startled as he glanced up from his desk to see Pierre de Montfort barge into his office, looking unusually grim. Pierre tried to appear calm, but he was set on escape and didn't want to bother with pleasantries. He said brusquely, "I have to get to Florida this afternoon. It's important."

"Delta and American can take you," Jack said with a laugh. "Any day, every day. How come you want *me* to get you there?"

"Look," Pierre said, "this is a last-minute thing. I have a meeting with a client and I can't book a ticket without it taking me out of my way. I don't feel like flying to Miami via Cleveland. I have to get there quickly. Can you do it or not?"

"It'll cost you."

"I'll pay cash," he replied. "Just get me to Miami."

"I'll have to file a flight plan."

"How quickly?"

"I'll file as soon as possible. How does five thousand dollars sound?"

"Fine," Pierre snapped. "Let's get moving."

Team Werewolf radioed the field that they were coming in for an emergency landing, and the pilot added a code gaining them official government status. This meant nobody would interfere with the chopper or its crew. As the helicopter settled down on the tarmac, blades still creating a downdraft, Walker unfastened his harness, flung open the door and ran out, followed by the others.

Jack McGee had just opened the door of his office to stroll across to the tower when a loudspeaker called out, "Pierre de Montfort, surrender now. We have a warrant for your arrest. Do not resist."

Stunned, the pilot stared at the party advancing on his office, guns drawn, faces grim. Paul took the lead. "Step aside," he ordered as he moved purposefully toward the office. "If you're sheltering Pierre de Montfort, understand you can be accused of interfering with agents of the law in pursuit of a criminal."

"Is Pierre in some kind of trouble?"

"This is government business. Is he inside? Answer truthfully, and you won't be charged with aiding and abetting a fugitive." It was a bluff that usually worked.

At that, the pilot put up his hands in a pacific gesture and replied, "He came barging in to ask me to fly him to Florida. I don't know anything about him being a fugitive."

"Then go about your business, sir," Catherine instructed him.

He didn't wait to be told twice. Jack McGee practically knocked over von Hoffman in his haste to get out of the way.

Walker and the driver raced around the back of the small office as Paul kicked in the front door. As he did, he saw Pierre's back halfway through a rear window. Paul charged forward, grabbed his prey, and flung him to the floor while Catherine immediately stuck the jeweler with a tranquilizer dart, making him scream with fury.

"I'll kill you bastards," he shrieked, scrambling to shake off his attackers. "I'll leave you all in shreds."

Heinz added his own contribution to the cause of science as he jabbed a second tranquilizer into Pierre, but not before the jeweler had begun his transformation. As Team Werewolf watched in fascination, Pierre's limbs started to grow fur and his body twisted in marvelous distortions before their eyes, the first time they had actually witnessed the alteration on the spot. Heinz whipped out his cell phone and caught it on video.

Sinking helplessly into a daze, the wolfman seemed to lose his motor abilities as the audience watched, enthralled by the transformation.

"Heinz, are you getting it all?" von Hoffman asked as he proudly watched his assistant. "What a glorious opportunity."

By this time, Walker and the driver had entered the small office, leaving a man standing guard outside to chase away any curious civilians. When the Americans observed the large silver wolf lying sprawled on the floor at Catherine's feet, they stood transfixed by the sight.

"Is he dead?"

"No, just sleeping."

"Be careful."

Paul turned and gave him a grin. "He's knocked out with enough drugs to keep him nice and quiet for the trip. This bad boy won't give us any trouble."

"Well, what are we waiting for?" von Hoffman demanded. "Let's get going. We'll fly south and meet up with our transportation. At that point we'll take on a steel cage and load him in it for the trip to Europe."

"You don't have one prepared?" asked Paul in surprise. "I thought you were going to arrange for one. What if he awakens during the trip south?"

"He won't. He's out for the count," von Hoffman snapped. "Besides, he'll be strapped into a straitjacket and secured with steel chains."

Heinz chose this moment to glance at his boss and say, "Are we really going to fly with an uncrated werewolf in the helicopter? That is madness." Sweat was beading on his upper lip. It was the only time he had ever questioned von Hoffman.

"Well," said Paul sarcastically, "if you're so uptight about it, you could take a bus."

"That tone really isn't necessary, monsieur. What you're proposing is contrary to all acceptable practices. It would place us all in danger."

Catherine and Walker kept their eyes on the werewolf as this discussion took place, with Paul and a nervous Heinz both getting angrier and louder, and von Hoffman attempting to calm down his assistant, fearful this would lead to blows. Catherine silently shook her head, but kept out of it.

"Who are you to speak to me like that?" Heinz shouted. "We're all here because of the Institut. You are not my superior!"

Walker pulled Catherine out of the way as Paul reached out and clipped Heinz on the jaw, exasperated by the tone and the attitude. Heinz staggered, nearly colliding with Catherine. Walker held on to her as something large and furry began to move, rising unsteadily to its feet.

"Paul! It's coming to."

Before the driver could unload another dart into its backside, the wolf gained strength, fixed the humans with a furious glare, and lunged at the first one in its path, Herr Doktor von Hoffman.

"Heinz!"

Paul and Catherine both pulled out their weapons, released the safety catches, and fired straight at the wolf, but not before he had his jaws around the old man's neck.

"Help me. . . ."

Paul responded in horror, "Shoot to kill! Save von Hoffman!"

A second volley of shots rang out as their boss's screams reverberated through the wooden office building. Blood spurted from several sources as the wolf chomped down on its prey and then looked down at its own wounds. It was hit, but it still had life in it. It was the last Montfort werewolf; it wouldn't go easily.

Von Hoffman's screams died in his throat as the beast knocked him to the ground in his last agonies. The old man fought like a demon to keep death at bay. He used every move he could to battle the unholy beast that had made him its target, but he lost.

Snarling, biting, clawing at its prey, the wolf extracted a demonic revenge on its human pursuer as it proceeded to rip open his throat, tearing flesh to shreds as if it were playing with a rag doll. With Paul and Catherine still shooting at him, hitting him in the chest and the body, the wolf flung his quarry aside and barged out the door, heading for the runway. They had never met a werewolf of such strength. He was terrifying in his capacity to withstand pain.

"Herr Doktor!" shouted Heinz, rushing to where he lay.

"Gone," Catherine said. "Let's get the wolf."

For an instant, Paul stared at the bleeding body on the floor. Then he raced out the door after her, intent on killing the predator.

# Chapter Forty-five

Teterboro Airport had seen its share of bizarre incidents, but nobody could remember a large silver wolf running across the tarmac, pursued by an armed posse. Employees backed away in response to the flash of badges held aloft and shouts to clear the way. Most onlookers sought shelter behind doors, except for a few young guys who wanted to see the action.

Catherine and Walker struggled to overtake Paul, who held the lead. A few of the men remained behind to deal with the civilians and keep them out of the way. Heinz, unnerved by the mayhem, remained behind with the corpse, stunned and speechless.

As the wounded wolf ran at a speed Catherine couldn't even calculate, she and Paul ran after it, peppering the animal with bullets. Suddenly it lost momentum, hesitated, staggered, and turned to stare at them, glassy-eyed as they closed in. With one final surge of energy, the great silver wolf attempted to leap at its pursuers, defiant to the end, fangs bared in one last display of bravado. It fell in a hail of gunshots and lay dead on the tarmac, heart and brain pierced by silver bullets as Paul and Catherine gave him the coup de grâce.

Suddenly a large shape appeared from behind and made its way slowly down the runway, a corporate jet ready for departure.

"Catherine! There's a plane coming. Watch out."

Paul grabbed his partner and pulled her aside as Walker heard the warning and veered off. The plane revved its engines and began to pick up speed as it hurtled toward them, the noise of its jets growing louder and louder, until the air was filled with a deafening roar.

As it lifted into the air, Catherine, Paul, and the American could see the wolf rise from the runway and get sucked into its engines like a piece of paper into a vacuum. Bits of bloody matter began to spew in a sickening pattern all across the tarmac, and suddenly the engine sounds changed to a horrible clunking as the plane aborted takeoff and made an emergency landing to deal with the debris that now clogged its jets.

"Son of a bitch!" Walker exclaimed as he holstered his weapon. "There isn't enough left of him to analyze."

That evening, after hours spent convincing civilians, law enforcement, and FAA agents that the beast killed on the runway had been a massive dog they were hunting in connection with the recent spate of killings, Paul and Catherine returned to New York and a reunion with Ian.

"Well, we weren't able to carry out von Hoffman's plan," Catherine said, "but we did take care of the Montfort. He's dead and the case is closed."

Ian bowed his head briefly. Then he smiled at his

guests and asked Vladimir to get some champagne. "We're going to toast your success," he said.

After a glass, Paul hesitated and said, "Ian, I don't want you to think I'm unappreciative, but there's a young lady I have to see right now so she knows I'm still alive."

"I understand," he replied. "Please give her my regards."

When Paul left, he turned to Catherine. "Now that you've terminated the beast, I would like to show my gratitude."

To her surprise, Ian reached into a drawer and extracted a square flat velvet case. When he handed it to her, she opened it and stood mesmerized by the sight. In the box lay a diamond necklace of nineteenth-century style, purchased at Tiffany in 1896.

"Ian, I'm overwhelmed. It's magnificent," she murmured.

"Let me fasten it around your neck so we can both admire it."

After he did, he stood behind Catherine as she gazed into the mirror, seeing only herself and the masterpiece around her throat.

"I love you, Catherine," he said softly. "I guess I will have to love you as a human since you refuse to convert."

"Ian! Is this a bribe?"

"No, my darling. It's a tribute," he said smoothly. "I would never stoop so low as to attempt to bribe you to do anything."

"You wicked thing," she replied. "You can be so devious."

"Perhaps we can discuss this in a more comfortable

place," he suggested. "We'll take the champagne into the bedroom, why don't we? And we can have all night to ourselves."

Julie's heart went thud as she heard the buzzer announce a visitor. Paul had called hours ago from New Jersey to tell her Pierre was dead, but she was desperate to see for herself that he was unharmed.

She pressed the intercom and said, "Paul?" She heard a low laugh in reply and immediately buzzed the door to let him in.

"Paul," she cried out as he emerged from the elevator and hurried to take her in his arms. "You're safe."

They held each other in what seemed more like a collision than an embrace. Somehow Paul backed her into the apartment, where they remained entangled in each other's arms all over again, laughing, embracing, kissing for the sheer joy of being alive and together again.

"How did it go down?" Julie asked when she could finally speak.

"Badly," he said. "We tracked him to Teterboro Airport, cornered him, and shot him with tranquilizers. Then he unexpectedly recovered and leaped on my boss. At that point it was shoot to kill. We must have fired dozens of rounds at the wolf, but he seemed impervious to the bullets. We lost Herr Doktor von Hoffman," he said sadly. "Despite all our efforts, the creature killed him. Then the wolf ran out onto the tarmac with Catherine and me in pursuit. Julie, we fired everything we had. We couldn't believe the creature's strength. Finally it all seemed to drain it and it stopped running, stared back at us, and leaped. . . ."

"Oh my God!" Her hand went to her throat.

"It was then that our bullets took him down for good, and we quickly administered the coup de grâce. A private jet came roaring down the runway and sucked the remains right into the engines. He's history."

"Finally," murmured Julie with a shudder. "Marie-Jeanne and all the rest of the victims are avenged."

Paul nodded. "Yes," he said. "What began more than a thousand years ago with Princess Sulame has come to an end. The Montfort werewolves are no more."

"Thank God."

"And you and I are here and alive."

Julie leaned toward him and kissed him tenderly. "Oh, Paul, I was so frightened today. It was surreal, sitting here with student papers and normal life all around me, but all the while distracted by thoughts of you hunting the werewolf. A real werewolf, for God's sake!" She leaned against him and sighed. "This past month has been incredible. I love you so much, Paul, but I can't help wonder if this is just some crazy extension of the pressure and the intensity of the hunt. I'm scared you're going to snap out of it."

Paul raised her face to his and said tenderly, "Never, Julie. Loving you isn't something I'll ever snap out of. That night, when I asked you to marry me and put my ring on your finger, that's forever." He paused, then said, "I know that your father has passed on, but if you can arrange it, I would like to formally ask your mother for permission to marry you."

Julie smiled. "That's so old-fashioned. It's lovely. I think she'll be speechless."

"I want her to know I'll take care of her daughter," he said. "Even if my work is a bit odd."

"Are you going to tell her you hunt werewolves?" Julie asked nervously. "I don't think Mom could handle that."

"I'm going to tell your dear *maman* that I'm a writer and researcher who loves her daughter very much and who wants to marry her. You can show her the engagement ring afterward."

"She'll be very happy," Julie said with relief.

"Then let's adjourn to a more comfortable place where we can discuss it."

When Paul scooped Julie up in his arms and carried her into the bedroom, she felt a fire in her blood that had been dormant all day, just waiting to be released. They threw their clothes on the floor and happily settled down on the bed, kissing, caressing, exploring each other's bodies as if they never wanted to let go.

"I would have died today if that thing had killed you," Julie whispered as Paul kissed his way down her breasts. "I was so frightened for you. To be so much in love and to have it taken from you . . . I don't think I could have survived that."

"Then it will be my pleasure to show you what you would have missed if the werewolf had gotten his way," he teased.

Paul's kisses descended even lower and Julie gasped as he probed the moist slit between her thighs. She moved urgently against him, pulling him toward her, desire building as they moved together. He raised his head and positioned himself to enter her, slowly, then quicker, moving in a sensual beat that left her nerve endings on fire.

"Oh, Paul," she gasped as his breath came in ragged bursts. She dug her fingers into his back as he moved inside her, sending her senses spiraling out of control.

They merged in a wild tangle of arms and legs, holding each other as if they were afraid to let go, taking their pleasure, unashamed and ferocious.

When Julie lay back on the pillows, too tired to stir, Paul wrapped his arms around her and kissed her gently on the lips.

"That's how much I love you," he said softly.

"May it last forever," she murmured as she caressed him tenderly.

The day after Paul and Julie announced their engagement to Ian and Catherine, Julie looked up from her desk at work in the history office of James Miller College to see a tall man in some sort of generic brown uniform standing outside the door and knocking on the glass. In his hand he held a small box.

"Come in," she said.

"Delivery for Professor Julie Buchanan," he announced casually as he placed the cardboard box on her desk and thrust out a clipboard with an invoice. "Sign please, to indicate delivery."

"What is it?" she asked, puzzled. "I don't remembering placing any orders."

"I just deliver the goods, ma'am," he said in a slightly Slavic accent. "It has your name on the label, so it comes to you. That's all I know."

When Julie took the package and glanced at it, she

saw no return address. Startled, she sat down and shook it, still rattled from her recent experiences with Paul's odd world, but when she looked up to ask where it had come from, the messenger was gone.

"Chuck," she called out. "Could you come out here for a minute and look at something?"

When her colleague ventured into her office, he glanced at the package on the desk and said, "Somebody sending you a present?"

"I don't know. Somebody just dropped it off and said it's for me. Things have been a little weird lately and . . ." She shrugged. "I think I'm afraid to open it."

"You think it's a bomb?"

"I don't know what to think."

"Let's call security. Maybe they can help."

When the head of security heard about the suspicious package, he came immediately up to the office, flanked by three subordinates who seriously advised calling the NYPD. When the police dogs and the bomb experts finished with the cardboard box, it had passed all the tests for toxicity and explosives but now looked as if it had been fished out of the dump after a downpour.

"It's harmless, ma'am," the security chief was finally able to report. "You might as well open it and see what it is."

"Thank you," she said, staring at the sodden mess. "I think I will."

She waited until she was alone with only Chuck as a witness and then gingerly, carefully, Julie peeled off layers of wet cardboard to uncover a second box, made of polished wood, somewhat the worse for wear.

"What is it, a Chinese puzzle?" Chuck asked.

"I don't know. Let me keep going."

Julie took a deep breath. Somewhere in the back of her mind, a memory surfaced, making her tremble with the uncertainty and the drama of the moment. No. She had no reason to think that, she told herself. It couldn't be.

Finally, she bit her lips and nervously lifted the lid. Inside lay a fine leather pouch, surrounded by a bit of old silk.

"Go ahead," said Chuck. "Go for it."

When she removed the pouch and held it in her hand, she was shocked by the weight of it. "It's heavy."

"And if you open it, you can find out just what's in there," he said impatiently. "Come on. Now you've got me curious."

"Okay," Julie said. "Here we go."

And with that she pulled open the strings of the little bag and beheld the glint of old gold.

"Oh my God! The coins!" She was so stunned, she dropped the bag on her desk. Then she spread the opening and stood transfixed by the sight as she turned it upside down and watched thirteen gleaming Louis *d'or* coins spill out onto her paper-littered desk. "I think I'm going to faint," she whispered. She sank down into her chair as Chuck stared at the golden treasures, struck speechless by the sight.

"Well, you'd better call your fiancé and tell him to get over here with a Brinks truck," he said finally. "I think you've got a fortune on your hands."

Pavel completed his assignment to perfection, changed into a fine cashmere sweater and slacks, and reported that evening to the gentleman who had entrusted him with the delivery.

"Did Professor Buchanan seem surprised?" Ian inquired as he graciously offered the Russian a glass of Stoli.

"Absolutely, sir. She wasn't expecting anything."

"I wish I could have been there to see her reaction when she opened it," he said with a smile. "But I'm sure I will hear all about it quite shortly."

"Are you going to tell Julie the why and wherefore?" Catherine inquired as she accepted a glass of champagne. "I think it's the least you can do."

"In time. Let's have the wedding first," Ian said. "After all," he added with a shrug, "she understands about werewolves. So why not vampires?"

Catherine smiled at her lover. "Paul says she wants a small, cozy affair, just family and close friends."

"Of course," Ian said agreeably. "Let her tell me where and when. Just so it's an evening ceremony with reception to follow. I'll pay for everything."

Catherine cleared her throat and gave him an amused smile. "Julie's mother would expect to pay for it," she reminded him. "This is how they do things in America."

"But my resources are so much more . . . vast," he protested. "We'll say Paul is footing the bill. She wouldn't object to that. He can certainly afford it."

"But, Ian," Catherine said, "what is this obsession with Professor Buchanan? I understand your, ah, family ties, but there's something else, isn't there?" she said suspiciously. "I know you. With you Montforts, there's always some devious business swirling just under the

surface. My mother told me about our ancestors' deal-
ings with you."

Turning to Pavel, Ian said politely, "Will you excuse
me? Vladimir has something for you for your services. I
must speak to Mademoiselle Marais right now."

When the Russian gave him a formal bow and left, Ian
turned to Catherine and said, "Come with me. I will
show you something no one has seen in over two hundred years. When you do, I think you will understand my
affection for Julie. And shame on you if you think badly
of it."

With champagne glass in hand, Catherine followed
her host into his study. She sat down as he went to an antique cabinet, carefully opened the two doors on the
upper half, and removed a cloth from a standing rectan-
gular object inside.

"This is the source of my love for Julie Buchanan," he
said quietly as Catherine rose to inspect what lay within.

When she leaned closer to take a good look, the
champagne glass crashed to the parquet floor, and price-
less crystal splintered into a hundred pieces. "Her portrait?"

Catherine looked first at the painting, then at Ian.
"Why is she wearing eighteenth-century costume?"

"She's not," he said softly. "This is my dear wife,
Marie-Jeanne LaVillette de Montfort, painted in 1788,
the year we married. When I look at Julie, I can see
Marie-Jeanne again. It's as though she's my own child,
the very image of her mother. You can't imagine the joy
she gives me simply by existing."

For a long time, Catherine stood staring at the painting. "It's difficult to compete with such a love," she said

at last, the corners of her mouth turning down, defeat showing in her face for the first time in her life.

"No," said Ian as he wrapped her in his embrace. "She's my family. That's a pure love, the love of centuries of our blood, our genes, our whole being." He kissed Catherine passionately on the mouth and led her away from the painting. "What I have for you is, of course, less pure," he said seductively, "but far more sensual. With you, I wish to pursue the limits of desire for quite a long time. Perhaps forever," he said with a tender smile. "We shall find out."

Catherine nestled in his arms, smiling at Ian's relentless quest to convert her.

"You make me feel like the most desirable woman in the world," she said with a sigh. "That's such a talent."

"No," he said as he kissed her and let his fangs brush her neck as she wrapped her arms around him. "It's merely the truth."

"Darling, you make me feel weak," she whispered as he drew a thread of blood and licked it quickly with his tongue, causing waves of lust.

"Then we should lie down," he said.

"Till morning," Catherine replied. "I think it would be best."

"So," Ian murmured as he guided Catherine out of the study and into his bedroom, "will you convince my descendant to let me take charge of her wedding?"

She paused, looked up at the ceiling in amusement, and said, "Jean de Montfort, you are a scheming, manipulative, obsessed, charming vampire. You have all the wiles of the Montforts that my dear *maman* warned me against."

"Is that a yes?"

"Of course."

"I knew you would agree with me. You are such a brilliant woman, dear Catherine."

"Take me to bed," she said with a smile. "We'll have plenty of time for talking later."

# About the Author

Before writing *Devour*, **Melina Morel** wrote two historical novels under a different name. She lives in the New York Metro area and spends time at the Jersey shore in the summer.

# Penguin Group (USA) Online

*What will you be reading tomorrow?*

Tom Clancy, Patricia Cornwell, W.E.B. Griffin,
Nora Roberts, William Gibson, Robin Cook,
Brian Jacques, Catherine Coulter, Stephen King,
Dean Koontz, Ken Follett, Clive Cussler,
Eric Jerome Dickey, John Sandford,
Terry McMillan, Sue Monk Kidd, Amy Tan,
John Berendt…

You'll find them all at
**penguin.com**

*Read excerpts and newsletters,*
*find tour schedules and reading group guides,*
*and enter contests.*

Subscribe to Penguin Group (USA) newsletters
and get an exclusive inside look
at exciting new titles and the authors you love
long before everyone else does.

**PENGUIN GROUP (USA)**
us.penguingroup.com